THE ART LOVERS

G N Lawson

First published in 2025 by Blossom Spring Publishing
The Art Lovers Copyright © 2025 G N Lawson
ISBN 978-1-917938-04-4
E: admin@blossomspringpublishing.com
W: www.blossomspringpublishing.com

1.

Well, I for one wouldn't dream of showing up there in a pair of those plastic whatsit shoes, yellow ones too, for goodness' sake. I'm surprised the corgis didn't go for his ankles. And, honestly, the brass neck of the man turning down a knighthood for just a silly old OM, mused Frank.

Something Max had said the week before prompted those thoughts, vain though they were, as Frank forced himself to admit. They had been bitching about Hockney getting a gong, and why actors and footballers seemed to get more recognition than artists. Then Max said that you only stood half a chance of getting one too if your work got plenty of the right kind of PR. He said that there was no such thing as bad PR, but Max hadn't said what he meant by "the right kind". *And what about that jeweller, Gerald Rat something* – Frank allowed himself a brief chuckle at the name – *hadn't bad PR killed off his business?* Although his portraits and the increasingly infrequent exhibition usually got a few lines in the art press, Frank simply couldn't imagine them getting any more coverage than that, so he gave up trying to think of how to get the right kind of PR, whatever that might be. But later in the week, Julian rang from The Snicket Gallery.

Yes, a title would suit me rather well, thought Frank, happy instead to continue with his daydream as the Sunday paper slid from his lap to the floor, one section at a time. Of course, she'd need a new hat and all the whatnots that seem de rigueur for a trip to the Palace, but nothing wrong with that. Max seemed to know a fair bit about the sort of perks one might get, but Frank had dismissed them grandly, telling him that recognition for his paintings mattered far more than a few baubles. Then again, if that young rogue she was seeing could be bothered to propose to her, an ennobled Frank could give away Georgia in St Paul's. *Now that would be worth having.*

Yes, Sir Francis Armstrong RA has a good ring to it, Frank thought to himself, as he looked through the French windows of 14 Exmoor Gardens SW15. The gamin silver birches trembled daintily above the studio roof, which needed re-felting. It was a glorious day and he had suggested they ate al fresco, but Louise insisted that, with the baby coming, it would be easier all round to eat indoors.

Louise brought a tray of glasses and a jug of water in from the kitchen. 'Frank, lunch,' she said but got no reply. She tried again, 'Come on, Frank, time to eat. Lizzie's arrived with Theo. Didn't you hear the door?' She paused before adding, 'Is there anybody there?'

He shook his head to end the reverie and turned. 'Sorry, darling. Miles away.' With a grunt, he bent down to round up the Sunday paper then, unsure as what to do with it, shoved it on the armrest of one of the sofas, only for it slowly to return to the carpet. Frank shrugged and made his way to the dining table.

Louise looked out of the window too. 'We really do need to get Mister Sweeney round to sort out the lawn and the beds. He could clear the Russian vine that's taking over too, and sort out the studio roof while he's at it.'

There was a clunk against the door, and their daughter Lizzie emerged, pushing a buggy that contained her second child, Theo. Tall and dark like her mother, Lizzie sat down wearily, and made a half-hearted effort to clear some half-eaten food from her dungarees. 'George says she's running late, stuck in traffic or something. Says we should start without her.'

Frank brightened at the sight of his grandson, 'Ah, how is the nipper? You and the boy getting much sleep yet?'

'That's the thing we humans do for eight hours every night to recharge our batteries, isn't it? Well, the answer's no.'

'It's always the way at that age,' said Louise, getting in before Frank could say anything unhelpful.

'I don't remember Polly being so difficult to get down. And, more to the point, stay down.' Lizzie rooted through her bag for a bottle then ran a hand through her thick hair to retrieve a large tortoiseshell clip that had come adrift.

Frank nodded solemnly, 'I suppose so.' Then, on seeing the lunch, spread out on the table, added, 'Oh no, not fish.'

'Yes, fish, darling. You know what Doctor Schwarz told you.'

'Right name for that blackhearted swine. He doesn't know everything, you know. Wish I'd never gone to see him. Really, I mean it. He's always such a misery guts, never has time for a chat. Not like old Barnett used to be. Now, he was a man you could have a proper conversation with. Anyway, I told you I wanted a roast with Yorkshire pud.'

'"Eat more fish," Frank, that's what he said.'

Frank looked morosely at the slices of cold salmon and cucumber that Louise had put out for him, and reached forward for the jug of mayonnaise.

'Oh, please Frank, not so much.'

He clattered his knife and fork onto his plate childishly, then picked them up with a sigh and began to eat. Frank looked at the water in the wine glass, held it up to the light and swirled it round, wishing it were Chablis.

Lizzie ate her salmon with one hand, and rolled the buggy back and to with the other, while Theo howled.

'I was talking to Julian the other day,' said Frank, knowing all too well that the lunch conversation would be all about babies if he didn't say something. Neither his wife nor his daughter replied, so he continued, 'And he said he's had a whisper about a commission for me.'

'You never said,' replied Louise, surprised since her husband never usually needed any prompting to tell her about his work, especially since she looked after all the admin. 'What's he got for you?'

'Well, I gather it would be rather a departure from my usual oeuvre,' he replied cautiously.

'Doesn't want you just to knock out a portrait of another minor aristo then?' said Lizzie.

Ordinarily, Frank would have reminded his daughter that the portraits had paid for her education and more besides. This time, though, he let it drop and replied with a small smile, 'Oh, nothing like that.'

'Well then, Mister Mystery, who's it for?' said Louise, pretending not to notice Frank helping himself to another large dollop of mayonnaise.

The two cats, rangy, all white and over-affectionate Titus and the diminutive half-Persian Saskia strolled in from the kitchen, seemingly aware that their owners were momentarily ignoring the salmon. The former attempted to jump on Louise's knee, but she swept him off, while the smaller cat sat neatly and stock still beneath the table, waiting hopefully.

'I don't know, darling. Julian just said it was for a commercial client.'

'Some banker, I suppose, or maybe a Russian oligarch this time?' huffed Lizzie.

'I have no idea, but,' Frank twinkled at his daughter, 'it's always nice to be asked.'

Louise cleared away the plates and returned with glass bowls of raspberries, keeping the cream jug as far from Frank as she was able. 'I assume you are going to find out a bit more and not keep us in suspense for ever?' she asked.

'Julian did say he'd call,' said Frank trying not to sound defensive about being put on the spot.

They had finished the fruit when their younger daughter Georgia bounded in, sunglasses wedged into her hair, wearing tight jeans and a striped shirt with the collar raised. She went straight past them, then returned from the kitchen with a doorstep of sourdough and Nutella, kissed Frank then Louise before launching into a diatribe.

'You wouldn't believe it,' she began, smiling through her irritation. 'Sorry I'm late, but it's taken two bloody hours to get here from South Ken. Football match, roadworks and a demo. Or so they said,' Georgia spluttered through a mouthful of sandwich.

'And how is young Tony?' ventured Frank.

'Toby, Dad.'

'Frank!' said an exasperated Louise.

'Sorry, sorry. Senior moment. Do forgive me.'

'No worries. He's fine, thanks. Oh, and I forgot to say, we might be off to Antibes this summer. His Dad's got a boat there, and he says we can borrow it for a bit. Not bad, eh?'

'How lovely,' smiled Louise.

'Yes, darling. Remember that wonderful fortnight we spent there. Cannes, Menton, Cap Ferrat, what simply gorgeous places. That perfect light.'

'He thought he was going to be the next Monet, didn't you dear?' Louise grinned.

'Before he found out there was no money in Monet, and moved on to portraits instead?' joined in Georgia.

'That's terrible, George.'

'Oh, and there was that funny little café by the quayside too, remember?' said Frank.

'I can hardly forget. You wanted to paint that girl there. You know, the one who was a…'

'Ah, well, yes, bit of a misstep, you might say.'

'You can say that again.'

'But it was a lovely holiday all the same.'

'Hmph.'

'Well, I'm sure that you and… and Toby, yes, you're bound to have a jolly time down there.'

'What does he do again, George?' asked her sister as Theo settled on his play mat.

'Oh, he's something in the City.'

'So's The Old Bailey.'

Georgia ignored her sister, and headed off to the kitchen.

The rest of them moved into the conservatory while Georgia made the coffee. After the conversation returned briefly to the sleep patterns of babies, the girls pored over their phones while Frank and Louise picked at the Sunday crossword. Feeling his wife start to nod off, Frank pulled the half hunter from his waistcoat and slowly rose from the sofa.

'Time for my constitutional,' he said, as he did every Sunday afternoon and, knowing there would be no takers, asked, 'Don't suppose anyone fancies tagging along?'

'Duke of York, as usual, Dad?' said Georgia, feet curled up beneath her on a Bergère sofa as she cradled a mug of coffee in both hands.

'Certainly.'

'You'd think they'd have had the sense to rename it by now,' said Lizzie, now holding Theo and trying to interest him in a squeaky toy.

Frank leaned down and kissed the top of Louise's head, as his paisley cravat flopped out from his shirt and into her face. Louise got up, straightened Frank's pony tail and accompanied him to the hall. He struggled into a voluminous tweed coat then pulled a wide brimmed felt hat from the rack.

'You aren't going out like that, for heaven's sake,' she said. 'You'll fry in it.'

'I'll be all right. Anyway, I like my old coat. It sets the right tone.'

'But not that hat. Really, Frank.'

'Why on earth not? It's a perfectly serviceable hat.' Frank plucked a gnarled knobkerrie from the umbrella stand. He kissed Louise again and, as he opened the front door, added, 'Shan't be long. Back before you know it.'

He stopped at the gate and looked back at his wife, framed by the leaded lights of the porch. *She's still so beautiful*, he thought, and gave her a small wave, receiving one the same size in return. He thought back momentarily to the first portrait he made of her, an oil sketch. Louise had been intrigued by the idea, but it was more than a year later before she agreed to pose in the nude for him. At the end of the road, Frank extracted a small box of cigars that he kept in an inside pocket and, checking no-one was around, lit up, puffing contentedly.

Although he had no real need for it, the stick took Frank's weight as he walked down to the Upper Richmond Road then, refusing to wait at the kerb, used it to halt the traffic, raising it imperiously at the cars that had no option but to stop. Frank then made his way through the backs, over the railway bridge, and down to the riverside. The light was lovely at that time of day, softer and the colours warmer, as the harsh midday sun had begun to sink, spreading and settling over west London like a great hen.

He liked his Sunday afternoon walk to the pub for a glass or two with his pals, usually at least three or four would be there: always Doug, usually Gerald, Max and Sean, and occasionally Martin, too. Frank had known Doug and Max from their days at the Slade, then Gerald since they'd exhibited together for years. Martin had been Frank's pupil, and Doug had taught Sean. But what he liked most was the fact that his friends all had to travel some distance to get to The Duke of York, whereas it was a mere ten minute walk for Frank. It gave him a sense of being the group's leader.

When they were much younger, Louise had met them all at boozy parties accompanied by the latest girlfriend, model or student then, as a measure of success came with age and marriages, at equally boozy dinner parties. And they were always at each other's previews, without fail. She referred to them as 'the stereotypes', but only to the girls and never to Frank, at first amused by the self-consciousness of the images they cultivated, but latterly feeling they should be old enough to know better.

Doug was the northern one. He still had his Wearside accent. No longer the athletic dancer, who played football well into his forties, he was overweight now, and moved like a shopping trolley with a wonky wheel. A widower for more almost ten years, these days, he seemed to subsist on sausage rolls and beer. Gerald was the rakish one, almost a caricature of Leslie Phillips or Terry-Thomas in his barathea blazer and brogues, and that untrustworthy moustache. Max was the exotic one, a dark and knowing eastern European who had come to England as a small boy in the fifties. He chain smoked, always holding his dark brown cigarettes between thumb and index finger. Louise wondered if he hammed it up, but thought they probably all did.

Of the former pupils, Sean was the Celtic one, voluble, always in chunky sweaters and boots, full of nonsense about 'Erin' despite being born in Woking. And Martin was the sensitive one, but so thin and pallid it was hard to imagine him even having the strength to wield a paintbrush. How slight he was, with those blue veins that seemed too close to the surface of his translucent skin.

Then there was Frank, perhaps more of a stereotype than any of them. Louise was appalled at the way he was always so willing to be flattered by Doug's perennial greeting 'Now here's a man who looks like a real painter'.

Oddly enough, though, Frank's paintings seemed less stereotypical than those of his friends, those meticulous portraits at odds with the bohemian image he liked to cultivate. Doug, on the other hand, continued to paint the bleak seascapes of his birthplace, dockyards with rusty cranes and glowering warehouses. Max, working on copper, created tiny gem-like images of mysterious scenes he claimed were based on the fairy stories with which he had grown up. Sean was a very late pop artist, whose work owed much to Jasper Johns and James

Rosenquist, while Martin's paintings were of finely crafted figures, almost always in a domestic setting. And then there was Gerald, whose early work had the art world heralding him as the next great British abstract artist after Hoyland, but who suddenly changed, producing the most conservative and accessible paintings of all.

Louise went back into the conservatory where Georgia fussed over Theo, and Lizzie was straightening up the contents of the baby bag.

'Out with the stereotypes again, eh?' said Georgia looking up with a grin.

'He really ought to be more sensible, Mum. I mean, at this age…' said Lizzie. 'Can't you get him to stop acting like a teenager? And you do know he's still smoking, don't you?'

Louise shrugged. She wasn't irritated, and couldn't help thinking that, for all Georgia's sweet nature, it was Lizzie that she would turn to in a crisis. 'Of course I know, darling, but you know how he is. The tiniest, weeniest clipping of his wings and he gets so… oh, you know, petulant.'

'Come on, Liz, cut the old man some slack,' came back Georgia.

'But you know as well as I do who'll have to pick up the pieces. It'll be us, just like last time,' replied her sister.

Georgia shrugged and went off to make a phone call, while her mother loaded the dishwasher.

In the saloon bar of The Duke of York, Doug, first to arrive, had commandeered a corner table overlooking the river and was finishing his pint when Gerald and Max arrived together. Despite living closest, Frank was last, as always. Max was at the bar and, spotting Frank walk in, added a glass of sauvignon blanc to the order. As Max ferried a tray of drinks over, Doug gave Frank his usual greeting, 'Now, here's a man...'

Breathing heavily from his walk, Frank draped the coat over a chairback and skimmed his hat onto a vacant seat. 'I take it we're quorate, Douglas?' he asked.

'Aye, we are that. Just the four us today, mind, Frank. The kiddiwinks are otherwise engaged it seems,' replied Doug, after a long slurp of his bitter.

'Actually, I heard that Sean has a commission. That young fellow seems to know how to have his bread buttered,' said Max.

'Quite right too,' put in Gerald. 'Keep your nose to the grindstone while you're young enough, and stash away the shekels. Gets a damned sight harder at our exalted age. Who's it for?'

'I am told it's for a rock group. A guitarist, in fact.'

'My giddy aunt.'

'Yes, I saw Sean out and around the environs I inhabit,' continued Max, reaching for his Bristol Cream. 'He told me the fellow has bought a rather enormous property and is seeking a fistful of large abstracts with which to bedeck its interior.'

'Saints preserve us.'

'Painting by the yard,' harrumphed Frank. 'Any news of young Martin?'

Doug shook his head, 'Not heard from the lad for a while. Still, there's always this and that wrong with him. Especially when he's working.'

'Ah yes, a most delicate flower of the hot house is young Martin,' added Max.

'Might not be a bad idea for one of us to call round.

See how he's doing, like.'

'As his tutor, Francis, perhaps you might…'

Frank was mindful of Louise's insistence that he should see Martin more often, but always seemed able to conjure up an excuse. 'Well, that was all rather long ago. But, yes, naturally, I should be the one, though I'm afraid something rather pressing has come up.'

Gerald gave a nonchalant wave. 'Never mind. I need to pop into town, so I'll call in on the young master and see what's what. Can't have him all pale and wan and slowly loitering in his garret, now, can we?' He pulled out a handkerchief and coughed loudly into it.

'Thought you'd given up the fags, Gerald?' asked Doug.

Wiping his face, Gerald nodded, before answering hoarsely, 'Did. Years ago.'

'You have his new address, Gerald, no?' Max fished out a small leather notebook from his jacket. 'He has gone somewhere up in the market, I understand.'

Gerald copied down the address, then added, 'Anyway, what's cropped up, Frank?'

Frank, glad of the opportunity to steer his friends away from Martin, and mindful of his recent visit to the GP, was equally determined to deflect them from a conversation on ailments. He let the group have the few details he had that constituted his news, 'Well, on to less morbid matters, it rather looks like I might have landed a nice little commission. Oh, and before anyone says anything, it isn't for a portrait.'

'Intriguing, Francis. How very curious, if I may say so,' said Max with an eyebrow archly raised.

'So, not within your usual bailiwick then, eh?' asked Gerald.

'Indeed not. Not all,' said Frank, glad to have control of the conversation, and happier still to be at the centre of it.

'Julian been pimping for you again, mate?' chuckled Doug, knowing he was the only one who could have got away with the remark.

'Certainly not,' said Frank with mock indignation. 'All I know is that it's for a commercial client.'

'No names, no pack drill, Frank?'

'Afraid not, Gerald,' said Frank, mildly irked by his friends' reaction to his news, and at not being able to furnish them with more details. 'Anyway, I haven't said yes yet.'

'But you will, of course, won't you?'

'Oh, I suppose I might, but I'm not so desperate that I need to agree to anything,' said Frank airily. 'It does rather depend on what Julian has in mind.'

Relieved that it was his turn to go to the bar, despite the fact he, too, had no idea of what Julian had for him, Frank allowed himself a slow smile at the prospect of keeping his friends in suspense.

It wasn't unusual for Martin to work at the weekend. As so often, he found himself working against the clock to complete the last few paintings for his forthcoming exhibition. It was the best possible excuse to avoid the trek across town for Sunday afternoon drinks at The Duke of York that for some reason he couldn't remember, he felt obliged to attend. Doug was friendly yet somehow intimidating but, apart from the fact Frank had once been his tutor, Martin didn't find it easy to get along with the others, especially when the conversation became competitive or bitchy.

On this day, however, he was joined in the studio by his husband, Dominic.

'Wow,' he said after Dominic unwrapped the parcel he had been carrying.

'A little present for your new studio.'

'But you've done so much already. You really shouldn't have.'

'It was a special day, remember?'

'How could I possibly forget? Pride ninety-seven, the day we first met.'

Dominic kissed him. 'I just thought it would be nice to have something that would always bring back that day.'

'My God, we drank a lot that day, didn't we?' said Martin.

'Pimm's, wasn't it?'

'Oh, that's right. And then all those shots too. We were so drunk.'

'Not that had anything to do at all with what happened afterwards,' smiled Dominic.

'No, of course not. Still, I don't know how we did it.'

Martin looked at the large photograph that Dominic had brought with him. The frame was much too gaudy for Martin's taste, and the image among a sea of rainbow banners rather blurred. *Still*, he told himself, *it's the thought that counts* and Dominic had put up the money for the new studio, though goodness knows where he was going to put the thing.

A Monday sun split heavy clouds that had glowered over SW15 ever since breakfast. The sudden warmth, and the harsh light that slanted across the drawing room had woken him up. Recumbent in an armchair, Frank felt overheated and cross that a lovely dream had been disturbed. Unable to remember it all, he did at least recall shaking hands with Joshua Reynolds and being elected President of the Royal Academy. He was not yet coming to and had begun to drift off again when the telephone rang. He waited for Louise to answer it then remembered it was her afternoon for yoga then looking after the grandchildren. Frank stretched out a weary arm. It took a few moments for Julian to check if anyone was there.

'Must I?' Frank wailed into the receiver. Being woken from one of his increasingly regular afternoon naps had made him testy.

'You seemed interested enough when I mentioned it the other day,' said Julian mildly.

'I know, I know. Sorry, sorry, sorry. I don't suppose you can come over here, can you? I can't really...'

'Well, I can't really leave the gallery, can I? How about we meet for a drink later, say The Windsor Castle at about six?'

'Oh, very well,' sighed Frank, mindful that this meant a trip on the hateful Tube, and at rush hour, too. 'I will see you then.'

Reynolds, Tom Lawrence and the other great academicians of the past would not be summoned again, so Frank gave up and lumbered into the kitchen to make a mug of strong tea and, Louise not being round, cut himself a thick slab of Dundee cake. He was at a loose end, but roused himself sufficiently to change into a lemon yellow seersucker jacket and cream trousers, then made his way against the tide of people coming out of the underground station.

Julian Furnell looked more like a retired bookie than the owner of an art gallery, in his usual beige suit that was always decorated with a different, brightly coloured handkerchief, or foulard as he preferred to call it, billowing out of his top pocket. He took a corner table in the shadowy bar, while Frank stomped his way out of Notting Hill Gate Tube station, dispatching burger wrappers and paper cups into the gutter with his stick as he headed towards Campden Hill Road. But Julian knew his man, and had a bottle of Chablis in a cooler and two glasses ready when Frank walked into the pub.

'Are you sure we couldn't have done this over the phone?' grumbled Frank.

'Well, we could have, I suppose. But I really need to show you what the client has in mind.' Julian poured them both a drink.

'So, a commercial client, you say?'

'Yes, well, a quango, to be precise.'

'It has a name, I suppose?'

Julian paused and coughed slightly, 'It's the Nuclear Development Commission, as a matter of fact.'

'Goodness me. Whatever next?'

Julian peeled a leaflet from his battered briefcase. 'They're building a place called The Net Zero Observatory. Just a fancy name, really, for a visitor centre to show people all about the new nuclear reactors they're wanting to build.'

Frank looked baffled, 'But where on earth do I come in?'

'They want a series of murals extolling all the virtues of nuclear power. You know, clean energy, good for the environment and all that sort of thing. Energy security so that we're less dependent on our friends and enemies. Putting something back into the community with lots of jobs. And very, very safe these days, of course. It's all here in their brochure.' Julian pushed the artist's impression of the Net Zero Observatory over to Frank.

'Hang on, Julian. I'm not about to look a gift horse in

the mouth, but why for heaven's sake would these people think that someone who's a portrait painter might be the man for the job?'

'Ah, look here,' Julian pointed to the caption beneath the illustration. 'It's in Cumbria, you see, just down the road from Sellafield…'

'So…'

'So, their funding and something to do with the planning application, requires them to use as many local suppliers as possible. They asked if I had any Cumbrian artists on the books, and then I remembered you were born up there, weren't you?'

'Ah, yes. Westmorland born and bred, that's me. Even so, I don't know the slightest thing about nuclear power, and am even less interested.'

Julian topped up their glasses. 'They seem to have obscenely deep pockets, you know.'

'Just how obscene?'

'Oh, they're offering 20k per mural, eight in total.'

'Good God, I assume that's before your hefty cut? Even so, no more living on beans on toast for me, eh?'

'Gross as usual, of course. And it would be excellent PR for you too.'

'PR, eh?'

'Doing your bit to fight climate change. All helps, you know.'

Frank took a long slug of wine. 'I think you'd better put me down for it, then. Sounds like an offer I'd be mad to refuse.'

'Good. Now, I assume you'd be willing to meet them and get a brief?'

'Of course,' said Frank grandly.

'There's a hotel they use for meetings, close by the

train station.'

'Train station?'

'Yes, Penrith. Next week, they said Thursday, ideally.'

'Penrith! They can't come to London, then?'

'Afraid not, Frank. They're flat out busy up there.'

'Oh well, a trip to the land of my birth I suppose it is then.'

They finished the bottle, and a dazed Frank made his way back to the Tube station, wondering if perhaps he should have inspected the equine dentistry more closely. It was his habit to explore every possible snag to any new scheme, and he spent the journey home trying to do just that, brooding in a half-full carriage as an empty drink can rolled back and forth. He found none and, reassured by the money and Julian's enthusiasm, Frank was in a more expansive mood as he made his way along Upper Richmond Road, and picked up a bottle of Pol Roger from the chiller cabinet in Mr Aziz's convenience store.

Would this be the "right kind of PR" that Max had mentioned, he wondered? Frank's mind turned to press conferences, chat shows even, and drifted further off to where they might lead. *The things we artists have to do*, he said to himself. *Making the world a better place in so many ways, yet all too often unappreciated. Yes, I'll have to put up with all manner of hardships, travelling the length and breadth of the country, but doing my bit for mankind not to mention the future of the planet regardless of the sacrifices.* He basked in anticipation of the plaudits that would surely come his way.

At the corner of Exmoor Gardens, Frank saw Louise coming the opposite way in her Toyota, and hurriedly disposed of the remains of his cigar. They arrived at the house simultaneously, and Louise greeted her husband with a broad grin.

'You really don't need to skulk about, Frank.'

'Eh?'

'The cigar. I saw you chuck it in the gutter. I know you have the odd one; I still have a sense of smell, you know. I'd much rather you didn't, but if you're going to have the occasional cigar, I'd rather you didn't feel the need to be surreptitious about it,' said Louise, leading the way into the hall.

Frank returned her smile with his own, one that was half guilty, half relieved.

'What's in the bag?' asked Louise, as she took off her coat.

'Oh, just some fizz,' began Frank before perking up. 'Ah, yes, I've some news.'

'Oh goody. Well, let me just get changed first. Theo had a little accident, and I need to sponge my blouse.'

Frank gathered a bowl of olives and one of peanuts, two glasses, and plonked himself down on the sofa. Ten minutes later, Louise came in, pulled a footstool towards her, and moved the peanuts out of Frank's reach.

'None for you, my boy. Champagne and a cigar, if you must, but no peanuts. Just the olives.' She ran a hand through her hair. 'My goodness, she's the sweetest thing, but Polly does rather run riot. I don't think we let our girls carry on around the place like that. I'm shattered.'

'We aren't as young as we were, darling.'

'Suppose not. Anyway, what's all this about?'

Frank filled the glasses, and rooted about in his jacket for the now crumpled brochure and handed it to Louise.

'Julian said I need to meet them, so I'll be popping up next Thursday. Penrith, of all places.'

'Goodness. How long must it be since we last went to

the Lakes?'

'Aunt Jem's funeral, I think. Oh, and I'll tell the girls all about it at the weekend.'

'They'll be thrilled, I'm sure.'

'Yes, of course, they can always rely on their aged P to bring home the bacon.'

'And it'll make a nice change for us, not having to hear you going on about how wonderful those chinless wonders all are,' said Louise, then yelped as Frank pinched her arm.

'Cheeky girl! Any more of that and there'll be trouble,' he replied with a gurgle, simultaneously scooping up a large handful of peanuts.

Louise marvelled at how Frank could sleep so long and so soundly. As the years passed, her weekend lie-ins were replaced by hours of padding round the house between coffee, a magazine and the washing machine. Still, on Sunday, Louise let him rest. He surfaced at ten thirty, yawning and stretching, and wearily made himself a mug of strong tea while Louise boiled two eggs and filled the toaster. She had the lunch prepared well in advance, reluctantly opting for a joint of sirloin as at least one way of maintaining the peace that she knew Frank and his son-in-law would all too easily disrupt.

'They're all coming?' he asked.

'Yes, darling. The girls, and Tom, and Theo, but Polly is with his parents. Ballet then something.'

'Tom too?'

'I know he rather gets under your skin, but do try to be friendly, Frank.'

He nodded and took the top off his egg. Frank aways considered Lizzie's husband to be a know-all, and was about to launch into his usual complaint: how could an account director at an advertising agency pretend to know anything whatsoever about real artworks? But he checked himself as Louise gave him a look.

Georgia was first to arrive, kissing both her parents, then disappeared to make a phone call. Lizzie and Tom then turned up, laboriously carting in Theo, his buggy, baby bag, and a one-eyed Teddy bear. On seeing Tom arrive in baggy jeans and an elderly cheesecloth shirt that had once been white, Frank was unable to resist saying, 'Well, I know we didn't stipulate formal dress, but really, Tom!'

Although his son-in-law ignored the jibe, Lizzie hissed, 'Oh, for God's sake, Dad.'

While Frank and Tom sat awkwardly on opposite armchairs, with cabernet sauvignon and Coca Cola respectively, Georgia laid the table, Lizzie changed Theo's nappy, and Louise let the sirloin joint rest, while she loaded up the dishes with roast potatoes and vegetables, and filled the gravy boat.

With a wholly otiose flourish, Frank sharpened the carving knife on a steel, and sliced the joint as plates were passed around the table. Georgia poured the wine, and Lizzie poured water for Tom and herself. Once everyone's plate was filled, Frank, rather as if he were saying grace, told the family about his commission to paint the murals for the Net Zero Observatory.

'Wow, get you, Pa, saving the planet. Frank Armstrong, eco-warrior,' giggled Georgia.

Frank's smile faded as Tom, looking puzzled, asked, 'Sorry, Frank, who did you say the client was again?'

'Ahm, the Nuclear Development Commission.'

'So, this all about getting a positive spin for nuclear power then?'

'I suppose it is,' said Frank warily.

'I see.' Tom returned his attention to the beef.

'And what is it that you see, Tom?' asked Frank, avoiding Louise's glare.

'Well, that it's all good PR, I suppose.'

'Indeed it is. Very good PR for my part, albeit a very small one, in doing my bit for future generations,' said Frank loftily.

'I didn't really mean that.'

'No?'

'Well, it's about getting good PR for the people wanting to build nuclear reactors, isn't it?'

'I daresay, but–'

'So, it's not really about saving the planet or anything like that, is it?'

'Every little helps, Tom.'

'Maybe so, but there are plenty of us who are really uncomfortable about nuclear power. I mean, it isn't exactly clean energy, is it? And is it really safe? For a start, there's all that toxic waste that has to be buried underground for millions of years. And what if there's a problem? You know, like Chernobyl.'

Frank poured himself more wine as his son-in-law got into his stride, and took a long sip before responding. 'My word, Tom, how the advertising world has changed. Time was when you'd have been all too pleased to take any client's shilling, regardless of what they did.' He gave Tom a nasty grin. 'Who'd've thought that advertising would suddenly develop a conscience?'

'Well, Frank, that's how it is in the twenty-first century. At least at SHM. We only work for ethical clients, and ESG marketing is at the centre of every campaign we run. And–'

Georgia interrupted her brother-in-law, 'Give it a rest, Tom. If I'd wanted a sermon, I'd've gone to church this morning.'

'Hang on,' joined in Lizzie, passing Theo to her mother. 'Tom's quite right–'

'But, Dad's not done anything–'

'Let me finish, George. Tom's right. I'm not at all keen on having nuclear power, and neither is Scotland or Germany for that matter. But it doesn't make Dad some sort of hypocrite either. He's just painting a few bloody murals, for God's sake.'

Tom cut up a potato sullenly, while Louise returned Theo to Lizzie and said, 'Well said, darling. So perhaps we can now enjoy our Sunday lunch together. Yes? Boys?'

Tom and Frank nodded their agreement, unaware that a distant organisation they knew little about would bring them together again in quite different circumstances.

2

A dirty sun hung over west London, criss-crossed by the vapour trails of aircraft coming to and going from Heathrow. It was going to be a humid day, and the workmen had already begun installing the concrete bollards to create what the local authority were calling a low traffic neighbourhood. The noise was even permeating the house's triple glazing. It was also going to mean a long detour to get to Sainsbury's for the weekly shopping.

Gerald Graham got up early these days. It was not just a function of late middle age, but had become a necessity, so that he could be sure of intercepting the post. After weeks of waiting, the brown envelope arrived with the news he had both expected and dreaded. The cough that persisted long after the pandemic and tests had shown it to be wholly unrelated to COVID had prompted him to see the GP. Gerald didn't tell his wife about having to have a scan, or what the doctor had said might be the implications of a worst case scenario. But, even before the letter confirmed it, he had made up his mind to refuse any kind of treatment. After all, these days, what was the point?

Gerald looked around the sitting room of his cosy semi in Ealing and grimaced as his wife placed the floral Royal Doulton cup and saucer on the side table next to his armchair, where he sat in cavalry twills, a tattersall check shirt and a tie adorned with pheasants. Betty sat opposite him in housecoat and pinny, smiling hopefully, though Gerald was at a loss to know what she might have been hoping for. Then, when no response came from her husband, she got up with a small sigh and went to mop the kitchen floor. God knows what she does with her time these days, Gerald thought, as he remembered her as the girl who could party all night and whose once blonde curls and Shrimptonesque figure had attracted the attention of more than one minor rock star.

The square unframed painting, a series of rough horizontal bands in acid reds and yellows, that hung incongruously above the tiled mantlepiece reminded him every day of what a reviewer had described as his "unrealised promise". The rest of his earlier work had been sold, apart from a handful of small sketches that languished in the attic. Betty once said she liked it, that last reminder of his more successful days, but Gerald had no idea what it was she could possibly have liked about it, and could barely remember what had prompted him to paint it. He kept thinking of taking it down, yet had never got round to it.

No-one was quite sure when the Damascene moment came, but the timing made most put it down to his daughter Andrea's fatal experiments with heroin. In the eighties, Gerald was the firebrand, the painter whose huge, dramatic canvases teetered between moody landscapes and wild abstracts. That was all in the past, and his output no longer attracted the attention of the art press: big game in the jungle, wartime scenes of Spitfires and Hurricanes, frigates and destroyers, tanks and artillery. At least Julian had stood by him, unlike some of the other galleries.

There were three elephants, two great big ones and a smaller one, framed by a bosky dell, more Bournemouth than Botswana. Gerald had been irked when Julian told him his paintings were valued by the number of elephants in them. Still, he thought, as he stood before the painting in the conservatory he used as a studio, at five hundred each it was easy enough money. He decided to take it round to the gallery in the morning as Betty called out from the kitchen that it would be fish fingers and fruit cobbler for tea.

After his breakfast, Gerald rang Martin's mobile. If he was working, Gerald knew he would be up early. Gerald and Martin had been the least close members of the group. Martin loathed Gerald's early work and his current output equally, but also disliked the older man's manner that could switch midsentence between condescending and bitter. Martin was surprised to hear from him, and even more so when Gerald asked if he could call round. Martin said he was too busy with work, but Gerald pressed him until he wearily gave in. The painting loaded into the Rover, Gerald drove across town to drop it off at Julian Furnell's gallery, tucked behind Lamb's Conduit Street, that a reviewer had once described as having a "certain, dingy charm that was worth making the journey from W1". The art dealer sat behind an incongruously vast and richly-carved desk, lit by a brothelish lamp with pink tassels and unconvincing Biedermeier base.

Julian's face, with folds a razor could not reach, appeared to have gone through the same process of being "distressed" as the burgundy leatherette captain's chair that enfolded him. Beneath his thinning hair, grey except for a more gingery lock that never let his forehead alone, Julian's eyelids were crenellated with skin tags. His long nose was accompanied by two moles on the left hand side, and sometimes by the half-moons on a lanyard that shuttled up and down between hair and chest. One and all would be greeted with the same genial, toothy smile.

From opening up at ten, often until gone six, the place was always busy, and every visitor, whether timewaster or prospective buyer, was handed a glass of wine – usually a middling Fitou – regardless of the hour.

Before the congestion charge forced them to take the train, Julian and his wife Joan went between their large, modern house in a leafy Hertfordshire suburb and The Snicket Gallery in an elderly Jaguar. He entertained their most valued customers extravagantly, taking them to long, drink-fuelled lunches. And Julian liked to show off his Rolex and the handmade shoes he bought exclusively, he insisted, from Crockett and Jones. If true, and Julian did spin some yarns, both watch and shoes were bought a good while ago.

Every month or two, Julian would hold a preview evening of the gallery's next exhibition, and his generous opening hours were extended further for the couple of dozen or so VIPs, as he liked to refer to the crowd that left him with dozens of empty bottles close to midnight. While Julian schmoozed his guests, beetling about with sheets of red and orange dots to stick on paintings that were sold or reserved, his wife Joan, moon-faced in loose, floor length robes, floated around the gallery with a bottle in each hand, topping up glasses without a word or any change in her expression.

'Bunch of tuskers for you,' called out Gerald cheerily.

Julian knew that his jibe about how to value Gerald's wildlife paintings had annoyed him and though no longer one of the more lucrative artists on his books, Julian treated him more kindly than most.

'Ah, good to see you, Gerald. Always glad to have a painting I know I won't have any trouble selling. Have you time for a glass?' Julian reached below the desk for a bottle.

'Sorry, Julian, another time. Must dash. But do let me know how you get on.'

Gerald wound his way through WC1 into EC1 to park in an NCP in St Cross Street. He dug out an old A to Z from the glovebox and traced the route to Martin's studio, a few hundred yards away in a narrow street behind Farringdon station. Gerald pressed the bell and heard Martin's voice echo foggily. The large, steel door opened with a slight click, and he made his way slowly up the stairs to the second floor. Pallid, with no sign of ever having needed to shave, Martin was still thin but early middle age had gifted him the beginnings of a pot belly. He let Gerald into the studio without a word. It was perfect, with good light and plenty of space, noted Gerald, enviously comparing it with the cramped conservatory where he worked. There were easels and racks along one side of the room, and two large tables in the middle, one with a mess of bottles and bric-a-brac, the other covered with an equally messy array of paint, brushes, pallet knives, jam jars and rags. It smelled like all artists' studios, a combination of linseed oil and damp.

'Like it?' asked Martin, seeing Gerald taking in the new studio.

'Well, it's a damned sight better than that place you used to have in Wapping or wherever it was. Don't know how you managed there. Hardly enough room to swing a cat.'

Wiping his hands on a rag and keen to get back to work, Martin asked, 'Anyway, now you're here, what can I do for you?'

'Oh, nothing really. Not having seen you for a while, the boys were just wondering how you were faring and, since I had to nip into town, I thought I'd just check that you're still in the land of the living.'

'Well, here I am.'

'And in fancy new digs too,' said Gerald, eager to find out how Martin was able to afford his new surroundings.

The kettle clicked and, irritated at knowing it would be rude not even to offer his visit a drink, Martin went over to put instant coffee into two Lorna Bailey mugs. Gerald was unable to detect the presence of any biscuits. 'Yes, well, I needed somewhere bigger, much bigger,' said Martin. 'And Dominic was left rather a lot of money. An aunt passed away...' Martin added vaguely.

'Lucky old Dominic, and lucky old you, for that matter.'

'Anyway, I simply had to find a new place. For one thing, there's the exhibition coming up, you see.'

'The exhibition...' Gerald began.

'Oh, sorry, yes, I should have explained,' Martin blew at his coffee. 'Yes, The Curzon have offered me what they're calling a retrospective. Well, retrospective isn't quite right, is it? After all, I'm still alive, aren't I? And there'll be quite a few new pieces too. It's less than a month away, but you know how I always take ages to finish anything, so I'm up against the clock with two that I want in the show.'

'Mind if I take a gander?'

Martin hated the way Gerald lapsed into old-fashioned slang. 'Well, I can spare a few minutes, I suppose.'

Gerald followed the younger man to the far wall, where he began carefully removing a dust cover from one of the pictures on the easels. Martin's paintings were painstakingly detailed and being painted on a white ground gave the colours an almost luminous quality. The first picture was of a young man in a harlequin costume against what looked like a backdrop of a window looking out onto the Thames. It was different from Martin's earlier work, but still recognisably his. Gerald looked at it closely and was about to ask what had led to him painting a harlequin, when his attention turned to the second, much larger painting that Martin was unveiling, of two men, naked and in a passionate embrace.

Much larger than the rest of the paintings in the studio, the large horizontal scene had a low viewpoint as if seen from the frayed rug that spread across the foreground. It was lit diagonally from a skylight that emphasised the faces of the two men. They were holding each other closely on a shining Chesterfield before a faint, but still discernible background with a half-completed portrait on an easel, a huge aspidistra, and a shelf lined with wine bottles.

It took Gerald a moment or two to return to his usual smooth, sardonic self. 'My, what a naughty boy you've been. Or, should I say, you've both been.'

'I hardly think that's fair. Still, it's the sort of thing you would say, isn't it?' bridled Martin.

'Now, now, calm down, dear,' said Gerald his demeanour fully-restored. 'It's only my little joke. Anyway, for what it's worth, I think it's really rather good.'

'Really? I don't imagine for a moment that it's to your taste.'

'Thank you, Martin, I do happen to recognise a decent painting when I see one. Even if decent isn't quite the right word in the circumstances.'

'It isn't finished yet. I need to sort out the foreground...'

'Looks fine and dandy to me.'

'No, look. I'm not sure about that bit where the rug finishes.'

They studied at the painting closely until Martin broke the silence. 'I've called it *The Art Lovers*. It's of–'

'Don't be silly, of course I know who it's of. Must have been a while ago, mind.'

'We took a photograph, you see. It was at The Slade…'

'Oh, that's very naughty indeed,' smirked Gerald.

'It wasn't *at* The Slade.'

Gerald peered at the painting. 'No, of course not. I think I recognise the place. The flat he used to have in Bayswater, if I'm not mistaken.'

Martin nodded.

'Well, of course there'll be ructions, if you're going to show it, that is.'

'Of course I'm showing it. Jane McNab wants it in the exhibition.'

'Good for Mother McNab. But I suppose you'd better be prepared for some flak, hadn't you?'

'It is 2024, Gerald.'

'And some of us won't see seventy again.'

Martin led the way to a couple of plastic chairs. He sat down heavily while Gerald stood. 'You think he'll be very cross?'

It took Gerald just a few seconds to see the advantages that might come from changing his mind about the picture. He rescued his coffee from a window ledge. 'No, I don't suppose he will. It's just that I was a bit taken aback. Sorry, not getting any younger. Oh, he might huff and puff a bit, but I'm sure it'll all blow over and you'll be pals again soon enough.'

'Really?'

'Sure as eggs is eggs. Don't worry about it.'

Martin had become less sure, but gave a tentative nod before saying, 'I don't know. Maybe I shouldn't include it if there's going to be trouble.'

'Look, if Ma McNab wants it, she must think it's worth showing. After all, it's her gallery.'

'I suppose so.'

'Anyway, you don't want to let her down if she's expecting it. Need to tread very carefully, laddie, in our dealings with the likes of Mother McNab, you know.'

'Oh, Lord, I hadn't thought of that.'

'Incidentally, what's she asking for it?'

'She thought five or six would be about right, I think.'

'Not bad, so you don't want to chuck that down the khazi, now, do you?' Gerald thought of the paltry five hundred he got per elephant. 'Less her usual percentage, I suppose?'

'Well, of course, but I can never remember exactly how much she charges.'

Gerald envied and marvelled at Martin's lack of interest in money. 'And, anyway, we don't just paint for the hell of it, do we? I know I don't,' he added bitterly. 'We've all got to earn a crust, even you. Stopping you from doing that amounts to nothing less than restriction of trade. So, show the thing, and stop worrying.'

'If you're sure.'

Gerald looked at his watch. 'Of course I am. Now, look, I'd better be on my way or it's another tenner for the car park. But, if you're bothered, by all means give me a tinkle.'

'Thanks, Gerald. Sorry about what I said before.'

'Forgotten already, don't give it a second thought.'

Gerald was at the door when a thought occurred to him. It was a long time since he had called in at The

Curzon. 'Do I need an invitation to come along to the preview?'

'I don't know. I suppose so,' said Martin absently. Then, taking the hint, added, 'Sorry, sorry, of course. Just a mo.'

Despite having to walk no more than a few yards into the studio, he returned sounding breathless, 'Here we are. Have a couple.' It was a small A5 booklet, with a price list of the paintings in the exhibition.

Gerald left Martin with a disconcertingly over-merry 'Cheery bye', and headed back to his Rover with a growing grin. Driving home, he wondered whether or not to tell Frank about the painting. They were known as the best of friends and had been each other's best man, appearing to turn on its head that saying about who one should keep the closer. Yet, their relationship endured or perhaps thrived on carefully balanced envies. Frank was envious of the critical acclaim Gerald's early work attracted and the confident suaveness that lasted even after his recent paintings became dismissed as little more than potboilers. Gerald, on the other hand, latterly envied Frank's RA, and his recognition among the rich and famous. There was another envy he had, which he was especially careful not to reveal. But back then, it was just a time when people were forever changing partners.

Each man knew why he envied the other, but had no idea why they were envied in return. Two overheard conversations, though, made both more wary and perhaps indicated the saying was right after all, that they needed to keep each other closer than the rest of their friends in the group. First, Frank was hurt at hearing Gerald say to Max that he simply couldn't understand what Louise was doing married to an oaf. Then, some years later as Gerald made his transition from abstract to commercial artist, he heard a drunken Frank saying to Julian Furnell that his more recent work was crap but, since his earlier paintings were too, he couldn't really blame anything on the death of his daughter.

By the time he had reached Shepherd's Bush, Gerald decided to pull up in a supermarket carpark. Gulls bore down on the remains of a sandwich, and a group of teenage boys lumped across the tarmac alternating between scoffing doughnuts and pastry-based snacks, and aiming kicks at each other. The drive had tired him, but an idea had occurred to him as he crossed town.

After a long coughing fit, he called Martin. 'Sorry to take you away from your labours again, but I've been thinking.'

'So've I.'

'Oh yes? Go on.'

'No, you first. You called me.'

'Well, since you were worried about the painting causing a bit of a to-do, I thought it might be helpful to have a chat with Frank about it. Thought I might be able to pour a spot of oil on troubled waters, that sort of thing.'

'That's funny.'

'Yes?'

'Yes. That's exactly what I was thinking, but I wasn't sure you'd be willing to do that. You are old friends, after all, aren't you?'

'Of course I'd be happy to do that, Martin. Any time.'

'That's so kind of you, Gerald. I really am very grateful.'

'Not at all. Think nothing of it.' Barely able to suppress a guffaw, Gerald quickly ended the call, then, in a spirit of what some might have regarded as friendship, he rang Frank.

'Busy with the brushes, Frank?' he began breezily.

'Always busy, Gerald. Clients, deadlines and all that, you know how it is,' Frank replied, putting down the Burlington Magazine next to his mug of tea and plate of chocolate digestives.

'Ah, that's a pity. Just been to see young Martin, you see. There's something I really think you could do with knowing before anyone else hears about it.'

'And what might that be?' asked Frank, his curiosity pricked.

'Well, if you're too busy…' Gerald was reeling his man in. He knew Frank could never resist gossip of any kind.

'No, just rather betwixt and between things right now, but do tell me.'

'Hmm, I'm afraid it's a rather delicate matter. Far better to have a chinwag man to man, I'd say. Look, it's still just about lunchtime. What say you we meet for a snifter at The Duke of York? I could pop over in about half an hour.'

With Frank well and truly hooked, Gerald set off through Hammersmith, speculating on what might be the reaction to the news he was about to impart. After a long search before finding a space just off Lower Richmond Road, Gerald arrived at the pub after Frank and found him on the empty terrace, smoking a small cigar.

'Good idea,' he greeted Frank heartily. 'More discreet out here.'

He went to get the drinks and left Frank wondering why they needed to be discreet.

'So, how is my former pupil? Thriving?'

'Oh yes, he's in the pink all right. Oops,' chuckled Gerald. 'Any chance I could scrounge one of your cheroots?'

'You don't smoke these days.'

'Well, the odd one doesn't do any harm now, does it?' he helped himself from the proffered tin.

'Now, Gerald, what's this all about?'

Trying his best to appear reluctant, Gerald fiddled with his moustache for a moment. 'Well, as I said when I rang, it is rather delicate, you see.'

'No, I'm afraid I don't see. Now, come on, it's not like you to be so coy.'

'All right then. Well, the lad has an exhibition in the offing with Mother McNab. And, well, he showed me some of the things he's been working on and…'

'Yes? Oh, do get on with it, Gerald.'

Gerald looked around the terrace, exaggeratedly checking they were on their own, then leaned forward and almost whispered, 'One of them is rather, shall we say, revealing.'

'Revealing?'

'Yes. It's of the two of you. Back when the pair of you were at The Slade.'

'Well, what's all this cloak and dagger routine about? I think it's charming of him to remember his old tutor.'

'You won't when you see it, I can promise you that.'

'Eh?'

'No, Frank. The thing is, you're both starkers.'

'What? Surely not.'

'I'm afraid so.'

'No! Starkers, really?'

'Mm. Having a bit of a cuddle, too.'

'Oh no. What is he trying to do to me?' Struggling

with the breeze off the river, Frank lit up another small cigar. 'He can't possibly show it. It would ruin me. My clients…'

'Not to mention The Slade…'

'How could he? And what does he hope to achieve by humiliating me like this? He mustn't, he really mustn't.'

Gerald nodded sombrely. 'Of course, you're quite right. I did try to talk him out of it.'

Frank breathed heavily, 'Thanks, Gerald, that was good of you.' He squinted as the cigar smoke went in his eye. 'So, what did he say to that?'

Despite knowing almost nothing about Martin, Gerald replied, 'Well, you know what the lad's like when he's made up his mind about something.'

'I see.' After a pause, Frank continued, 'Yes, there's no alternative.'

'No alternative to what?'

'It's obvious. I shall have to beard him in his lair. I cannot possibly allow him to show this painting.'

'He's called it *The Art Lovers*.'

'Oh, good God. Right then, tomorrow morning, I will make him see the error of his ways.'

'Hadn't thought fisticuffs were quite your style, Frank.'

'Oh no, I shall rely utterly on nothing more than my own sweet reason.'

It was an attribute that neither Gerald nor any of Frank's friends and family had ever recognised in him. 'Well, if you say so.

'Wasn't there something about him moving to a new studio? I suppose you'd better let me have his address.'

Gerald restrained his eagerness, knowing reluctance would make everything he said more plausible, 'Well, if you're sure about it…'

'My mind is made up.'

'Oh well, I'll scribble it down for you. Now, if there's anything else I can do to help, old boy, just say the word.'

'Of course, and I really am most grateful to you, Gerald.'

He pulled on his string-backed driving gloves and set off for Ealing, while Frank mooched up the slope towards home, remembering that Louise was out and that there was the remains of a chocolate cake in a cupboard somewhere. Heading over Putney Bridge, Gerald said aloud, 'They'll both be hopping about like mad. Wonder what they'll do next?'

Back in Exmoor Gardens, Frank was disconcerted to find Louise's car in the drive. Her reading group postponed meant that so was the possibility of any cake for him. He went across the back garden, having to push aside the climbing rose that all but barred the door to his studio, and sat on an old Windsor chair that was missing more than a couple of spindles. The cobwebs that masked the windows and the damp patch that had spread across the ceiling were ignored as Frank set his mind to deciding what to do about Martin. There was an old cigar box in the cavity behind the bottom drawer of the filing cabinet that housed Frank's sketchbooks. He hauled himself out of the chair, and reached for the box. There had been photographs, letters too, but Frank had destroyed them before the children were born. Still, it didn't hurt to check. He was relieved to find the box was empty, and went back to thinking about Martin.

What if sweet reason on its own were not enough? Oh, he had said that to Gerald confidently enough, but he couldn't help doubting the likelihood of its success. There was money, of course, and Martin took so long over his paintings that he never seemed to make anything like enough to live on. But hadn't Gerald or one of the others mentioned that Martin's husband had come into money? *If the blasted painting were to go in the exhibition, then the only thing to do would be to go away for a while.* He could stay up in Cumbria to paint the murals for the Net Zero Observatory. *That was the answer.* But he couldn't stay there forever. What would happen when he had to come back to London? He scrubbed the idea.

Frank tried desperately to think of something, anything, that he had that Martin might want. Nothing came to mind. He found a flask in a drawer which still had a drop of brandy in it. He swigged a mouthful and then it came to him. That was it, he would buy the painting from him.

While Betty polished a pair of EPNS candlesticks, Gerald sat in the conservatory where half a leopard – or was is a jaguar? – eyed him coldly. He went over Frank's options, and came to a similar conclusion. Frank would have to buy the painting. Yes, it would cost him a few bob, but Frank was far from short of money. If the painting weren't to appear in the exhibition, Gerald suddenly realised, then that was that, he'd have been wasting his time. No, he needed to do something, and that was make a call to Jane McNab.

Everyone knew Jane. She had run The Curzon since the seventies, inheriting from her father what had been a dusty antique shop. The gallery had indeed once been in Mayfair, not exactly on Curzon Street but just at the entrance to Shepherd Market, so close enough. In its heyday, Jane McNab sold paintings to the most fashionable clientele, but spiralling rent forced her to move. It had kept the name, but was now in a less salubrious part of Fitzrovia, just off Cleveland Street, that was still awaiting gentrification. It was in a former ironmonger's, wedged between a Greek restaurant and a nail bar. Jane was now in her mid-seventies, but still a beauty, defiantly grey hair wrapped in a French pleat above the profile that had appeared in painting after painting by her admirers in the second generation of the Euston Road School.

It was a good many years since they had last met and Gerald thought Jane had probably forgotten him. He had been hurt when she refused to show a pair of his paintings for a mixed exhibition of contemporary British artists, soon after turning his back on abstraction. He was glad to have been too upset to confront her at the time, since he certainly did not want her to remember him now. 'Two birds with one stone,' he said to himself with a mirthless smirk at the big cat on the easel.

Gerald's wristwatch read almost five o'clock. The Curzon would still be open, but he was tired after the day's adventures, and the phone call could wait. In any case, he wanted to prepare for it. Walking stiffly to the bookcase, he plucked out a monograph on d'Hondecoeter, and took it back to his rattan chair and table that looked for all the world as if Gerald had tried to recreate the last days of the raj in west London. He skimmed through the plates, each one an avian slaughterhouse for a blood-lusting aristocracy. The leopard or jaguar or whatever it was could wait, he suddenly liked the idea of painting a brace of inedibly old and butchered fowl, even if dead birds would probably only fetch a couple of hundred quid for the pair. He knew Frank was always a late riser, having heard him say on many occasions that he never did anything before eleven, so a call to Jane McNab at ten would be well before Frank went to see Martin, assuming nothing in the meantime changed his or Frank's mind.

Checking that Louise was in the drawing room, Frank went into the bedroom and picked up the extension. Gerald was not entirely surprised to get the call, but could barely hear him.

'Frank, you'll have to speak up, it's a dreadful line.'

'I said, how much does he want for it?,' hissed Frank.

'How much he wants for the picture, d'you say?'

'Yes. How much?'

'Oh, I don't know. But I think he mentioned that Jane McNab would be pitching it at about five or six. Something along those lines, but why...'

Frank ended the call before Gerald could finish the question, hearing Louise's footsteps on the stairs. It didn't matter to Gerald; he had guessed correctly what Frank would do. The bedroom door opened.

'Did I hear you on the phone to someone?' asked Louise.

'Oh, just Gerald. He was going round to see Martin today.'

Apparently satisfied, Louise went off to tidy up what looked set to become a spare room since Georgia was hardly ever at home these days, although she still managed to create havoc in just a single night there.

Frank pulled his cheque book out of a drawer. Knowing that, after Jane McNab's commission, Martin would be left with about two and a half thousand, at least Frank wouldn't have to offer him the full five or six thousand. But Frank kept just a couple of thousand in his current account. He would need to transfer funds from the joint account, or maybe the business account, but how to do it without Louise finding out? She kept a close eye on the money, handling all the invoices. Frank wondered if Martin would be willing to let him pay for the painting in instalments, that would be easier to sneak through. If not, perhaps Gerald would give him a loan. Still, it irked Frank to have to hand over all that money to someone who appeared to be going out of his way to ruin him.

Then again, what if Martin refused to sell him the picture? The thought preyed on Frank's mind. So far, he had no alternative scheme. The only other possibilities were simply too embarrassing to contemplate. Frank had thought of calling his brother, the QC, to see if his legal mind might come up with something, but he quickly discounted the idea, knowing how Robert would react. After the initial disapproval would follow a lifetime of jibes and knowing glances. Of course, he could go to another lawyer, but how on earth would he cover up the heavy costs involved?

He was taciturn over dinner and seemed distracted, but Louise merely put it down to Frank being in one of his "funny moods". He went over and over what he would say to Martin in the morning, sweet reason swiftly giving way to fury. Not being allowed a second drop of Scotch did not improve his humour. For once, Frank didn't sleep well that night. When, at last, he drifted off, it was just before Louise, disturbed by his tossing and turning, got up to make coffee for herself.

In the heavy sleep of early morning, he saw a group of stone figures slowly emerge and recognised it as the Laocoön, except that Frank himself was Laocoön, and the two other figures were Martin and Tom, his son-in-law.

To his horror, he found the serpent that was about to set its fangs in his side had Martin's head, too. The marmoreal scene then evaporated into thick, grey clouds of smoke rising above him. Looking down, Frank was surprised to see he was a small boy wearing shorts and a sailor suit, standing on a blazing tower that overlooked the sea.

Over strong Assam in a Spode cup and a bowl of granola, Jane McNab looked out over central London from her small, tidy flat in Belsize Park. After all her years of selling paintings, she understood better than most how temperamental artists could be, from raging tempers to plummeting depths of despair. She had learned to be phlegmatic, firmly of the belief that worrying about them could achieve nothing. And yet, this morning something troubled her. Martin Robertson was a lamb compared to some of the other artists on her books, but he took so long to finish his paintings, seeming to agonise over every brushstroke. When she called him earlier in the week to find out how he was getting on, Jane could not help feeling anything but reassured when Martin told her that, with a bit of luck, they should be ready on time.

She sighed, and washed the cup and saucer by hand. In a short, cream raincoat and carrying a slim leather briefcase that doubled as a handbag, Jane made her way to the Tube station. After five stops on the Northern Line, every day she made minor variations to the route that led to The Curzon, yet always remained under the looming bulk of the BT Tower. While most people found the unloved and long-disused tower an oppressive presence, Jane saw it more as a gentle giant that watched over her. She liked it best of all in the evenings, when its red eyes shone through the growing dark, as if to light her way.

The gallery wouldn't open for another hour, Jane had long determined that there was no point opening before ten. It was a peaceful time, for planning and getting some paperwork done, before Chloe arrived with complaints about her partner or hints about a pay rise. In her office at the back of The Curzon, she checked the bank account. Martin really did need to come up with the goods; sales over the last few months had been patchy at best. Jane took a turn round the gallery and looked at the few red dots, no more than half a dozen, placed on the canvases that had been sold. The shop bell rang and there was a clunk at the door as Chloe, her assistant, walked in with her rucksack, earbuds and a litre water bottle in her hand.

'Bonnie still won't let us have a cat,' she grumbled, as Jane switched on the track lighting.

Before Chloe could get into her stride, Jane was relieved to hear the phone ring, and quickly retreated to her office.

'This is The Curzon Gallery?' an imperious yet strangely high-pitched voice demanded.

'It is…'

Before Jane could finish, the voice continued, 'I thought you were in Mayfair.'

'Oh, that was some years ago. We've moved since then.'

'I see.' The response seemed needlessly icy.

'May I help you?'

'Indeed. I understand you'll shortly be holding an exhibition of paintings by Martin Robertson, is that right?'

'Yes, quite right.'

'And you haven't sold any yet?'

'No, nothing. We seldom sell anything before the exhibition opens.'

'I'm glad to hear it. Now, my employer has seen a list of works for sale, and there is one he is interested in acquiring.'

'May I ask which one?'

'The title of the painting is *The Art Lovers*.'

'And your employer wishes to buy it?'

'That is what I said.'

'But doesn't he wish to see it first?'

'Oh no, that won't be necessary. If you will please reserve it, I shall arrange for your remuneration once the exhibition opens as I have been charged with inspecting the painting before payment is made. I take it that is acceptable to you?'

It was not the first time Jane had been asked to reserve a painting unseen, but not for a good many years. She withheld her surprise at the request. 'Yes, perfectly acceptable. And, so that I can make a note of it, your employer's name is…'

'I'm afraid I cannot divulge that. My employer is a very private man.'

'I see.' Jane had also sold numerous paintings to intermediaries on behalf of individuals who wished to avoid being known, but had been let down on too many occasions by buyers who backed out. An advance sale was extremely tempting, but years of experience had taught Jane to be wary. 'The painting is listed at five thousand five hundred–' she began.

'I am aware of that. And I daresay you are wondering about the possibility of our giving back word with regard to the sale. Yes?'

Jane had not expected that. 'Ahm, well, it can

sometimes happen.'

'Of course. My employer is a generous man. He is willing to offer more than the asking price in order to secure it. And if, for any reason, it is decided not to proceed with the acquisition, then you are naturally at liberty to make it available immediately. I am sure you understand.'

Jane was not sure that she did entirely. 'Perhaps you could tell me how much your employer is willing to pay?'

'I am instructed to offer six thousand five hundred pounds.'

Jane considered the position and decided that the opportunity of an extra thousand pounds more than outweighed the risk. While the preview night was always the best time to sell a picture, when the gallery was full of people, if the sale fell through, she would still have the painting.

'That would be fine,' she said at last, 'Mister…?'

'Melchior. M E L C H I O R,' Gerald spelled it out. 'Thank you. I look forward to seeing the painting the day after the opening night.' Wheezing heavily, Gerald put the phone down. 'Should get a bloody Oscar for that,' he said to himself. He felt cold, but still needed to wipe the sweat from his forehead. Betty put her head round the door to the conservatory, curious to know who her husband had been speaking to. She had heard him on the phone while she was dusting the dining room and yet it hadn't sounded like Gerald. *Perhaps he's coming down with something*, thought Betty.

In the gallery, Jane wondered who Mister Melchior's employer might be and why he was so keen to buy *The Art Lovers*.

But, whoever he was, if indeed he really existed, a sale would be very welcome. She realised that another call to Martin was unavoidable. As it turned out, Martin was to call her first.

3.

After his restless night, Frank woke in tangle of sheets, with sweat pouring off him. He turned to look at the alarm clock and groaned at seeing the green numerals indicate it was gone eight. At length, he dragged himself out of bed and made his way unsteadily to the shower. Barely refreshed, he picked out a pinstripe suit and white shirt, then added a crimson bow tie, before replacing it with a navy blue polka dot tie. Dressed and in need of tea and breakfast, he went downstairs to find Louise chatting with Georgia.

Looking at the clock on the mantelpiece, Louise exclaimed with a chuckle, 'My goodness! What are you doing here? I can't remember the last time you surfaced before ten.'

Frank ignored her and went into the kitchen.

Georgia giggled, 'Looks like Dad has been in the dressing up box again.'

'I haven't seen him in that suit for donkey's years,' said Louise with a baffled shake of the head.

When Frank returned with a mug of tea and slices of toast spread with Patum Peperium, Louise asked, 'Now, Frank, all dressed up and barely nine o'clock. I think we deserve an explanation.'

'An explanation?' said Frank through a mouthful of crumbs.

'Yes, darling, what are we supposed to make of this extraordinary behaviour?'

'Oh, very droll,' said Frank pettishly. 'I am often up with the lark, thank you very much. Anyway, after a lifetime of hard graft, how can anyone begrudge me an occasional lie-in?'

Louise got up and gave her husband a kiss. 'We're only teasing, darling. No need to take it to heart. It's just unusual to see you up and about so early.'

'Come on, Dad, spill. We want to know what's with the suit,' pressed Georgia.

'I have some business to attend to in town,' said Frank airily.

Louise looked at him quizzically. 'You never said anything about that.'

Irritated at having backed himself into a corner, Frank tried to think quickly, 'I thought I'd pop into the RA. It's always as well to let them know one's still alive, you know.' Then he added hastily, remembering it was something Louise had been on at him about, 'Oh, and I thought I'd call in on young Martin. I ought to see his new studio.'

'Well, it's about time. You have rather neglected him, you know.'

Rather than protest, Frank finished his toast in silence, relieved that he had managed to deflect Louise from asking any more questions.

It was almost ten by the time Frank was ready to leave.

'What's the old man up to, d'you think?' asked Georgia as the front door closed.

Louise shrugged, 'He has been rather mysterious lately, hasn't he? I'm afraid your guess is as good as mine.'

Frank finished a small cigar by the time he reached the Tube station. To his relief, it was quiet, the rush hour all but over, though he still chose to hide behind his copy of The Telegraph. He felt a pang of guilt as the train left Earls Court, where he would have had to change platforms were he to pop in to the RA as he had said. He remained oblivious to the comings and goings before alighting at Edgware Road and transferring to the Circle Line for Farringdon. He treated himself to a bacon sandwich at a café by the station and went over Gerald's instructions as to how to find Martin's studio. A howling wind had got up and eddies of litter skittered around Frank as he peered at the street sign.

When the bell rang, all Martin could see on the screen of the entry phone was a collar and tie, then he heard a voice he knew well.

'Hello, hello. Anyone there?' there was a pause. Then it continued, 'How do these bloody things work?'

The morning hadn't begun well for him. Martin had been struggling to finish his last two paintings, and now he was more agitated than ever. What if he pretended to be out? But the bell ran insistently.

'Come on, Martin, open up. It's blowing a gale out here.'

Martin tentatively pressed the button to let Frank in. With a wholly unnecessary swirl of his mac, like an elderly and clumsy matador, Frank finally draped it over a chair and looked sharply at his former pupil.

'Would you like a cup of coffee?' asked Martin meekly.

'No thank you, Martin. There is a matter that we need to resolve first,' said Frank haughtily.

'Oh yes?'

'Yes, Martin. I need you to promise me something.' Frank strode past Martin to where *The Art Lovers* stood on its easel. With his hands on his hips, he looked at the painting with growing discomfort, leaning on a chair back to steady himself.

Trying to remain calm, Frank continued, 'You cannot, must not put that... that painting in your exhibition. Do you understand?'

'But I have already promised to–'

'Never mind that. I cannot let you exhibit it, and that's final. Now, to business.' Frank clapped his hands together.

'Business?'

'Yes. Now, as you very well know, I am not an unreasonable man, and I daresay we can come to an agreement about this.'

Martin looked at Frank silently, starting to find this side of his former tutor more menacing than one of his angry outbursts.

'I am prepared to buy this painting from you so that it will never be seen in public,' said Frank grandly. 'I can offer you three thousand pounds. And that's more than you'd get from La McNab if someone is foolish enough to purchase it from her.'

Martin stiffened. 'No, that's not enough.'

'Well, I believe I am being more than generous. But tell me how much you do want.'

'You make it sound like blackmail,' said Martin furiously.

'Don't be absurd. Everyone has their price. Even you.' Frank said nastily. His attempt at sweet reason had barely lasted five minutes.

'Well, I don't. And it isn't about the money.'

'What on earth do you mean?' Frank was astonished. 'All right then, what will it take for you to withdraw the painting from the exhibition?'

Martin sank into a chair wearily. He'd known that, despite Gerald's assurances, Frank would be livid. He hated arguments and Frank was an old and special friend.

At last, he spoke quietly. 'All right, I will sell you the painting, but with one condition.'

'Name it,' snapped Frank.

'I want you to tell Louise about us.'

'Us?'

'Yes. That we had been lovers.'

'Lovers! We were nothing of the sort. It was just a fling, a dalliance, or–'

'Frank, you told me you loved me.'

'Don't be absurd. I said nothing of the kind.'

'I assure you, you did.'

'Well, even if I did, it doesn't mean we were lovers as such. All right, yes, perhaps I did say that. But I never said I was in love with you. There is a difference.'

'Sophistry, Frank, nothing more to it than that,' sniffed Martin. 'You and I were lovers, and that's that.'

'But–'

'I want you to tell Louise that we had been lovers. I think she'd be impressed by your openness. And we were lovers, there's no denying it. And this is my tribute to one of my very first lovers.'

'You can't expect me to tell her that.'

'I can and I do.'

'Oh no, you're outing me!'

Martin shrugged, 'I'm not outing you, I just want you to be honest with yourself. Take it or leave it. Never mind the money. A thousand will be enough. Tell Louise and you can have it, or the picture's going in the show.'

Frank stomped out of the studio and retraced his steps to Farringdon station. The Telegraph stayed unopened on his lap as he pondered on what to do. *Max was completely wrong*, he said to himself, *there is such a thing as bad PR*, and he would be a laughing stock if that painting ever saw the light of day. At Baker Street, two young men got on the train, holding hands. They sat opposite Frank and he was momentarily taken aback as one of them grinned at him. He wondered if the young man had picked up some kind of signal from him. Frank shook off the idea, dismissing it as nonsense, straightened his tie, and brushed cigar ash from his mac. While he waited for the train to Putney, Frank rang Gerald, but Betty told him her husband was out. He tried Doug and was relieved to hear his Wearside accent.

It was gone one o'clock by the time he reached Doug's untidy flat off Fulham High Street. His friend cleared a pile of old newspapers from a sofa for Frank to sit down. Doug had been a widower for most of a decade and had thought, on many occasions, of returning to his native Peterlee but, on reflecting that there was hardly anyone left up there who might still know him, stayed put.

'So, what's to do, Frank? You sounded proper bothered on the phone.'

Frank leaned forward, and the sofa creaked sympathetically. 'I most certainly am bothered, Douglas.'

'Well, d'you want to talk about it over a few jars?'

Ordinarily, he'd have welcomed the idea of going for a drink, but he decided the privacy of Doug's sitting room was more important. Frank shook his head. 'Not this time, if you don't mind. Something's, ahm, come up.'

Frank told Doug about meeting Gerald, and his own visit to Martin's studio that morning, then asked, 'So, what the hell am I going to do?'

Doug looked at his friend curiously, 'Well, I knew you and the lad were always rather matey, but I didn't realise…'

'We were very young. I suppose I was curious, but there really was nothing more than that.'

'I suppose so. Different times, and all that.'

'But what am I to do?'

Doug wiped some paint off his jumper with a rag before replying, 'Want me to go and see the lad?'

Frank took a deep breath, 'I don't know. What would you say to him?'

'I might find a way, you know, man to man, like.'

'He seemed pretty adamant.'

'Well then, it looks like your options are pretty limited, mate.'

'So…'

'So, I reckon you'll just have to tell her and hope for the best.'

'She'll hit the roof, you know. I just know she will.'

'Now, Frank, it was all a long time ago. Throw yourself on her mercy. Take flowers, chocolates, you know, something to sweeten the pill.'

'She'll see right through that.'

'Well, it's either that or Martin puts this picture of his in the show. My advice is just to bite the bullet. The sooner you do that, the sooner it's all behind you.'

'And my marriage will be, too.'

Back in his conservatory, after picking up a stack of pre-stretched canvases and the acrylics he now favoured, Gerald snapped the album shut as he heard Betty opening the door with his afternoon coffee. After she retreated to the sitting room, he opened it again, flipping past the black and whites, then blued photographs until he reached the one he was looking for. It was of Sean's wedding to Siobhan, the young artist looking uncomfortable in suit and tie, with the guests lined up outside a church somewhere in Kilburn.

All of The Duke of York crowd were there with their partners. There was a dark-haired woman almost a head taller than the other women in the shot. He had had a copy made of it years ago, but, discarding the rest of it, cut out the woman's head and kept it tucked away in his wallet. Gerald looked at her, then angrily closed the photo album, before opening it again and studying it for several minutes.

Frank's visit had rattled Martin. Even though he'd been unable to concentrate on finishing his paintings after Frank left, he knew he had to call Jane McNab, and that worried him, too. She was not going to be best pleased at having him withdraw *The Art Lovers* from the exhibition. Pacing up and down the studio didn't help so, finally, he picked up the phone.

'Jane? It's Martin. Martin Robertson.'

'I'm glad you rang, I was going to call you.'

'Well…'

'Those last paintings are nearly ready, I hope.'

'Ahm, not quite.'

'But you're making progress?'

'There's not much more to be done, but, the thing is…'

Jane detected the note in Martin's voice that meant there was a problem. 'But they will be ready in time, won't they?' she asked.

'Well, yes, I suppose so. But that's not what I'm ringing about.'

'What then?' She was alarmed now.

'It's just that I can't include *The Art Lovers* in the show, you see…'

Jane was astounded. 'What?'

'No, you see, someone's offered to buy it today.'

It was hardly the first time that Jane had had to deal with one of her artists wanting to sell their work themselves. She settled back on her office chair, summoning up her years of experience to ensure Martin would do as she told him. 'I see. Now that's a bit of a coincidence, Martin.'

'Oh yes?'

'You see, I've already promised it to someone else.'

'But you can't have, the exhibition hasn't opened. I mean, the picture isn't even finished yet…'

'I sell a good many paintings unseen,' exaggerated Jane. 'And my buyer made his offer yesterday, not today,' she lied reluctantly, 'so I am sure you'll agree that they should come first, shouldn't they?'

'Yes, but–'

'No buts, Martin, that's all there is to it. Now, you need to get it finished and round to me by the end of next week. Okay?' Jane was not a bully, but she ran a business and knew that that came before sentiment.

'Well. Yes, I–'

'Thanks for ringing, Martin.' Jane put the phone down, far from certain that her sale of *The Art Lovers* was guaranteed.

It was mid-afternoon by the time Frank, unable to face the Tube again, trudged glumly over Putney Bridge towards home, where he knew a half bottle of Picpoul in the fridge was waiting for him, but he stopped off at The Feathers first for a large Johnnie Walker. He rehearsed in his head a series of introductions and, on finding one that seemed to fit the bill, went over it again but quickly stopped as a young couple at the bar began to giggle as he mouthed the words silently. Frank thought about another, in case the girls were still at home, but knew he needed to be on top form for what he had to do. At the corner of Exmoor Gardens, he flicked what was left of his cigar into a grid.

He opened the front door quietly, as if returning from one of the drunken sessions of his younger days, instead of yelling 'Anyone at home?' as he usually did. He removed his hat, coat and stick, and gently opened the door to the drawing room. Louise had her feet up and was between dozing and reading the paper, but jumped up with a start when she saw Frank. 'Didn't hear you come in. Nice time?' she said, stifling an afternoon yawn.

'Hmm, yes,' replied Frank guardedly. 'Girls around?'

Missed Lizzie and Theo, I'm afraid, but Georgia's probably still at work, or galivanting somewhere. What time is it?' Louise paused, slightly curious. 'Something you want them for?'

'No, oh no, nothing like that. No,' said Frank. 'Have you got a minute, darling?'

Louise nodded sleepily. 'How was the RA? See anyone we know?'

'Eh?' Frank had momentarily forgotten the lie he'd told her. 'Oh, no. Change of plan.'

'Oh.' Louise was still coming to.

'I need a word…' Frank felt ridiculous, still standing in the middle of the room. He went across to join Louise on the sofa.

'What about?'

'You know I went to see Martin today?'

'Yes, of course. And about time too. I've been telling you– began Louise.

'I know, I know, darling, but…' Frank hesitated.

'What, then?'

'He's got an exhibition. The Curzon…'

57

'I know. You said.'

'Well, there'll be a few of his new works in it as well as some of the older stuff.' Frank had all but forgotten how he was going to broach what he needed to say. 'How about I get us a nice glass of something?'

'Now, Frank.'

'All right. Never mind. I just thought…'

'Oh, come on, you're like a cat on hot bricks, Frank. What on earth is the matter with you?'

Frank took a deep breath, ran a hand through his scraped back hair. 'I do love you, Louise.'

'And I love you too, Frank, but do get on with it, whatever it is.'

'I love you very much. I really do. I always have.' Frank began, not knowing whether to feel pleased or awkward as Louise reached across to hold his hand. 'I'm afraid there's no easy way to put this, darling, but one of Martin's new pieces is rather, ahm, compromising. Yes, well, compromising is perhaps not quite the–'

'Compromising?' Louise was fully awake now.

'It's a study of two nudes. Two men, you see. And one of them happens to be…'

'It's you? Really? Martin painted you in the nude? So, who was the other chap?'

'Ah, yes, he did. The other one is… Well, it's Martin.'

'You boys!' chuckled Louise. 'What larks you get up to! I assume it wasn't done recently?'

'Oh no, God forbid. It's from an old photo, back in the eighties.'

'Very risqué! And rather risky too, since you were his tutor back then.'

'Yes, well, that's one thing. But, you see, they're, ahm, they're embracing, too…'

'You and Martin are embracing each other?'

'Mmm.'

'Well, so what?'

'Yes, well, if he puts the damned thing in the exhibition, everyone will know it's me, won't they? And then, well…'

Louise shrugged.

'But, darling, can't you see, it would be beyond embarrassing for me?'

'Perhaps, perhaps not. Anyway, have you decided what to do about it?'

Frank exhaled loudly, then measured each word as carefully as if he were angry, 'Martin said that he would only leave the painting out of the exhibition if I told you that we were…'

'That you and he were lovers?'

'Oh no, we were never anything like that. It was just one of those things that happen. I mean, we'd probably both had lots to drink.'

'I see.'

'I'm so sorry, darling. It was before us, you know, but I simply couldn't risk telling you.'

'Oh, you are silly, Frank. Of course I knew there was something between the pair of you. It wasn't very difficult to put two and two together. I mean, it was obvious the way Martin used to look at you with those cow eyes, and how that always made you so uncomfortable.' But Louise did not say anything about the looks she got, thankful that Frank's friends were so self-absorbed as to be unobservant about such things, though she did wonder if Betty might have noticed something.

'Oh, Lou. You knew all along? So, do you forgive me then?'

'Of course I do, you idiot,' Louise leaned across and kissed her husband. 'And there really isn't anything to forgive.'

Frank returned the kiss, but Louise carried on, 'And, quite honestly, Frank, there are a good many things far worse than that that I've forgiven you for. You got horribly drunk at Daddy's funeral, for one, remember?' She smiled and gripped Frank's hand, while he gradually deflated with relief.

'Do you think any of the others know?' he asked at last.

'Maybe one or two of the girls. I don't know. But not the boys. You're always too busy showing off and trying to outdo each other.'

'I wouldn't mind a bloody drink now, you know.'

'And that's another thing, Frank.'

He smiled at Louise, and stroked a loose strand of hair that had made its way across her forehead.

'Oh, and by the way, he said we can have the painting for a thousand pounds too.'

Louise's expression appeared to cloud over. 'I see.'

Frank was puzzled by the sudden chill in the atmosphere. 'What?'

'Now, let me guess,' Louise began slowly. 'Gerald told you about the painting after he saw Martin yesterday, right? Hmm. So, that's why you went round to see him in such a hurry today. And you offered to buy it so that it wouldn't be in the exhibition, but Martin only agreed to let you have it if you told me that the two of you had been lovers…'

'I told you we were never lovers…'

'And so, you wouldn't have got round to telling me if it'd been just about the money. That's more like it, isn't it?'

'Well, I suppose so, but–'

'But you were horrified that people would see the picture, weren't you? Come on, admit it Frank, you know you are.'

'Well, it would be embarrassing, of course, but–' blustered Frank.

'So why else would you want to buy it, apart from wanting to avoid telling me about you and Martin, and making sure it didn't go on show? Honestly, the last thing you could possibly want would be to buy it, and have it here as a constant reminder.'

'I thought I'd just destroy it, or paint over it, that's all.'

'And throw a thousand pounds down the drain just to protect your vanity?'

'Oh, please don't let's argue, Lou.'

'Well, it would have helped if you'd told me the full story from the start.'

'I know I should've. I'm sorry. Truly, I am.'

Louise sighed, 'I just wish you'd been straight with me.'

Frank nodded, cursing himself for being so foolish mentioning the money. 'Stupid of me, I know. Sorry, Lou.'

'You're hopeless when it comes to stringing people along, you know. Georgia and I knew you were up to something this morning. All that silly nonsense about going to the RA, indeed.'

'But how?'

Not wishing to prolong the matter, Louise said, 'Never mind about that. Now, let's move on. But if you end up buying the blasted thing, it'll be a thousand pounds of your money, and not from the joint account. Okay?'

'Okay. Thank you, darling,' Frank breathed heavily. 'And it would be all right if I give Martin a ring to tell him that I, ahm, did what he asked?'

'Go on, Frank. Otherwise you'll only end up fretting all evening and being a complete pain.'

Frank took himself off to what he called the study, which was really just Louise's office, and rang Martin. It went straight to voicemail, which rather threw Frank.

'It's Frank, here. Frank Armstrong,' he began stiffly. 'I have done as you asked and spoken with Louise. So, I hope that's that.' He was about to finish the call, but added as an afterthought, 'Oh, yes, and if you need proof of that, you're welcome to ring her yourself. Right. I think that's everything.'

Frank slumped back in the chair then, hearing his wife go upstairs and run a bath, sneaked into the kitchen and poured himself a glass of wine. At least, he had done his part of the deal and, while not exactly happy to pay the thousand pounds Martin had asked for, he reasoned it would be worth it to protect his reputation.

After a long afternoon of childminding and glad that she had prised out the truth from Frank, Louise relaxed in the hot water. *Frank had been foolish because he'd panicked*, she told herself, *so there was little to be gained from staying cross with him over what was really nothing more than a silly attempt at deception*. Even so, she resolved to keep a close eye on what her husband chose to do next.

What Frank did might have surprised her. There had been a piece in the paper that morning about the Net Zero Observatory, and an interview with the minister. She justified it costing tens of millions by the number of young people it would attract to work on renewable energy projects, and be a place she described as a "world-leading centre of excellence". The journalist pressed her, saying that it was really just a PR stunt to promote nuclear power, since it was being paid for by the Nuclear Development Commission, but the minister insisted that, by attracting visitors and being used also as a conference centre, it would end up paying for itself. *More PR, eh?* mused Frank, *and spending millions on it to boot.* He rummaged in the pockets of the jacket he had been wearing when he met Julian Furnell, and found the crumpled brochure by for The Net Zero Observatory. He was due to meet them the following week and tried to imagine what they might be expecting from the murals he was due to paint. When no clear idea came to him, he picked out an atlas of the British Isles and turned the pages to Cumbria, looking fondly at the places he had been to as a boy. With everything that had gone on that morning, he decided there was perhaps something to be said for spending some time up there.

Across London, the light was fading and Bishopsgate had begun to fill up with people heading home. In his office at Sidwell, Hillier and Morrow, heavy-set and feeling too hot in his suit, Tom Wilson sat gloomily at his desk as Bobbi, his account executive broke the news that the Conch Telecom account was up for a re-pitch.

'What do they want to go and do that for?' he asked, hands supporting his bearded cheeks.

Bobbi leaned against the door jamb and shrugged. 'Just said they wanted a more traditional kind of campaign.'

'What do they mean by that?'

'All I know is they said they want more of a focus on their price points.'

'Don't they want to promote their environmental credentials? How else do we separate them from the pack? We told them that it was dead right for their demographic. It's all in the research.'

'I know, but they've got some new people in their comms team, so maybe…'

'I could really do without this right now,' Tom sighed. 'Still, I'd better ring them and find out what the hell's going on.'

'I don't mind doing that,' said Bobbi.

'No, they're my biggest client. You'd better leave it with me.'

Bobbi detached herself from the doorway and sauntered back to her desk as Yannick Morrow walked into Tom's office. He sat down opposite Tom, stretched out his long legs, revealing dark brown ankles and cream loafers without socks, and flicked his heavy black pony tail over the back of the chair. The youngest of the agency's main board directors, Yannick's star had risen rapidly since leaving a small agency in Belfast for London. He smiled at Tom and pushed a brochure across the desk. 'I think I've got something here that you're going to like,' he said.

Tom didn't need to pick it up to see that it was a brochure for the Net Zero Observatory.

'We're on the pitch list,' grinned Yannick. 'And, since you're the ESG lead, I think this one's for you.'

Tom nodded dumbly.

'What's up? I thought this sort of stuff was right up your street.' Yannick looked puzzled.

'No, yeah, of course, absolutely. Yeah, that's great,' Tom picked up the brochure and opened it, summoning up as much enthusiasm as he could muster.

'If you're sure.'

'Oh, yeah, sure. Sure I'm sure. Just had a few things

on my mind today.'

'Work or home? Anything you need from us?'

'No, no, it's fine. It'll all get sorted. No worries.'

'Good. Right, now pull in a couple of creatives and media buyers. We'll be getting eyes on the brief in a day or two while you get your team together. They say they're in a rush.' Yannick smiled. 'Hey, but don't all clients, right? But this is Government, so maybe they mean it. Anyhoo, we'll need the concepts Usained. Then we'll murder room them with the guys. Okay?'

'Sure, yes, thanks, Yannick. I'll get on to it.'

Yannick left Tom's office, not wholly convinced his account director was as enthused about the pitch as he had expected, or needed him to be. Conch Telecom were courteous, but adamant in insisting to Tom that the account had to be re-pitched. On the train home from Blackfriars to Denmark Hill, Tom thought glumly about his day, unable to decide whether it was worse having to fight to keep the Conch Telecom account or face the derision of his father-in-law about the possibility of him also working for the Net Zero Observatory. His mood did not improve when Lizzie informed him that her parents were coming round at the weekend to celebrate Polly's fourth birthday.

The surly ping of the microwave summoned Doug into the kitchen. He put the container onto a tin tray which bore a worn Sunderland FC logo, and took it into the sitting room where he placed it on the coffee table alongside a bottle of brown sauce and a half-full pint glass of brown ale. Despite blowing on his meal, it was still too hot, as it always was. He thought about the conversation he'd had with Frank, and wondered what

Gerald had discussed with Martin. Relations between Doug and Gerald had always been cordial, but both men were wary of each other. Doug was well aware of Gerald's sharp tongue, and Gerald knew that Doug had once been handy with his fists if someone irritated him, so a sort of détente existed between the two men that made them unusually observant of each other. Doug had long suspected Gerald of not being quite the best friend of Frank that everyone in the group imagined him to be. And, even if the others weren't aware of it, he certainly knew of one very good reason for that.

It was well past six by the time Martin closed the studio door and caught a bus to the tiny terraced house on the northern edge of Islington where he lived with his husband, Dominic. Head of department at a north London comprehensive school, Dominic sat at the kitchen table surrounded by piles of papers and a red striped water bottle, his tall, thin frame hunched up into an S shape and a pair of round, steel-framed glasses rested on the top of his bald head.

'I've a ton of marking to do, so dinner won't be for a while,' said Dominic, poring over his year eight's maths homework, as Martin walked in.

The lack of any response prompted Dominic to look up. 'My God, what's the matter? You look like you've seen a ghost.'

Martin sat down opposite.

'Don't tell me, it's to do with that bloody painting, isn't it?'

Martin nodded silently.

'I hate to say I told you so, but I did say it would cause a whole lot of trouble, didn't I?'

'I know, I know.'

'So, what's happened now?'

Martin explained how Frank had turned up at the studio and that now Frank and Jane McNab were both annoyed with him. 'And then Frank rang and left a message just as I was finishing off. He said he'd done what I asked him, and told Louise that we'd once had a bit of a…'

Dominic pushed his marking to one side. 'Well, it looks to me like you're between the proverbial rock and a hard place. So, what are you going to do?'

'That's the trouble, I don't know what to do. I'll end up pissing off one of them whatever I do. Or maybe both of them.'

Dominic thought for a moment. 'I think it would be more harmful if you were fall out with Jane, don't you? I'm sure Gerald was quite right, and Frank'll calm down eventually.'

'But what if he doesn't?'

'It was all ages ago, wasn't it? And it was only a fling, and not as if you were lovers, was it?'

'Well, no, but...' Martin began hesitantly. 'No, I just can't bear the idea of Frank being angry with me. He was my tutor back then, and, well…'

'Okay, then you'd better call Gerald and see if he can get Frank to be reasonable.'

'You're right, of course. Yes, that's exactly what I should do.'

'Good. Now go and get changed, you're covered in paint. And I need to get on with this marking too. You can put the pasta on if you like.'

Martin was anything but reassured by Dominic, as he took off his overalls. Putting them into the laundry basket, he stopped to look at the little painting at the top of the stairs of the beach at Barceloneta, back when Frank had hoped to make a living as a landscape painter. It was simplistic and a little crude, painted outdoors, but Martin loved the warm colours of the sand, the flecks of light on the water, and more besides. The picture took Martin back to that wonderful trip to celebrate his graduation from The Slade, when they spent the days swimming and painting, drinking sangria, and he had calamari for the first time. They had stayed in Sitges, then Barcelona and Girona, and Martin couldn't remember ever being quite so happy or at peace with the world.

But Martin's brief feeling of contentment faded all too soon as he recalled Dominic's earlier remark, reminding him that he had never been completely open with his husband about how he had once felt about Frank.

4.

Gerald bought a brace of pheasants from the butcher and placed them carefully on a side table to look as if they had not been artfully arranged but simply dumped there. It would be easy enough, he decided, for him to make them look anything but edible. He was thinking about the kind of background that would best set them off when Betty walked in.

'Urgh,' she grimaced. 'Hadn't I better put them in the fridge?'

'I didn't buy them for us to eat. I'm going to paint them.'

'I'm glad about that. I had pheasant once and didn't like it one little bit. There was a piece of shot in mine.'

She was about to leave the conservatory, but Betty hesitated by the door, 'Gerald, what about when they start to go off?'

'Well, you can just be glad it's not an elephant I'm painting, can't you?' snapped Gerald. 'I'll have the bones of it done today, so you can bin them later on if you like. Okay?'

Betty disappeared and Gerald, humming *Alouette*, began positioning jugs, bowls and a Persian rug behind the birds when the phone rang.

'Yes?' he answered, always irritated at having his work interrupted.

'Gerald, thank God you're there. It's all gone horribly wrong–'

'Slow down, Martin, what's all gone wrong?'

'I knew it would happen. I just knew it. Frank was furious and then said he wanted to buy the painting so it wouldn't be in the exhibition, but Jane McNab called and told me she'd already got a buyer for it…'

Gerald could barely suppress his glee at discovering that both Frank and Jane had taken the bait. 'We talked about that, Martin, didn't we? You can't go round upsetting the woman who sells your paintings, now, can you? How would you be expected to make a living if you can't show your work, answer me that?'

'Yes, but you see, Gerald, I haven't told him what Jane said. And if, as you're saying, I have to let her have the painting, then he'll be even more angry, won't he?'

'No, just as I said, Frank was always going to blow up, but he'll calm down before long. So, stop worrying.'

'But, what do I do? Shall I tell Frank that Jane had already promised the painting to someone? Otherwise, he'll see it in the exhibition, and then…'

Gerald had delighted in throwing a large pebble into the water, but now he was more interested in seeing where the ripples would end up, rather than having to deal with Martin's problems. But it was too early to step away from what he had begun, and risk the painting being withdrawn. 'I suppose, you could tell him,' he began cautiously. 'But I'd be tempted to leave it. Anyway, you never know, he might not come to the gallery.'

'Oh, but he'll find out soon enough.'

'Well, it's up to you. But think, Martin. What good will it do, telling him now, eh? If I were in your shoes, I'd leave it up to Ma McNab to do the explaining. Just say it was nothing to do with you, completely out of your hands.'

'I don't know.'

'Oh, come on, Martin. All's fair in love and art.'

'But Frank was my tutor, and…'

'I bet he wouldn't have given a fig about you, if the

boot were on the other foot.'

'Oh no, I don't think so, Gerald. I'm sure he wouldn't do anything like that.'

'Trust me. Not everyone has your finer feelings. Now, Martin, deep breaths, hold your nerve, and get that painting finished and over to The Curzon. Right?'

'I suppose so. All right, yes. Thanks, Gerald.' Martin was no happier after putting down the phone, but decided it was probably best to follow the older man's advice and got down to finishing off *The Art Lovers*.

Gerald, satisfied with his composition, took several photographs of the two pheasants, which he then picked up and deposited on a worktop in the kitchen.

Frank, too, had visited the shops that morning. He returned home, pink and out of breath, but beaming as he put down his acquisitions on a coffee table.

'Oh, Frank, not more paints and brushes,' complained Louise. 'You got them for her last year, remember?'

'Did I?' Frank answered breezily. 'Oh well, you can't have too many paints, can you?'

'That's the trouble with you men,' she said, putting down the crossword. 'You just can't help yourselves, can you? Always wanting to get children to do the things you're interested in. Daddy was just the same. Why on earth did he think I'd want to go fly fishing? And you wonder why the girls always find an excuse not to come to any of the previews. If you push too hard, it just puts them off.'

'Well, it's too late now. I suppose I could get her some chocs...'

'Oh no you don't. You know how Lizzie feels about giving them sweets. They're strictly rationed.'

Frank looked crestfallen.

'Anyway, it doesn't matter. It's nice that you remembered,' said Louise gently, patting Frank's arm. 'And I've got Polly something from both of us that Lizzie told me she wanted.'

'But I can still give her the paints, can't I?'

'Of course, you can.'

On Friday afternoon, Martin listlessly wrapped up *The Art Lovers* and *The Harlequin* in bubble wrap, and booked an Uber. He lugged the two paintings down to the street, and sat in the back of the car, unable to think of anything other than how Frank was going to react. Jane McNab was relieved as she saw him carry the two pictures into The Curzon Gallery, and gave Martin a kiss on both cheeks. She put the artist's silence down to Martin probably having worked for most of the night trying to finish them on time. He caught the Tube home, convinced everything was bound to go wrong. If only he and Dominic could get away for a little while, maybe Paris for a few days. But Dominic's half term break was weeks away, so there was no point even thinking about it. Still, he didn't have to go to the preview, did he?

Later that afternoon, Yannick emailed Tom the brief for the Net Zero Observatory pitch. Tom had been brooding on it all week, and it was everything he had expected but hoped it wouldn't be. Yes, there was plenty about the NZO's role in promoting solar, wind and tidal power, but the theme that ran through the entire brief was the need to communicate the importance of nuclear power as an equally clean source of energy. Tom ruled out any idea of producing a poorly executed pitch to avoid winning the NZO account, especially since if he also failed to hang on to the Conch Telecom account it would ruin his career, not only at SHM, but at any other agency in town. Wearily, he set up a meeting with the team he had assembled. He called in Donna Radford to handle the media buying, and Fran Simpson and Mo McLintock to look after the creatives. Bobbi Sammels, Tom's account executive, sat in to take notes. None of them shared his concerns and Tom was left feeling very much the odd one out. He wondered if he was overreacting. Perhaps he was, but he would still have to find a way of keeping Frank from finding out he might be working on the account, or endure his father-in-law's scorn.

After coffee and scrambled eggs, Frank took the box of paints and brushes that Louise had wrapped for him and another parcel wrapped in pink paper with leaping unicorns and bouncy rainbows out to Louise's Toyota. It was a chilly morning, but not cold enough to justify the thick coat that contained his box of small cigars. While Louise finished putting on her make-up, he tucked the cigars into a pocket of his rumpled cream safari jacket.

'Shouldn't we be bringing a bottle or two?' asked Frank hopefully.

'She's only six, for goodness' sake. Anyway, I daresay Lizzie will have something,' replied Louise turning into the Upper Richmond Road.

'Suppose so. I just thought…'

It was gone eleven by the time they arrived at Denmark Hill. The front garden of the thirties semi had been block paved, with enough room for Louise to park alongside Lizzie and Tom's old Volvo. Polly dashed down the stairs to see her grandparents, grabbing first Louise then Frank by the legs, more affectionate than ever, knowing they had come with presents.

Lizzie ushered them into the drawing room. 'She's so excited. I think we'd better do presents first.'

Tom sat at the far end of the room, dandling Theo. He half stood up to greet his parents-in-law, then concentrated on interesting the baby in a bottle.

Louise handed the presents to Polly, who tore at the wrapping paper to reveal an outfit, comprising a long blue dress and a silvery train. The little girl pulled it out, held it against herself and twirled round delightedly.

'What on earth might that be?' said a puzzled Frank.

'It's an Elsa outfit,' explained Lizzie.

'Really? Doesn't look like the sort of thing Elsa Lanchester might have worn.'

'No, it's *Frozen*.'

'Eh? Well, if she were to wear just that on a day like today she certainly would be frozen,' said a still-mystified Frank.

'It's the name of the film.'

Tom put on a DVD, and the music from *Frozen* blared out. Polly joined in the song, dancing along to it.

'Oh, I see. Whatever next?' Frank felt rather left out, seeing his present remaining unopened on the sofa.

With Tom not about to mention the NZO pitch, and Frank keen to avoid any snarky comments from his son-in-law, Polly's birthday passed off peacefully enough. Cake was eaten, Frank's present was finally unwrapped and his granddaughter, seemingly having forgotten what he gave her the previous year, gave him a big kiss and let him paint with her. Louise was pleased and said so on the drive home. 'Well, Frank, you have been a good boy. Let's get a bottle of something nice for this evening.'

The following day, as usual, Frank strolled down to The

Duke of York to meet his old friends. As last week, it was just the older members, with Sean too busy and Martin nervous about seeing Frank again. He found himself standing next to Doug in the gents.

'How's the missus?' asked Doug over the rattle of the hand dryer. 'Everything all right at home?'

'Yes, thank God. Louise seems to be surprisingly sanguine about it all.'

'You're a lucky bugger, Frank. I know what my Kath would have said about it.'

Back in the saloon bar, Max asked, 'You know a little more about your mysterious commission, perhaps, Francis?'

'Indeed I do.' Frank was glad, as ever, to have the chance to hold court. 'A series of murals for the Net Zero Observatory.'

'The what?' asked a puzzled Doug.

'It's a place they're building up in the land of my fathers. Cumbria, to be precise. And the murals they want me to paint are to celebrate the benefits of, ahm, green… Yes, green energy instead of coal and what not.'

'Portraits of the founders of Greenpeace, rainbow warriors, folks like that, is it?'

'I rather doubt it, Douglas. But I'll know more when I meet them later this week.'

'So, not necessarily portraits, then?' Doug sipped his pint, then rubbed his chin in a confused sort of way.

'So, you've got to flog all the way up there then?' said Gerald.

'Oh yes. I'm meeting them in Penrith on Thursday.'

'And I daresay you'll be having to spend a bit of time up there then?' Gerald was barely able to conceal his delight at the prospect. *Time for a last hurrah, perhaps?*

he said to himself.

'Well, I suppose I'll be up and down a bit, but you never know.' Before Frank came up with the idea of buying *The Art Lovers* from Martin, the idea of staying in Cumbria to paint the murals had seemed a wise option, but now he had done what Martin asked and told Louise, he was relieved that now it seemed there would be no need for him to run away from London.

On Tuesday afternoon, Tom and his team got together to discuss the NZO pitch. Donna Radford kicked off with the research she'd been doing. The location of the observatory, on the Cumbrian coast, meant that visitors other than the locals would have to travel some distance to get there. While the brief stressed the need to appeal to a youngish demographic, she felt that some of the spend should be targeted at holidaymakers in the Lake District. The campaign, therefore, should be a combination of social media, local press, and flyers in visitor attractions and tourist information centres across the county.

'What about broadcast?' asked Tom without any real enthusiasm.

'We could, I suppose, but I reckon we might try and PR that instead. I was thinking that our friends at Vaessen and Price might handle that for us.'

Tom nodded. Discussing the media spend was just about bearable, but the creatives were another matter. Fran Simpson stood up her laptop on the desk, and went through a series of straplines. Green and pleasant land. The wind of change. Sunrise on clean sources of energy. Tom didn't much like any of them. The first was too old-fashioned and would mean nothing to anyone under forty, the second sounded meaningless. Maybe the third would do, even if "clean" didn't sound quite right to him.

Mo McLintock took over and showed the team the designs she'd been working on. It was hard to make solar panels and wind farms look particularly interesting, but she had cleverly combined them with images of people using the power they had generated. Her final slides were what Tom had been dreading: nuclear power stations in all their glory. When she showed a row of cooling towers with fluffy white steam coming out of them, Tom kept quiet. It would show nuclear power for what he believed it to be, anything but clean.

Then Fran interjected, 'Ahm, Mo, they don't have them anymore.'

'Eh?'

'It's the towers. Nuclear power stations don't look like that these days.'

'Ah, no problem, I'll take them out. Trouble is, though, without them they don't really look much like anything other than some great big factory. Ah well, I'll think of something. Back to the drawing board,' said Mo with a good-natured grin.

Tom said they should go with "Sunrise on clean sources of energy", and if Mo could get the images amended by Thursday, he'd send them over to Yannick.

On Thursday lunchtime, the cabbie looked his passenger up and down on the forecourt of Penrith station before saying, 'It's less than half a mile, mate.'

'I do have a case, you know,' replied a tired Frank with his usual imperiousness. After another taxi ride at what he considered the unearthly time of eight in the morning, he had caught the nine thirty train from Euston, first class, after checking with Julian that expenses would be paid, and dressed in an ancient tweed suit like one of Gerald's castoffs, topped off by a grey trilby with a large feather in the band. Country garb, as he explained to Georgia, who couldn't stop giggling at her father.

The meeting was at two, so, case stowed in his room, Frank settled down to a ploughman's and a large glass of rioja at the far end of the bar, from where he could see the main entrance and all its comings and goings. He fished a sheet of paper from an inside pocket and his reading glasses from the breast pocket, unfolded the former and placed the latter unevenly on the bridge of his nose. Julian had kindly furnished him with a few details of who Frank was due to meet, one Julia O'Leary, Communications Director for the Nuclear Development Commission, and Barney Brady, Director of the Net Zero Observatory.

Frank left the pickled onions, got the meal put on the bill for his room, as he saw a tall woman in her thirties walk in accompanied by a roundish man about ten years older with a shiny pink face. The woman remained standing, turning to scan the room, while the man sat down heavily and peered into a briefcase. As Frank emerged from the gloom of the bar, the woman's face lit up. 'Mister Armstrong?' she asked, regarding his tweeds curiously.

Frank gave a small bow and put out his hand.

'Thank you for taking the time to meet up with us,' said Julia. 'Can I get you something to eat? Coffee perhaps?'

'No, no thank you. Most kind of you, but I'm quite replete.' Frank couldn't work out the woman's accent, not quite English and not quite American. Of course, O'Leary, Irish.

'Coffee, Barn?' she asked her colleague.

'Can I get a flat white?' he demanded, not looking up.

The man apparently known as Barn, awkwardly half standing, shook Frank's hand, and introduced himself. He was American. Julia returned, having placed the order for the flat white and her latte, and Frank, on a hard chair, found himself a good six inches higher than Julia and Barney, who had taken the sofa. He wasn't sure if it was to his advantage or not. Yes, he was higher than them, but he still felt like the interviewee.

After a few words on train travel in the UK, Julia broached the purpose of the meeting. 'We at the NDC need to–'

'The NDC?' asked Frank.

'Sorry, it's acronym soup round here. Yeah, so, we at the Nuclear Development Commission need to generate... Hey, see what I did there, Barn?' she tipped her head back and laughed loudly. 'So, we need to generate some really really positive PR for the NZO. And that's why we need you, Mr Armstrong.'

'Frank, please.'

'Thing is, Frank, not everyone quite gets nuclear power, but building a new fleet of small, plug and play reactors is the only way we'll get close to net zero.'

Barney Brady spoke up, 'We kind of downplay the words "nucular power", Jools. "Green energy" has better traction with stakeholders.'

'Sure, Barn, but we're paying for it, so it's the NDC's name on the publicity. Right?'

'I guess. Can't help thinking a rebrand would be a good call.'

'Well, the Minister is going to green light that any time soon.'

'So, let me see if I understand,' said Frank. 'You need

me to come up with artworks that celebrate nuclear power, green power or whatever you call it., but not to mention that it's really about nuclear. Is that right?'

Barney spoke up, 'Yeah, I guess that's right, Frankie–'

Frank interrupted him, 'Frank, if you don't mind. Only two people have ever called me Frankie, my mother and my wife. And only when they're cross with me.'

'Okay, sorry, Frank. Jeez, you should hear what my wife calls me when she's pissed about some little thing.' Barney smiled at Julia. 'Right, so you're the artist, so it's kind of up to you how to make this work. But, first we need a theme. Okay? We need you to rough out a few ideas for us to kick around…'

'By "kick around", do I take it you mean…?'

'Yeah, you know, preliminary stuff for us to check out and give you our input. Okay with you?'

'Fine. I think.' Though Frank was less than sure what he was agreeing to.

'Yeah, we need to be kept in the loop with this. The NZO is costing us a packet. Well, costing the good old British taxpayer, that is,' said Julia. 'So we can stay involved with what you'll be doing, we kind of need you around. Right?'

'I live in London, you know.'

'Yeah, I know, but you could rent some place up here, couldn't you?'

'I suppose so, but–' Frank began to protest.

'Great, so it's all settled. We've arranged to route the money through your pal, Julian Furnell, since he put us in touch, and he'll pay you. Okay?'

Frank hauled up a small portfolio he'd brought. 'You don't want to see any of my work?'

'Nah. Thanks, I already checked you out on the web,

you being a member of the Royal Academy and all. Anything you need to ask?'

'Um, can't think of anything off hand.'

'All righty, I'll diary a meeting for us and send round a Doodle poll. Sometime soon. Couple of weeks, maybe, to come back with a theme. That sound okay?'

'I imagine so,' replied Frank, wondering what on earth a Doodle pole might be and why she would want to send him such a thing, but glad the meeting appeared to be coming to an end.

'Okay, great. Barn, I think we're done.'

Julia got up, shook hands with Frank while Barney fiddled with his briefcase and followed her out of the hotel. It was that funny hour of the afternoon, between lunch and dinner. A bit too early for a drink, and too tired to do much else, so Frank went to his room and doodled in an A3 sketchbook. He didn't really want to spend the night in Penrith, but had reluctantly decided that Cumbria and back in the day was a bit too much for him. After half an hour or so of fruitless sketching, Frank mooched into town. He looked around the remains of the sandstone castle, the parish church, and popped into a couple of bookshops.

He was exhausted by the time he reached the hotel again and decided it really was time for a drink. After his second glass of Chablis, he thought that maybe Doug was right. After all, he was a portrait painter, so why not include some images of the men behind nuclear power? There was Ernest Rutherford, of course, but no other names sprang to mind. Then he remembered the man who had put out the Windscale fire back in the fifties, Tom Tuohy. It had all happened when he was very young, but people in Cumbria talked about it for years afterwards.

He scribbled a note to himself and, satisfied that he had done quite enough work for the day, ordered Herdwick hogget, followed by sticky toffee pudding and custard.

'It's just kind of flat, Tom. Right media, wrong creative. Didn't blow anyone's frock up when we murder roomed it, so it's going to need a rethink. You've got to differentiate our offer from the pack,' said Yannick on Friday morning, smiling and stretching out on the chair across from Tom's desk.

Tom wasn't surprised, and felt his lack of enthusiasm for the NZO pitch was probably the problem. 'I think we've struggled with putting nuclear power and green energy in the same campaign. They just don't really seem compatible.'

'Hey, if the NDC are okay with it, then so are we. Look, I know you're the ESG guy, but you can't let the E get in the way of what the client wants. Come on, Tom, you need to kick some life into the pitch.'

Tom nodded sullenly, and Yannick looked quizzically at him before continuing, 'Okay, so something tells me you don't feel totally comfortable about it, is that it? Okay, I get that, so I don't like peanut butter but does that stop us from having the Sunnygold account? No. We aren't the ones to decide what's right and wrong, we're here to make a profit. You know that. And what if some anti-nuke outfit chucked a shit load of cash our way? We'd work for them, wouldn't we? Look, any case, you've gotta admit nuclear's better than coal. Right? I can't do all the thinking for you here, man. Figure it out. And quickly, too.'

Yannick left the office wondering whether or not to hand the pitch over to one of the other account directors, while Tom resigned himself to sharpening it up, knowing the Conch Telecom account was still in the balance.

It was a weary but pensive Frank that dumped his bag in the hall of Exmoor Gardens. He was glad to be home and to have some ideas for the murals, but wasn't altogether sure about the expectation of his having to leave the comforts of London for Cumbria. Louise was out, but Georgia was curled up on a sofa with a laptop.

'Not at work, darling?'

'I can work from home since COVID, Pa, remember? I'm saving a packet on the commute, but it's just a bit too close to the fridge. I must have put on half a stone,' she said, sticking her stomach out. She went into the kitchen and made mugs of coffee, and brought a pile of Biscoff biscuits with them.

Frank leaned back heavily in an armchair, then suddenly remembered what had been puzzling him. 'Oh, look, could you help your aged P with something? Would you have the faintest idea what a Doodle bug, no, that's not it. No, yes, a Doodle Pole. That's it. Do you know what one of those things is and what I'd be supposed to do with it if I were to be given one?'

Georgia grinned. 'It's online, Dad.'

'Eh?'

'A Doodle poll's an invitation to a meeting. The organiser sends round a list of possible dates, and you have to let them know which ones you can make.'

'Oh, doesn't come through the post or anything then?'

'No, Dad. They'll email you.'

Frank nodded, not entirely clear, 'Well, I suppose your mother will pick it up when it, ahm, arrives here.'

The following Tuesday afternoon, it was gone five

before Louise returned with Polly and Theo in his buggy after a walk round the park in an attempt to settle him, and an hour later, Lizzie turned up to collect the children, following a doctor's appointment. Since his meeting in Penrith, Frank had spent the time sketching ideas for the murals. Either because Frank was too lazy or felt it beneath a great artist such as himself to beaver about looking for information, Louise had come up with more names of people he could include. Although he always liked to act as if he didn't want people to see his work before it was finished, Frank could never resist leaving his sketches out so that no-one could possibly avoid looking at them. He had left four on the dining room table.

'More portraits, Pa?' said Georgia, as she strolled in with a laptop under her arm.

Lizzie passed the baby over to Louise and joined her younger sister. 'I thought you were working on those murals for that nuclear place,' she added.

'And so I am.'

'But these are just a bunch of old geezers, Dad,' queried Georgia.

'They, my dear, are the great men that made nuclear power possible,' said Frank grandly.

'I don't recognise any of them.'

Frank pointed at each in turn, 'Dalton, Faraday, Rutherford and Tom Tuohy.'

'Do you think that's what the sort of thing they're looking for?' asked Lizzie.

'Certainly. One must always understand the history of things, you know.'

'Yes, but…'

'The thing is, Dad,' said Georgia, 'they're all just a bit PMS.'

'What on earth are you talking about?' asked Louise from the sofa. 'They're all men, darling. What could premenstrual syndrome possibly have to do with them?'

'Not that kind of PMS, Mum,' chuckled her younger daughter. 'No, these men Dad's drawn, well, they're all pale, male and stale, aren't they? Not much diversity here, is there?'

Louise, more intent on defending her research that Frank's ego, replied, 'Well, I think it's a jolly good idea for a theme, and your father's quite right. The visitor centre is about educating people, so surely the context is important?'

'I suppose so,' said Georgia without much enthusiasm, while her sister got a bottle from the baby bag.

At last, Frank spoke, 'Anyway, since you're both here, there is something else I wanted to mention.'

The girls waited.

'Well, it seems they need me to be, ah, based up there for the job.'

Louise spoke up first, 'Your father and I have discussed this. It'll only be for a few months and he won't have to be there absolutely all the time, will you, darling? And I'll pop up at the weekends too.'

'Long way to pop, Mum,' said Georgia solemnly. 'So, I suppose there'll be no more Sunday lunches then?'

'Only for a while, darling.'

'I thought a flat with a little studio in Grasmere would be rather nice,' said Frank. 'I've always had a soft spot for the place ever since I was a young lad…'

'Here we go, off down memory lane again,' whispered Lizzie audibly to all, but unable to stop Frank's flow.

'Yes, we'd ride all the way there on our bikes. Mine was a Claude Butler with a lovely lightweight frame. We were fit as fleas in those days. You know, we'd have just a bottle of pop and some gingerbread. That's all we needed back then. There was none of that endless supping from bottles of water. Yes, we'd ride there, and we'd even do Helvellyn then ride all the way back. And over Dunmail Raise to boot. Great fun, but that climb's no picnic, I can tell you.' He leaned back in his armchair and sipped his tea, smugly enjoying both the presence of a captive audience and a topic which avoided a discussion about all that was wrong with white, middle aged men.

Strictly speaking, with the exception of one camping weekend when they did cycle there, Frank and his boyhood friends would catch the bus from Kendal to Grasmere and, while some of the camping party had indeed scaled Helvellyn, Frank had cried off, complaining of blisters. But he was the last person to let the bald facts ruin a perfectly good tale, albeit one his family had heard on rather too many occasions still to be enthralled by it, if they ever had been.

5

Frank formed a rigid diagonal from head to toe in his old leather armchair, somewhere between sitting and lying. He clasped both hands to his forehead and said hoarsely, 'I can't possibly go. I'm in agony.'

'No, you aren't,' replied Louise, fiddling with the clasp of her pearls.

'How could you possibly know how utterly debilitating this headache is?'

'Oh, come on, Frank. We'll be late.'

'Lou, I can't, I really can't.'

Louise removed one of Frank's large hands, and looked him straight in the eye. 'Yes, you will, my boy.' She tapped his forehead, 'Hasn't it got through to you that your absence will create far more chatter than Martin's picture, not that anyone will know anything about it? After your little deal with him, he isn't even going to show it, is he?'

'I suppose not, but all the same, I just can't bear to see him.'

'If you promise to be good, I'll let you take me to that nice little bistro in Charlotte Street afterwards, and we can have steak frites and a bottle of wine.'

'Oh, very well, if I must,' said Frank hauling himself slowly from the chair.

Taking his time to get ready, and then with traffic through Fulham and Chelsea almost at a standstill, Frank and Louise were the last to arrive at The Curzon Gallery.

Golden light from the tracked spotlights bounced off the scrubbed floorboards and white walls and streamed into the street. Frank pushed Louise forward at the door, and hung back. She grabbed his wrist and he followed, hesitating in the entrance. They were surprised to see how few people were there. A young couple mooched along in front of a row of Martin's earlier work. A few had red or orange dots on them. But the gallery didn't appear to be empty, as a hubbub came from the far end. Louise ventured forwards, to where the gallery extended round a corner into what had once been the shop's sales counter. It now contained a large desk, a table set out with bottles and glasses, and bookshelves with old catalogues on them.

There was a large group standing around, with glasses of white wine. Feeling more confident now, Frank saw some of his friends and a few journalists he knew, and went to join the throng. At the end of the room, to his horror, he saw *The Art Lovers*. It was clearly what had attracted the group's attention, and had already been given a red dot. Frank detached himself from Louise and marched across to Martin, who was helping himself to a drink. 'You bloody bastard,' Frank hissed. 'I thought we had agreed…'

Martin's face was expressionless as he turned to Frank; the nervousness he had been feeling at seeing him confront the painting again had completely evaporated. As Dominic had said to him, the expectation is nearly always worse than the reality of a situation.

'I think you're overreacting, Frank,' Martin said blandly. 'And, anyway, it was completely out of my hands…'

'But you promised…'

'I'm afraid Jane already had a buyer for the painting before you asked to buy it. I had no idea.' Martin gestured towards the gallery owner who was half-horrified and half-delighted at the confrontation, as she thought of the publicity it would generate for The Curzon.

'And this is how you repay an old friend is it, by humiliating me like this? I was your tutor, you know, if you can remember that. *The Art Lovers* indeed. How pathetic,' spat Frank.

'Yes, Frank,' said Martin raising his voice too. 'Yes, it's called *The Art Lovers*, because we were lovers, if you can remember that too.'

'We were nothing of the kind.'

Martin pointed to the painting, 'I think that suggests otherwise, don't you?'

The room's harsh acoustics made Frank's outburst audible to all. Everyone turned as Frank carried on, 'I could wring your bloody neck, you absolute shit. You'll pay for this, Martin…'

Louise pulled her husband away. 'Not now, Frank. Time and a place. Come on.'

Not before glaring furiously at his former pupil, Frank allowed himself to be led away. Outside the gallery, he said angrily, 'I suppose the steak frites are off, since I haven't been a good boy.'

Saying nothing, Louise took Frank's hand, and directed them towards Charlotte Street. At the door of the bistro, she finally turned to him. 'You've been an idiot, having a tirade like that. It won't have done the slightest good. Quite the opposite, in fact.'

'But…' blustered Frank.

Softening a little, Louise patted his arm. 'Look, I understand you're upset. I do know that. But we do have to eat. Come on.' She strode ahead of him and they sat at a table for two in a quiet alcove.

Frank remained silent until the menus had been deposited in front of them. 'I am going to have to take this up with him, you know. I shall beard him in his lair.' He slurped down some wine. 'And don't try and stop me, Lou.'

With a half grin, Louise answered him, 'Oh, I don't think I could even if I tried, could I? At least you've saved yourself a thousand pounds.'

'To think I was prepared to pay the bloody man, not to mention risk my marriage by having to tell you…' began Frank, then gave up as the wine arrived. 'Oh, what's the use?'

Meanwhile, Gerald, feeling weary and not in the mood to join his friends at the Yorkshire Grey for an evening's drinking, slipped away and caught the Tube home. He was uncertain as to how successful he had been. 'Just need to be patient,' he said to himself, repeating the phrase several times between Tottenham Court Road and Ealing Broadway.

In their taxi back to Putney, Louise was quiet too. Frank had drunk most of the wine, and lolled sleepily against the door. She had been too busy calming down her husband to think about what Martin had said, but in the silence of the back seat it came back to her.

Had he and Frank really been lovers? she wondered. *It didn't really matter*, she told herself, since it was so long ago, and anyway it was before she and Frank got together. *But what if it didn't end then?* The thought nagged away at her. Yes, her husband was capricious, selfish too, but he had been a good husband too, at least for most of the time. She dismissed her doubts, cross with herself at reacting to them so childishly, and helped to pour her husband out of the cab as it pulled up in Exmoor Gardens.

It was late by the time Martin and Dominic headed back to Islington, leaving Jane McNab and Chloe to tidy up the gallery, put the glasses in the dishwasher and a couple of dozen empty bottles in the recycling bin. Martin was still on a high after standing up to Frank, and because eight of his paintings had been sold at the preview. He was curious about who had bought *The Art Lovers*, but nothing could dampen his happiness. Dominic, though pleased at his husband's success was unusually quiet, but Martin did not notice it.

'There's some cava in the fridge,' said Martin as they arrived home. 'I'm in the mood for celebrating.'

Dominic yawned extravagantly, 'Sorry, I'm absolutely knackered. Busy day tomorrow. You have some if you like, I need to get some sleep.'

Jane McNab did not sleep well. Martin's preview had been a great success and it had boosted her finances too, but the row between him and Frank Armstrong had bothered her more than she'd expected. It wouldn't get any useful PR for The Curzon at all, quite the opposite; people would be talking about Frank and Martin, not the exhibition. What was most responsible for keeping her awake, though, was the anticipation of the six and a half thousand pounds that the mysterious Mr Melchior was about to pay her for *The Art Lovers*. She arrived early at The Curzon Gallery that morning, looking forward to meeting him, and to seeing the cash in her bank account.

Gerald, meanwhile, settled down to add paint to his drawing of a brace of pheasants, telling himself that he really must do nothing for the time being. The consequences of his plans would unfold one way or another, and he would discover how and when soon enough. The important thing was not to show his hand, or make a move of any kind, if the result he hoped for was to be achieved. He must remain at a remove from the action, and appear to be no more than an honest broker who had nothing to do with any of it, who had only tried his best to help two good friends.

Martin, though, had a lie-in. The last few weeks of frantically finishing his paintings for the exhibition, the excitement of the preview, and the half bottle of cava he had drunk were enough for him to barely wake as Dominic left for school. He finally surfaced a little after ten and, after a slapdash brunch, remembered that Jane McNab had asked if he could let her have some of his preliminary sketches, as the success of the preview had made her confident she could probably sell them too. At twelve, he dressed wearily, texted Dominic to say he was going to the studio, and caught the bus to Clerkenwell.

For all his fury the previous night, Frank slept no worse than he usually did, emerging dozily at half past ten. The refreshment he habitually looked forward to from his first cup of tea only served to remind him of what had taken place at the gallery. He groaned at the thought of it. Louise was sure it was a day for handling him with kid gloves. He needed to get on with his sketches for the NZO, but Louise knew she would get nowhere by nagging him. She thought about sitting with him in the dining room to see if he was all right, but something made Louise decide to keep her distance. Instead, she picked up a small garden fork and a trug from the utility room, and decided to have a go at the weeds that were sprouting up through cracks in the patio.

Not seeing his wife around, Frank put on his old coat

and left Exmoor Gardens to risk yet another Tube journey. At the entrance to the station, he called Gerald, who had turned his phone off as he painted the dead pheasants.

'Gerald. Oh, blast the bloody thing. Gerald, look, it's me, Frank. I just wanted to let you know that after that debacle last night, I'm on my way to see that swine, Martin, and I'm going to sort him out good and proper. Gerald, are you there? No? Oh well, that's all. Cheerio.'

Frank had no clear idea of what he might do to Martin, but 'Surprise is of the essence,' he said to himself, seated grimly in a carriage packed with young schoolchildren on a trip into town, seemingly unable to be kept quiet by two harassed-looking teachers. When he visited Martin's new studio, he had noticed there was a pub on the corner; it would be the perfect vantage point. From a seat by the window of the Black Lion, he was able to tuck into a shepherd's pie and a glass of Shiraz and see the comings and goings from the building where the studio was. At just before one, he saw the slight figure of Martin enter through the heavy steel door. It was busy in the pub, with a horde of young, casually-dressed office workers talking loudly. Frank finished his lunch and crossed the street. Two young women were by the door of the building and held the door open for him, before disappearing into a web design studio on the ground floor.

Frank gave a sharp rap at the door of Martin's studio and, when the latter finally opened it, surprised that apparently someone in the building should be on the other side, barged past him.

'Frank,' said Martin coolly.

'Right, you know why I'm here, don't you?'

'I suppose it's obvious.'

'We had a deal or, rather, I went along with your extremely unreasonable demands. Yet, you chose to give back word on it. So, I want you to tell me exactly what you think you're playing at.'

'I told you, Frank, Jane McNab already had a buyer before you offered to buy the painting.'

'So, why didn't you tell me that beforehand, you damned coward?'

'I have been rather busy…'

'Busy, my eye.'

'And, anyway, I was encouraged by a friend to include the painting in the exhibition. They thought it was rather good.'

'Encouraged by whom, might I ask?'

'No-one you'd know,' lied Martin warily.

'Come on, who?'

Martin shook his head.

'Well, let me tell you, young Martin, you haven't heard the last of this,' shouted Frank.

'Oh, Frank, I don't want to fall out with you,' said Martin gently. 'I really don't. And I am sorry about how it all ended up.'

'Sorry! You think that just saying sorry will do?'

'Please, Frank, surely we can stay friends.'

'You must be joking. Friends indeed.' Frank grimaced nastily, 'You're sure you don't want us to be lovers?'

'I'm married now, Frank, and so are you.'

'I damned well hope I'm still married but, after that, that pantomime last night, God knows.'

Frank swirled around in his voluminous coat and strode to the door. 'You are a treacherous bastard, Martin, and I'll make you suffer for this,' he yelled. He slammed the door shut and headed down to the street, as people in the building swiftly retreated back into their offices. He was exhausted and found a bench outside Farringdon station, where he sat down and lit a small cigar. Frank pondered on who might have encouraged Martin to put the painting in the exhibition. *Who had seen the painting before the preview night? It could only be Gerald, couldn't it? He was the one who had been to see Martin, but why would Gerald want to do such a thing? No, it couldn't be him*, Frank told himself. *Who else? It must be that bloody McNab woman*, he eventually decided.

Taking a break from the painting, Gerald turned his phone back on and listened to Frank's message. He thought about calling Martin, but remembered what he had told himself earlier. *No, far and away the best thing was to do nothing and keep shtum. After all, whatever Frank might do now would surely only make things worse. Another row with Martin would make him look foolish and achieve nothing, and making the peace with him would have everyone wondering if he still had the same feelings for Martin that he appeared to have all those years ago.* Gerald smiled at the cleft stick he had created and in which Frank now found himself.

After lunch, Louise gave up on the weeds and decided instead to do a spot of admin. There were a few bills to pay, and she checked her emails. A Doodle poll had arrived from Julia O'Leary at the Nuclear Development Commission, wanting to arrange a meeting with Frank. According to the diary, he could make all of the suggested dates. For a moment, she considered going with him, but there was always Theo and Polly to look after, and then yoga and the Book Club.

Hoping Storm Frank would blow itself out, as Gerald had said it would, Martin got out the sketches Jane McNab wanted and cut a length of brown paper to wrap them. The sun suddenly disappeared, casting the studio into darkness as the heavens opened, so there was nothing for it but to stay put for the time being. Jane would just have to wait for them a little longer. He was surprised, then, when Dominic emerged at four thirty, his anorak soaking wet and with a tiny brolly that had turned inside out. Dominic tried briefly to fix the brolly before discarding it on the floor of the studio. He draped his anorak over a chair and went over to his husband.

'You got my text?' asked Martin.

'Well, I wouldn't be here if I hadn't got it, would I?'

'I suppose not. No kiss?'

Dominic ignored him.

'What's the matter. And why are you looking so angry?'

'I've been thinking about what you said at the gallery last night.'

'What? I was talking to lots of people.'

'Oh, come on, Martin. You know what I'm talking about.'

'I don't, honestly.'

'So, you can't remember saying that you and Frank had once been lovers?'

With all the heady excitement of the preview, it had escaped Martin's mind until now. 'Oh God. Well, I only meant…'

'I don't care what you meant. You told me that you and Frank had never been lovers. And after everything I've done for you, this studio, supporting you to get the paintings finished in time, and…'

'I'm so sorry, Dom, I never meant…'

'Well, it doesn't matter. I need to get my head round all this, so I'm going over to stay at Charlotte and Tony's for a while.'

'Please, Dom…'

'And when I'm back, if I come back, you can get rid of that horrid little painting of his on the landing.'

Martin went over to try and take his husband's arm, but Dominic turned his back, pushing him away as he marched out of the studio. As the door was closing, Martin tottered backwards, slipping on the wet floor, then fell, catching the back of his head on one of the long tables.

Apart from a couple of art history students looking to scrounge catalogues that they'd probably put straight on eBay, no-one called into The Curzon Gallery. At five, Jane McNab sent Chloe home. She made herself coffee and brooded at her large desk. Where the hell was this Mister Melchior? And did he really exist? It certainly didn't look like it. She kicked herself for not even asking for the man's phone number. Why on earth hadn't she done that? She washed up her cup having waited until seven, then closed the gallery for the night.

Louise had printed out the Doodle poll and showed it to a weary Frank. 'There's nothing in the diary, so what day shall I let them know you'll go up there and meet them?' she said dully.

'Oh, I don't know,' replied Frank. Then, realising that, after the exhibition, being away from London for a while might be a good idea, he added, 'Well, I suppose, it would be best to make it as soon as possible. And I could see about getting somewhere to rent up there while I'm at it.'

That evening, after most of the tenants had gone home, the cleaners had made their way up to the second floor to hoover the landing when they heard a low, moaning sound from the other side of the door to Martin's studio, and saw a shaft of light that spilled out from under it. They called the landlord's building manager and carried on with their cleaning, while they waited for her to arrive with keys to the studio.

Seeing Martin sprawled on the studio floor, Lauren Kennedy, the building manager, asked the cleaners to ring for an ambulance while she covered him with a rug. He was barely conscious, and there was a great deal of blood on the floor, but Lauren did her best to keep him awake. Martin couldn't speak or respond to her questions with even a nod, but the cleaners confirmed that this was Mister Robertson, the tenant. It took thirty minutes for the ambulance to arrive and the lead paramedic called the police. By the time the ambulance reached the hospital, Martin was no longer conscious.

Lauren sent the cleaners home but stayed in the studio and, while she waited for the police, she found Martin's Filofax and rang his home number. There was no answer. There was a catalogue for his exhibition, and Martin had scribbled a mobile number on it. It was gone ten o'clock when DC Errol Kelly arrived. Lauren went through the last few hours as he took notes. The DC checked what might have been touched, and took photos of where Martin had been found and the edge of the long table where he found traces of blood. He took the Filofax and the exhibition catalogue and Lauren locked the studio.

Late the following morning, Frank forced himself to take another trip on the hateful Tube, this time to The Curzon

Gallery. He breezed past Chloe, whose ear buds kept her from hearing his arrival and who was peering intently at her laptop, and found Jane McNab at her desk. She waited for Frank to speak first.

'I suppose you put him up to it,' he said at last.

'Put who up to what?' replied Jane calmly.

'Oh, don't come the innocent with me, Miss McNab. You encouraged my former pupil to have that horrible painting in his exhibition.'

'Of course I wanted him to include it, because I have a buyer for it.'

'And because you thought it was rather good?'

Jane shrugged, 'I'd seen a few sketches for it, but I didn't see the painting until he delivered it just in time for the preview.'

'You do realise how humiliating this is for me?'

Jane shook her head. 'Oh, I hardly think so, not in this day and age. Anyway, it's still for sale, that is, if you still want to buy it. I think my buyer appears to have dropped out.'

'Dropped out, eh? Well, well, how convenient that is.'

Jane carried on, maintaining the same even tone, 'Well, I gathered, last night, that you'd wanted to buy the painting from Martin. I suppose that was to keep it from being seen. That's right, isn't it?'

'It's rather too late for that now, isn't it?' said Frank sardonically. 'Pay six and a half thousand for that daub, when the last thing I want to do is line that swine's pockets, or yours, for that matter?'

Frank and Jane looked at each other silently; it seemed there was nothing more to be said. At length, Frank turned and left the gallery, having, for the second day, wasted his time, put up with a Tube journey, and achieved nothing whatsoever.

The following Monday morning, Frank got to work on finishing his sketches for the murals to take to his meeting with the NZO. He drew each of the four figures, Dalton, Faraday, Rutherford and Tuohy, within an arched frame, not unlike an early Italian fresco. Each one was set in a Cumbrian landscape, with an expanse of lake and a panorama of mountains. He was in a quandary as to whether or not he should include a wind turbine or a solar panel, but decided that, for the time being at least, he might as well leave them out. Satisfied that they would do, he sprayed them with fixative and left them to dry.

Co-incidentally, that morning, his son-in-law was looking over a revised approach to the agency's pitch for the NZO account. Mo McLintock had come up with a series of "what if we didn't have it?" graphics, showing people living without light and heat, mobile phones, televisions and washing machines, while Fran Simpson had rethought the key messages along similar lines with bold statements such as "without renewable energy sources, we could end up back in the Stone Age". Tom felt a mixture of relief, that what the team had produced was a good deal better than their first efforts, and discomfort that it might end up being successful.

Jane McNab was surprised to see two tall men in suits enter The Curzon Gallery. Hoping one of them might be Mr Melchior, she came round from her desk to greet them, and was more surprised still when they pulled out their warrant cards. They introduced themselves as DS Brian Davis and DC Errol Kelly. She had had few dealings with the police since a rock star and a minor Royal were caught smoking cannabis at the gallery when it was in Mayfair.

The grey-haired DS, the older and taller of the two, asked if there was somewhere they could talk. Jane asked Chloe to go for a coffee, then put a closed sign on the gallery door.

'Miss McNab? We understand you know a Mr Martin Robertson, Miss McNab. Is that right?' asked Davis.

'Yes. I know him well. These are some of his paintings,' said Jane pointing round the gallery.

'I wonder if you might know the name of a wife or partner…'

'Martin's gay. His husband's name is Dominic something. I'm afraid I don't know his surname.'

'I see. That's most helpful of you, Miss McNab. Just one more thing. Perhaps you could tell me when you last saw Mister Robertson.'

'Yes, it was the day before yesterday. We had a preview evening for his exhibition.'

'And you didn't see him yesterday?'

'No. Why? What's happened?'

'I'm afraid Mr Robertson has been taken to hospital.'

'Oh, my goodness, what happened?'

'It may well have been an accident, but…'

'What sort of an accident? Oh, how awful. Tell me, how is he?'

'He was found on the floor of the place where he works and subsequently lost consciousness. We'll know more about what happened in due course. That's all for now, thank you, Miss McNab, but if you can think of anything, anything at all that might be relevant, do please call us.' Davis handed Jane a card.

'Oh, that's awful. Poor Martin. I can't believe it. Is there anything I can do?' Jane was puzzled, 'But, tell me, since the police are involved, are you saying that this might not have been just an accident?'

'We aren't ruling anything out at this stage.'

'But there's a possibility that someone... someone deliberately tried to harm Martin?'

'As I say, we can't be certain yet. So, if anything comes to mind...' Davis and Kelly made their way to the door.

'Wait a moment. There is something you should probably know.' Jane swept away a strand of grey hair that had come loose from her French pleat. 'In any case, you'd be bound to find out soon enough. The thing is, there was the most almighty row in the gallery that evening.'

'Oh yes? And what was it about? Do you know?'

Jane explained how angry Frank had been at seeing *The Art Lovers* in the exhibition.

'And do you have an address for this Mr Armstrong?'

Jane rooted through her Rolodex, 'I don't have his address, I'm afraid, but he's a member of the Royal Academy, so they should know. I think he lives south of the river. Barnes or Putney rings a bell, but I'm not sure.'

'Thank you, Miss McNab. We'll be in touch if we need anything further.'

Jane didn't think to change the closed sign on the door, and went back to her desk. She knew all too well how volatile artists could be, but surely Frank Armstrong wouldn't do anything violent, would he? The bell rang and Jane was disappointed to find it was just Chloe returning, and not Mr Melchior.

DC Kelly rang the mobile number on the exhibition

catalogue from Martin's studio. The DS had told him not to reveal anything about what had happened there, and just find out who the person was and if they had visited Martin recently. Gerald was surprised to hear from the police, and confirmed that the last time he had been to the studio was a few weeks before the exhibition. He explained that, as he had been in town that day, he had called in on Martin to find out how he was since none of The Duke of York group had seen him for some time.

Then, Kelly leafed through Martin's Filofax. Among a handful of names and numbers, there was nothing under F or A, but he found a mobile number for Dominic. He called it, but it went straight to voicemail, as Dominic was teaching. Kelly left a message for Dominic to call him as soon as he could. At the same time, Davis's phone rang. The call was from the hospital, telling him Martin's condition had deteriorated overnight and that he had been put in a medically-induced coma.

While Kelly contacted the Royal Academy to get Frank's address, Davis returned to the studio to talk to the other occupants of the building. He started at the web design studio on the ground floor. A young woman who worked there confirmed that, around lunchtime, she had let in a middle-aged man with a pony tail yesterday that she hadn't seen before, and that shortly afterwards she had heard shouting from one of the floors upstairs.

After receiving Tom's email, Yannick Morrow took less than an hour to go through the revised pitch. Seeing him come into the office, Tom waited anxiously for the verdict. Yannick gave him a broad smile.

'Yeah, we can go with it. Nice and edgy this time.'

'Edgy?'

'Sure. It's nasty, it's high risk. We're not giving them nicey nice, we're giving them the shock factor. I like that. Maybe we could put something in the mix about nuclear being good value for money too. I dunno. Let's just see how it goes.' And, with that, Yannick swept out of Tom's office, leaving the latter feeling a little more secure in his post.

At just after three, Dominic picked up DC Kelly's message and called him back. It was the first time that Kelly had had to break the news of a serious accident to a spouse, but his training proved more than adequate. No, Dominic told him, he did not need details of organisations that could help him, and yes, there were people he could talk to. First, though, he wanted to see Martin and find out what had happened to him.

It was nearing five when DS Davis arrived at Exmoor Gardens. Louise was shelling peas with Polly, and Frank was napping after his labours on the murals for the NZO. The second ring of the doorbell sent Louise to see who it was. She led Davis into the dining room, asked if he wouldn't mind waiting a few minutes while she saw to Polly, plonking her in front of the television to watch CBeebies, whose songs and squawks were wholly unable to wake her grandfather.

'How can I help you, officer?' Louise said at last.

'I'm here to see Mr Armstrong, if he's at home.'

'Oh yes, he is. But is there anything I can help you with? He's having his afternoon nap, you see.'

'If you'd be good enough to wake him, I'd be much obliged.'

'Certainly. Yes, of course. And would you like a cup of

tea, or coffee perhaps?' Louise knew she was gabbling, but couldn't help it. Davis shook his head. *What on earth could the police possibly want with Frank?*

She went into the drawing room, and gave Frank's shoulder a gentle nudge then, when that didn't wake him, a hard shove.

Frank was predictably irritated at being disturbed. 'Goodness' sake, leave me in peace, Lou,' he growled.

'There's someone to see you,' Louise hissed. 'The police.'

'The what?' said Frank, as he started to come to.

'There's a policeman in the dining room, and he wants to speak to you.'

Frank was wide awake now. He saw his granddaughter cross-legged in front of the television, and envied the innocence and simplicity of her life. Frank dragged himself out of the armchair and followed his wife.

'Shall I…' began Louise, making for the door.

'I understand that you were with your husband at The Curzon Gallery the night before last?'

'Yes, I was…'

'Well, in that case, it might be best all round if you're here too.'

'What's this all about?' asked Frank gruffly, wiping the sleep from his eyes.

Davis told them both that Martin had been found on the floor of his studio, and that he was now in a critical condition in hospital. Facing the policeman, Frank and Louise sat completely frozen, then Louise held her husband's hand.

At last, Frank spoke softly, 'What was it? A heart attack? We all knew that Martin, Mister Robertson, was never in the best of…'

'No, sir, not a heart attack, but we'll know more soon

enough. But my reason for wanting to speak to you is that I understand there was some sort of altercation at the art gallery the night before last. You were there, sir, weren't you?'

'Yes, I was, officer, but how can I…'

'And the altercation was between you and Mister Robertson? That's right, isn't it?'

'Well, yes, but you see…'

'And that was the last time you saw Mister Robertson, was it?'

'It was. We went for a meal afterwards and then we came straight home,' said Louise.

'And you, sir? You haven't seen him since?'

'Well…'

'Mister Armstrong?'

'Well, as a matter of fact, I went round to see him yesterday. You see, I was still very upset after what happened at The Curzon, and wanted to sort of clear the air, as it were.'

'Oh, Frank,' said Louise wearily.

'And you were able to clear the air with him, as you put it, were you?'

'Well, no, not really. It didn't go quite according to plan.'

'In what way didn't it, sir?'

'Oh, I don't know. This is all too terrible. I just don't know,' Frank gulped. 'We argued…'

'Did it perhaps get out of hand? And end up with more than just words being exchanged?'

'What do you mean?'

'Well, sir, maybe there was some sort of a struggle? Was that what happened?'

Frank was shocked, 'What are you saying? I never laid

a hand on him. I would never even think of doing such a thing. And Martin had been my pupil. We've been friends for years.'

'Friends, hmm, yes.' Davis flipped open his notebook. 'And yet, Mister Armstrong, you said to him at the art gallery that you could wring his bloody neck, didn't you?'

'Did I? Perhaps I might have done, but I was angry. No, I was upset.'

'I see. Now, I need you to take me through your movements yesterday, starting with what time you arrived at Mister Robertson's studio.'

His mind completely fogged by the news of Martin being taken to hospital and then by Davis's questions, Frank did his best to remember. It seemed to take an age, as Davis took down notes then seemed to want to check what Frank had told him again and again. At last, the policeman got up. 'That's all for now, sir, madam. We'll need to speak to you again in due course.'

Louise saw Davis to the door while Frank studied the patterns on the carpet. She resumed her place next to him and said, 'What have you done, Frank?'

She was puzzled. Frank was never violent. Yes, he'd been very angry with Martin, but she couldn't believe him capable of carrying out any of things he'd said that night. *But, what if it was something else that had led to passions getting out of control? Surely not a lovers' tiff? No,* she told herself, *these are silly thoughts. No, they're worse than that, they're selfish and unworthy. What if Martin doesn't regain consciousness?* Louise plucked a hankie from her sleeve and began to cry. She wanted someone to comfort her, but wasn't sure that she wanted Frank to do that. Drying her eyes, she turned to her husband.

Frank sat stonily silent, this man who ordinarily wept so easily. *It was*, she wondered, *as if mere tears might somehow cheapen his distress at what had happened to Martin*, but then again she couldn't help thinking it could equally be due to something else, perhaps something Frank hadn't revealed. Louise could tell that he was moved in a way she had seldom seen, though, and put her own feelings temporarily to one side, and took his hand again.

The weekend was a sombre one, relieved for Louise only by the day to day necessities of household chores. Frank spent most of Saturday in his studio, doing very little. Sunday lunch with the girls was cancelled, but Frank ventured down to The Duke of York. He felt some need to justify it and told Louise that Doug had called and suggested they get together to raise a glass to Martin. Dominic had called Doug, a fellow northerner and the one member of the group he liked, who had called the others. Louise was glad to have some time on her own to try putting her thoughts into some sort of order.

At the pub, all were present, including Sean. Max gave a toast, but the conversation soon faltered. They were all chary about bringing up the argument in the gallery. Frank was not about to tell his friends of his visit to Martin's studio. Gerald, too, said little. He had mixed feelings. Surely he wasn't really responsible for Martin ending up in a coma, was he? And he was uncertain as to what to do next. His decision to do nothing was clashing with his impatience. He was aware that the police already knew about it before they called him, but Gerald wondered if he should let them know that Frank had rung him to say he was going to have it out with Martin. That would be too much of a risk and could all too easily backfire. How would Louise react if she were to find out that he had helped to implicate her husband?

6.

Davis closed his laptop. 'Bloody reports. They never get any easier, and this one's going to be a bugger too,' he said, looking at DC Kelly.

The younger man shrugged. 'Just an accident, wasn't it?'

'Well, ordinarily, that's what I'd have said. Slipped on the wet floor, fell and cracked his head on the table and passed out. But, you see, here's this married man, seems to be doing all right for himself, and then there's this argument they had about that picture. You know, the one with him and Robertson…'

Kelly nodded. 'Could hardly miss it.'

'Yes, well, it's got me wondering. I can't help thinking there might be more to this.'

'You mean, you don't believe this chap, Armstrong?'

'Not sure. Still, it wouldn't hurt to have another word with him. You know, go through it all again a few times and see if he slips up. You know how it is.'

Louise had all but dismissed her suspicions about Martin and her husband, not so much because of what had happened to Martin, but due to a sense of personal embarrassment that she should even have been thinking them after something so shocking. Yet, while they flickered occasionally like a faulty lightbulb, she did her best to dispel any sense of unease.

'I think, perhaps, I should cancel my trip to meet the NZO people, or even cancel the whole thing altogether,' said Frank sadly.

'I know what you mean, but postponing it might be a better idea than cancelling it altogether.'

'Oh, I suppose you're right, Lou. Then again, maybe it would be best to get the thing over and done with. Dragging it out won't help. I suppose I'll have to catch that blessed early train again.'

Each afternoon after school, Dominic headed down to University College Hospital to see his husband. Martin remained in the induced coma and the doctors were unable to give Dominic any kind of reassuring prognosis. Seeing him there unconscious was distressing enough, but what also troubled Dominic's vigil was that their last words had been such a bitter argument, and that Martin had been the one who had wanted to put things right. Back home, Dominic felt guilty every time he crossed the landing and saw Frank's painting of the beach at Barceloneta. *It would remain exactly where it was*, he vowed, telling himself it was time he ought to grow up. Or even better, perhaps he could move it to a better spot downstairs. *Yes, that would be the right thing to do for when Martin came home. And if he wasn't going to come home*, he said, *then he would hang it there anyway*. So what if there had been more between Martin and Frank than his husband had let on? He loved Martin and he believed Martin truly loved him, too.

Yannick emailed Tom to say that a date had been fixed for the NZO pitch. It was to be in Cumbria the following week, and he should get the team prepped for it. For every pitch Tom had led, there was always a debate between whether to go mob-handed or not; it could either intimidate the client if they felt outnumbered or make them feel the agency wasn't taking the account seriously enough if only a couple turned up. Tom opted for the former, feeling certain that the NZO people would be bringing along a whole host of stakeholders, and told Fran, Mo and Bobbi they were needed and should get the presentation finalised for his approval.

Frank was still wondering about Georgia's comments, that his sketches for the murals might not hit the mark, but decided it was too late to change them now and that in any case they were only his initial ideas. He decided to take a break, and was about to help himself to tea and chocolate biscuits when the doorbell rang. Forgetting that Louise was out, he ignored it at first, but since the ringing didn't cease, went to see who it was. DS Davis stood there smiling amiably.

'Oh, it's you.'

'Mr Armstrong? I'm sorry to bother you, but there are one of two things I'd just like to check with you, if you don't mind.'

With a silent but theatrical sweep of his left arm, Frank gestured the policeman to come in and led the way to the drawing room where, with another sweep of the arm, he indicated to Davis where he might want to sit down.

'If we could just go over your movements on the day you visited Mister Robertson the day after your, ah, discussion at the art gallery?'

'I must confess to being puzzled as to why you need to ask me all these questions.'

'It won't take too long. We just need to be clear of the facts.'

'I am rather busy, officer...' Frank sighed, then weakened. 'Oh, very well then.'

It was painfully slow, even more so than the first time,

and Frank did his best but failed to prevent his impatience from showing. He noticed that the policeman had now dispensed with the nicety of addressing him as "sir"; perhaps it had just been for Louise's benefit. This time, after going over it all at least twice, Davis wanted more details of what Frank did after leaving Martin's studio.

'You then walked to Farringdon Tube station, yes?'

'Yes, as I said, I sat outside and had a cigar. I needed to collect my thoughts.'

'And that would be about what time, Mr Armstrong?'

'Umm. Well, I wasn't at the studio very long at all, so, ahm, perhaps some time just before two, I suppose.'

'You're quite sure of the time?'

'Well, I can't be absolutely certain of the exact time, but, yes, it was about then. Certainly no later than that.'

'And, then, what time did you get home?'

'About three, I'd say. That's right, I remember the kids were coming out of school.'

'Thank you. That's all for now. But you will be available if we need to speak with you again?'

'Well, yes, but I have to go to Cumbria next week. I'll be away for a couple of days, for work you see. So...'

Davis smiled, 'That's all right, Mister Armstrong. We have your phone number, just in case there is anything.'

Frank saw the policeman to the door, feeling more unsettled than ever, and starting to welcome the thought of his forthcoming meeting with the NZO. He settled down in his armchair, feeling he deserved a nap, but the telephone rang before he could drift off. It was Doug.

'Just giving everyone a bell about Martin, Frank.'

'Oh yes, how is he doing?'

'No change. The waiting's doing Dominic's head in.'

'I'm not surprised.'

'Anyway, that was all. I'll let you know if there's any change, all right?'

'Hang on, Douglas. Ahm, have you by any chance had a visit from the police?'

'No. But what the hell would they want to speak to me for?'

'Well, they've been to see me. Spoken to me twice, in fact, asking all kinds of questions…'

'Well you and him did have a bit of a barney that night, didn't you?'

'I know, but for goodness' sake, Douglas, it's as if they're accusing me of, well, of…'

'You didn't do anything to him, did you? You were bloody angry enough, you know.'

'Yes, I know I was, but you can't seriously imagine I would do anything to harm him, could you?'

'No, course not. So, why have the bobbies got a bee in their bonnet about it, then?'

'Oh, I don't know. It's very upsetting, you know.'

'Yeah, of course. Look, I said I'd call the others, so I'd better go. All right?'

Gerald was finding it difficult to settle down to painting the pheasants, and his impatience was in danger of getting the better of him. He had picked up the phone to call Frank several times, but had managed to restrain himself from ringing the number. He thought about trying to contact Dominic, but that would mean getting his number from Doug. Yes, he could say that it would be just to find out how Martin was doing but, since Doug was the one in touch with Dominic, what if he just said that he'd let them all know as soon as there was any news? And anyway, Doug had only called him that morning. The idea was a non-starter. His usual constitutional around the Common had exhausted him, but it had given him the idea of changing the painting's background from a domestic scene to a landscape, filled with rocky outcrops, and a large boulder in the foreground. That gave him the perfect title for it: *Two Birds, One Stone*.

Back at Islington police station, DC Errol Kelly handed the scene of crime officers' report to the sergeant.

'So, Armstrong didn't trip himself up on anything then?' asked Kelly.

'No. Got a bit hoity toity with me at first, but stuck to his story. He admitted to arguing with Robertson, but he's still saying that he never laid a hand on Robertson. I'm still not sure about him, but let's have a look at the SOCO report.'

'They took their time over it.'

'Yeah well, Errol, they're busy bees right now. Those two shootings up in Canonbury, and that lad with that got knifed before the Spurs game. I suppose this isn't exactly high priority for them.'

'So, what they saying?'

Davis tapped the report, 'They've looked at footprints that were next to that puddle of water on the floor. There's two lots, one heading towards the door, and the other going backwards. The first are of a pair of size tens with a patterned sole, probably trainers, but the others match the ones Robertson was wearing. But here's the thing. SOCO are saying that, if Robertson had slipped on the water, his footprints would have just slid forwards as he fell, but instead there's also a row of little backward steps before his feet go from under him.'

'So, they're saying he didn't just fall?'

'Well, they can't be sure, but they're saying the footprints are more consistent with him being pushed before he fell.'

'Hedging their bets, then? But what do you reckon, sarge?'

'Don't know for sure. But I think another chat with Mister Armstrong is in order.'

Louise had booked two nights at the hotel for Frank. He piled his sketches into a large, maroon portfolio and caught the train up to Penrith. This time, Julia O'Leary had booked a meeting room. There was a message at reception for Frank, telling him where to go, and he was surprised to find it was a bedroom. Julia sat on the bed, cross-legged, with a mobile phone pressed to her ear, while Barney Brady had taken a tub chair and was peering furiously at his laptop, not registering that Frank had walked in. She gestured to Frank not to say anything while he looked around the room for another chair and, finding none, sat down on the far end of the bed.

Eventually, Julia finished her call with a diminuendo of "byes", and Barney deigned to look up from his laptop. Frank felt uncomfortable, balancing his portfolio on his knee and having to look over his shoulder at the others. The preliminaries swiftly completed, Barney moved to the bed, and let Frank have the chair and the small coffee table.

'So, whatcha got for us, Frank?' he began.

Frank undid the ribbon of his portfolio, and placed one of his sketches on the table. Julia and Barney came over and peered at it.

'Okay, Frank, talk us through it,' said Julia at last.

'It's of a very great man, a hero indeed, and without whom we would probably not be sitting here,' said Frank grandly.

'He looks like some kinda old fashioned politician, right?'

'It's Tom Tuohy,' replied Frank, not without a touch of hauteur.

'Don't know the dude.'

'He's the man who prevented the Windscale fire from spreading.'

'No shit? Windscale… is that near here?'

'It's what they call Sellafield today.'

'Can see why they needed to give it a rebrand, eh, Jules?' Barney grinned.

Julia looked at Frank quizzically, 'Okay, so the guy's a hero, sure. But what's he got to do with the NZO?'

'Well, but for Tom Tuohy, there probably wouldn't be an NZO.'

'I'm not sure we want to remind people of what happened way back when. I mean, we don't want people to think nuclear power isn't safe, right?' she said.

'All right.' Frank pulled out his sketch of Ernest Rutherford.

'Is that E M Forster? Lloyd George, maybe?' said Julia.

'Ernest Rutherford, the man who split the atom.'

'Oh, sure. Hmm. But isn't having him in it just going to make people think of Oppenheimer?'

'Oppenheimer?'

'Yeah, like in the film. You know, The Manhattan Project.'

'I haven't seen it, I'm afraid.'

'The atom bomb.'

'Oh no, I hardly think so. One must credit people with some intelligence, you know.'

'Thing is, Frank,' said Barney, 'there is one other little

thing you need to know.'

'Oh yes?'

'You better tell him, Jules.'

'Sure, Barn. We've got this other little difficulty.' Julia recrossed her legs awkwardly. 'Not everyone feels that same way we do about nuclear power…'

'You can say that again, Jules, I'm also a bit, you know…'

Ignoring Barney, she carried on, 'We've had a few protesters camped out near the site. The last thing we wanna do is give them any mixed messages.'

'Mixed messages?'

'Yeah,' said Barney. 'We need to keep the focus on renewables…'

'But keep nuclear in the mix, as part of our commitment to clean energy,' added Julia.

'I suppose I could add a few of those wind turbine thingies and perhaps a solar whatchamacallit or two.' Frank laid the other sketches on the table.

'Mm, not so sure, Frank. I'm starting to think it needs a rethink. These pictures of a bunch of old dead guys don't really cut it for me. You, Barn?'

'Nah. I just can see people being turned on by them.'

'But aren't you trying to educate people about it and, if so…'

'Educate, sure, but through edutainment, not a history lesson.'

'Eh?'

'Not the usual old school stuff, you know. We need images that engage people. Make 'em interested, not bore them stupid.'

'Well, I'll see what I can come up with,' said Frank, packing away the sketches.

'Good man,' said Julia. 'Check out our publicity material. It's all on the net. Might give you a better steer. Oh, and we'll have more soon, once we've got the agency on board.'

'I'll certainly look into it,' said Frank unconvincingly.

'And you've found a little place to work up here?'

'I'll be looking into that tomorrow, too.'

The meeting broke up, and a disconsolate Frank tramped off to his room. There was a voicemail message on his phone from DS Davis, asking him to call back as soon as possible. After his meeting with Julia and Barney, the last thing Frank felt like having was another conversation with the police. But, knowing he couldn't put it off indefinitely, he returned the call.

'More questions, sergeant?' he asked querulously.

'Just one, Mister Armstrong, if you don't mind.'

Of course I mind, Frank said to himself. 'So, what do you want to know?'

'Would you mind telling me what size shoes you wear?'

'My shoes?'

'Yes, sir. What size are they?'

'I take a size eight, if you must know.' *At least, he's addressing me as "sir" again*, thought Frank.

'Not tens?'

'Certainly not.'

'And do you own any that have a patterned sole?'

'A what?'

'A patterned sole. The sort that you'd find on boots and trainers. Do you have a pair like that?'

'Sergeant, I wear shoes with leather soles. I have never had a pair of training shoes in my life, and it's many years since I went fellwalking.'

'I see. Thank you. Well, I'm sorry to have bothered you.'

That evening, he did not savour the beef stroganoff, or the glasses of Pomerol he had chosen to accompany it. His thoughts were wholly consumed with anger at and contempt for anyone under forty, and puzzlement at why the detective had wanted to know what shoes he wore. He slept badly, sneering at voices that kept repeating the simply awful syntax he had endured at the meeting. Even the hefty breakfast that he would never have been allowed to get away with at home failed to lift his spirits. He was in no mood to go searching for a place to live up there. He scanned the local paper. There was nothing remotely suitable. Eventually, he dragged himself off to scour the town's estate agencies. At Marwood's, he saw nothing in the window, but forced himself to enter and risk being exposed to yet more fractured language.

A slim young man in owlish spectacles blinked as Frank plonked himself in a chair across his desk. 'Are you looking for anything in particular?'

'Yes, I am. Nothing too challenging, and all very straightforward for you, I'm sure. I simply want to rent a small studio with living accommodation in Grasmere.'

'Grasmere?' the young man's eyebrows rose.

'Indeed. It really must be in Grasmere.'

'Well, that may not be quite so straightforward, I'm afraid.'

'And why on earth not?'

'The trouble is very little accommodation in Grasmere ever comes to market. You see, it's a very small place, and…'

'I know Grasmere extremely well and I cannot believe there is nothing available.'

'We've nothing at the moment, but if you'd like to leave me your details, I'll contact you if anything does become available, though I don't think it's likely to be for some time.'

'Oh no, I can't possibly wait that long. I'll simply have to try elsewhere…'

The young man shook his head, 'I don't think you'll have much luck.'

The cup of Frank's patience was almost down to the dregs, 'Well, what do you suggest then?'

'You could try broadening the radius of your search area.'

'The what?'

And now the estate agent's patience was ebbing too. 'Well, sir, how far from Grasmere would you be prepared to live?'

'Oh, not far at all. My heart is set on Grasmere, you see.'

There was a large map of Cumbria behind the estate agent's desk, and he pointed to it. 'We do have some properties within just about a ten mile radius, if that would suit you.'

'Such as?'

'Well, there's Keswick…'

'Oh, far too touristy.'

The young man sighed. *And Grasmere isn't touristy?* he thought to himself. 'And there is a cottage in Portinscale that might suit you, but…'

Frank whipped out a pair of half-moon glasses from his jacket pocket and looked at the sales brochure that the estate agent put in front of him.

'Well, I daresay that would do.'

'There is just one thing, though, sir.'

'And what might that be?'

'There is a local occupancy clause with the property.'

'A what?'

'It just means that the property is restricted to people who are employed in Cumbria or have lived in the county for the last three years.' The estate agent doubted that, given his accent and his age, Frank would be able to meet either requirement.

'I am coming here to work,' said Frank proudly.

'Very good, sir. And you would be able to provide the name of your employer?'

'I will not be an employee. I am an artist and I work for a great many clients.'

'I see. I'm afraid that might be a problem.'

'Young man, I was born in Cumbria, Kendal to be precise. So what could possibly be the problem?'

'But you haven't lived here for the last three years…'

'Oh, for heaven's sake!' expostulated Frank.

The two men trawled through a pile of brochures until they found the only one that was both suitable and in which Frank would be eligible to live. It was a converted garage with an upstairs bedsit on the northern edge of Penrith.

On the train north from Euston, Tom sat with his team around a table in first class. They ran through the presentation one last time, then devoted the rest of the journey to making calls, much to the irritation of the retired couple across the aisle from them, and answering emails. Meanwhile, Frank, tired of it all, wanted to get back home. He cancelled his second night at the hotel, and went to catch a late morning train to London.

Fran, Mo and Bobbi emerged from the underpass beneath Penrith station and headed for the taxi rank.

Tom's mobile rang, so he hung back to take the call. Outside the station, Frank had just lit a small cigar as he awaited the arrival of the London train, when his phone rang.

'Lizzie, that you?'

'Yes. I need to talk to you, Dad.'

'Just a mo.' As a goods train hurtled southwards, Frank juggled the phone, his cigar and the portfolio that was under his arm, then turned and saw a man who looked just like his son-in-law following the other three passengers towards the taxis. 'Surely not,' he said to himself then, on hearing a tall, Black girl, call out, 'Tom!' and, after he whispered something, put her arms around him, muttered, 'Good grief.'

'What?'

'Eh? Oh, nothing. Now, that's better, what's the matter, darling?' Frank was still getting over his surprise at seeing Tom across the station forecourt.

'It's about Mum.'

'She's all right, isn't she?'

'No, she isn't. We're very worried about her.'

'What is it? She isn't ill? Hasn't had an accident, has she?'

'No. She's told us all about what happened at the gallery, and then the police coming round. It took us ages to get her to tell us, but she thinks you're keeping something from her and that's really upset her.'

'Oh, your poor Mum. I really must…'

'Never mind that, Dad. When you get back, I want you to tell her what's going on.'

'Lizzie, darling, there's nothing going on.'

'There must be something. Mum isn't stupid.'

'Of course not…'

'So, whatever it is, I want you to promise that you'll let her know whatever it is you aren't telling her.'

'But…'

'Promise.'

'Well, look, darling, my train's pulling in. I'll have to…' lied Frank.

'Promise.'

'I'll talk to your mother when I get back. Yes, I promise.' Frank took a long drag of his cigar after Lizzie ended the call, as the station announcer informed him that the service to Euston was running fifteen, one five, minutes late. Frank glowered in his window seat. He had been rebuffed by a pair of ignoramuses who didn't know the first thing about the great men who pioneered nuclear power, let alone about art; there was to be no charming little studio in Grasmere, and he had been forced to put down a deposit for a shabby billet that he knew he could never grow to love; and now his eldest daughter knew all about the business with Martin and had given him a piece of her mind. His mood wasn't improved by the quality of the complimentary wine and moist sandwich, and having to pay extra for catching an earlier train.

Tom and the others checked into the hotel and arranged to meet for drinks at six. His call outside the station was from Jake Selley, Conch Telecom's newly-appointed marketing director. The news was bad; SHM was not being invited to re-pitch for the account. Jake simply said they needed a completely new change of direction, and wanted fresh ideas from a new agency. Tom sat glumly in his room, knowing that if he failed to win the NZO account, his career would be in freefall. He began to read the brief again, and some of the background research. He read a briefing on nuclear safety, if only to confirm his suspicions, but was surprised to find how different it was these days. Perhaps lessons really had been learned from Chernobyl and Three Mile Island. Another paper explained what "base load" is, and how nuclear power provided the only consistently reliable minimum source of electricity that is always in demand. He found himself admitting that perhaps it did have a role to play alongside wind and solar power.

In the cab back to Putney, Frank went over what to say to Louise. After Lizzie's call, he knew he had to say something, *but exactly what, and how much?* His thoughts kept drifting, though, as he wondered what Tom was doing in Penrith, *and with that pretty, Black girl, too*. Crawling through the West End, he wondered if seeing Tom might be a good place to start, and perhaps divert attention from what he needed to explain to his wife. He was tired, hungry, in need of a drink and feeling miserable. As he had on too many previous occasions, though, Frank had underestimated Louise.

He dumped his case and portfolio in the hall, and tentatively opened the door to the drawing room. Louise was reclining on the sofa, with Titus curled up on her lap, and Saskia playing with a toy mouse.

'I didn't expect you back so soon,' she said by way of a greeting.

Frank nodded, 'I didn't think there was anything to be gained from another night up there.'

'Good job they're paying the bill.' Louise watched Frank walk over to the sideboard and pour himself a hefty Scotch but, to his surprise, made no attempt to remonstrate with him.

'You'll never guess, I saw Tom this afternoon. In Penrith.'

'Oh yes.'

'With a rather pretty Black girl, too.'

'That'll be Bobbi.'

'Bobbi?'

'She's his assistant, or something. Honestly, don't you remember him telling us that he'd recruited her, and that she'd been in the same year as Georgia?' She paused, 'No, of course, you don't listen, do you? That's the trouble.'

'But what were they doing in Penrith, of all places?'

'Lizzie said something about it being quite the coincidence that Tom had a meeting up there too.'

'Did she now? Well, the thing is, the two of them…' Frank knew it would be futile to carry on, and let the sentence peter out.

'So?'

'So?'

'So, did what did you do?'

'Do what?'

'Oh, for God's sake, Frank. What did you do to Martin?'

Frank was taken aback and took a large gulp of whisky. 'Nothing. I didn't do anything to him. Lou, surely you can't imagine I'd do any such thing.'

'Well something happened to him, and you went round to see him. So, what happened?'

'All right. We argued a bit, yes, I admit that. But he was fine when I left him. Honestly, Lou.'

Louise did believe him, knowing Frank was a coward at heart and just full of bluster. But she also knew her husband was not always straight with her, and there also remained the matter of his relationship with Martin. She sat up, sending the cat scuttling off across the floor. 'The trouble is, Frank, if you will insist on keeping things from me, it makes it very difficult to believe you when you are telling the truth.'

'But, Lou, believe me, I never touched Martin. Yes, of course I was angry with him. Wouldn't anyone be?'

'All right. Let's say you didn't...'

'I didn't...'

'But that doesn't explain why you weren't able to be honest with me about your relationship with Martin...'

'It wasn't a relationship...'

'Well, whatever you call it then, it was certainly a good deal more than you had led me to believe.'

Frank knew he had backed himself into a corner. He breathed heavily. 'The thing is, Lou, it had been just a little fling to me. Just fun, you see. But it seemed to mean rather more to Martin. When I mentioned wanting to break it off, he went into such a tizz that I was terrified he might mention our, ahm, friendship to the Prof. So, you see, I had to go along with it for much longer than I wanted. I had no choice.'

Louise nodded. 'And that's the truth, is it?' *Yes*, she thought, *that's exactly what Frank would have done to save his skin. Poor Martin.*

'I promise. That's everything, honestly. Oh, I do wish I'd told you before now.'

'So do I.'

Frank was in two minds whether or not to mention it, but thought he might as well get hanged for a sheep as for a lamb. 'Oh, there was one other thing.'

'Go on.'

'That blasted policeman called me while I was up

there. Asked me about my shoes, of all things.'

'Shoes?' asked Louise, thinking the dialogue was beginning to sound like something by Pinter.

'He wanted to know what size I wear and if I possess such a thing as a pair of training shoes.'

Louise almost laughed. They sat silently, facing each other. At last, Louise brought it to an end. 'So, that's everything then? Now, Frank, you're going to have to be more open with me in future. That's what married life is supposed to be about. I mean to say, if I don't know what's going on, how can I help you? And if you keep things from me, you must see that it's more than likely I'll suspect the worst.'

'You're right, Lou. Course you are. Sorry.'

'Right. Now, top up your drink, and bring me a glass of wine. There's some Sancerre in the fridge. You'd better tell me how you got on with the NZO people.'

Tom was the last to arrive. The team were already in the bar with drinks in front of them. As he walked in, their conversation stopped abruptly. He got himself a pint of cider and joined them. The only one who's heard the news, Bobbi looked across at her boss sympathetically.

'It's okay,' said Tom. 'Yeah, Conch Telecom has binned us off, but it wasn't as if there was anything we could do about it, was there?'

'Suppose not, but you'd think they'd show a bit more respect, us being the incumbent and all,' said Fran. 'You sure you're okay, Tom?'

'Yeah, fine. Well it is what it is. So, we'd better be on form tomorrow.'

'Sure, but do you know who we're going up against?' asked Mo.

'Well, I did see Rupert Storey's Beemer in the car park. Don't know why the silly sod has a personalised plate,' said Fran.

'Hmm, so they're sending in a heavy hitter,' said Bobbi, then added after a mouthful of Coke, 'Maybe Yannick should be here too.'

'We'll be fine,' said Tom, disgruntled at the idea that he might not be sufficiently senior to lead the NZO pitch.

The team dispersed after dinner for an early night, but Tom reread the brief and thought about the approach he'd take to present SHM's offer. As Yannick had said, he needed to differentiate them from the competition.

With a mild hangover exacerbated by tiredness and the events of the previous day, Frank shambled into the dining room shortly after ten thirty, yawning expansively and in need of his morning mug of strong Darjeeling. He was not at all sure what to expect. Things with Louise had been sort of resolved with the help of a few drinks, but even Frank knew better than to expect everything to be exactly hunky dory again. Louise looked up from her coffee at her unshaven husband, and just said, 'Barrack gates are open, Frank.'

'Eh? Oh, lord,' he replied, quickly doing up the buttons on his pyjamas fly.

'Good job the girls are out,' she said with a faint grin.

Back with a mug of tea, Frank sat opposite Louise. "I've been thinking,' he said at last.

'Well, that's a start.'

'It's these blasted murals. I'm not going to do them. I'm a portrait artist when all's said and done.'

'And that's because they've asked you to make some changes, I suppose?'

'Well, yes, of course. But, I'm also starting to wonder if young Tom might have a point.'

Louise nearly choked on her coffee. 'My God, I never thought I'd hear you say that.'

'Yes, I mean to say, he's quite right about one thing. This Net Zero Observatory idea really is just about trying to persuade people to like nuclear power and get the antis out of their hair. And they're doing it in a really sneaky way, by putting it alongside all that green stuff as if it's all the same thing.'

'And that's what you honestly think, is it?' Louise's astonishment had risen another notch on the scale.

'Indeed it is. Those people really are quite cynical, you know.'

'I see. My word, Frank, you are full of surprises today. There must be something in the water up there.'

'It's a matter of principle,' said Frank grandly.

'Oh, I daresay, but aren't there a couple of things you've forgotten?'

'Such as?'

'For a start, Julian will be livid. After all, he got you the commission.'

'He'll get over it.'

'And you've already paid the deposit for the studio, haven't you?'

'Hardly a studio, Lou. It's a bloody converted garage, that's all.'

Louise reached across the dining room table, and put her hand on Frank's. She was impressed to think that Frank's decision to abandon the murals had been prompted by his curious and newfound principles, and that they appeared to matter more to him than the very large amount of money the NZO was prepared to pay, or the need to disappear from view while the investigation continued into what had led to Martin ending up in hospital. But, she also knew how capricious her husband could be, so she said to him gently, 'All right, Frank, but there's no need to make any hasty decisions, is there? Let's sleep on it, and see how you feel in a day or two.'

At eleven, Tom and the team assembled in the hotel lounge, and made their way along a corridor to a meeting room with a high, vaulted ceiling. Julia O'Leary and Barney Brady were already there at one end of a long table on which stood four half full glasses of water and a carafe from the previous agency's presentation. Tom had not slept well, but had spent the early hours deciding on what tack to take. While Mo rummaged beneath the table for the lead to connect her laptop to the large screen, Fran ran over her presentation and Bobbi sat poised, ready to take notes. Tom introduced himself and the team to Julia and Barney.

His colleagues had seen Tom in presentations before, and knew him to be articulate and thorough, but not perhaps the most inspiring speaker. They were surprised then, when he abruptly closed Mo's laptop, crossed the room to switch off the television screen, then turned off all the lights in the room. Fran and Mo exchanged anxious glances.

'Right, now let's begin. Our message is a very simple one. Without the vital role of nuclear power in securing the base load we all depend on, renewables alone will be insufficient to meet the needs of the public. Without it, we would be where we are right now. In almost total darkness, with zero connectivity. Without it, we would be asking the public to give up a quality of life to which they have long become accustomed. Put simply, we are asking the British people to make a choice. Accept nuclear power or do without so much that you take for granted,' Tom spoke clearly, and much louder than usual.

He got up and gave hard copies of the presentation to Julia and Barney, then added, 'I don't think there's anything more to be said. Here are the details of how the campaign would be run, with all the costings. We'll leave you to read them at your leisure. Thank you for inviting us to pitch. We would be especially delighted to work for the Net Zero Observatory, given its enormous importance in safeguarding the future of everyone in this country.'

And, with that, he put his notes in their folder and led the way out. The team hesitated before gathering their bags and following him. Tom held the door open to let the three of them leave ahead of him. They made their way back to the lounge in silence.

'Bloody hell, Tom, what was all that about?' said Fran.

'Yannick said all along that we needed to do something that would stand out,' Tom replied quietly.

'Maybe, but you've taken a hell of a risk just leaving it like that.'

Mo shook her head, 'And, I mean, we didn't even show them the presentation.' She tapped her laptop ruefully.

Tom knew how much of a risk he'd taken and did his best not to show how nervous he was. The mood of the team was subdued on the train journey back to London, and not the usual hopeful euphoria that follows a pitch to a prospective client.

The following day, Frank agreed to carry on with the murals. Louise was partly relieved, believing it to be for the best, but the readiness with which he changed his mind nevertheless made her wonder if her husband really had told her everything about what had happened to Martin, that he had realised that his anger at being asked to change the designs of the murals was less important than staying away from London for a while. 'So much for principles,' she said to herself.

7

'Well, for one thing, there's his shoes. They don't match the footprints, but that might not mean anything. They could belong to one of the cleaners. But then something Armstrong said has got me thinking. You see, he said he left the place about two, at least no later than that, and then stopped to have a smoke before catching the Tube home.'

'So, what's wrong with that?'

'Well, he wouldn't have done that if it had been pouring down, would he? And, remember that big puddle of water on the floor? Right, well, I've checked the weather report for that day, and it didn't start raining until well after three.'

'Might have just spilled a glass of water or something?'

'No, I don't think so. There was that broken brolly on the floor next to it. So, either our Mister Robertson went out in the rain sometime later, or the brolly belonged to someone else. Either way, that would be after Armstrong left, wouldn't it?'

'He could have come back.'

'It's possible, but then he said he was back in Putney by three, so it doesn't seem very likely.'

'I suppose not. So, are you saying that puts him in the clear? That is, if you reckon he's telling the truth.'

Davis nodded slowly, 'Yeah, it looks like it. But there's still something about him I can't weigh up. I, oh I don't know, maybe it's just that I'm not used to dealing with these arty types. Maybe it's just the way they come across.'

'So, we're not saying that it was definitely an

accident, then?'

'Well, it probably was, but we might know more if Robertson can tell us anything when he comes out of this coma. If he does, that is. Let's just sit on it for now. We're not short of stuff to be getting on with, and there's no need for us to jump to any conclusions. At least, not yet.'

There was an awkward atmosphere at the Bishopsgate offices of SHM, with account executives and creatives seeming to tiptoe around Tom Wilson, who busied himself with a few of his smaller clients, doing more than usual to keep them warm now that the Conch Telecom account was gone. It was one of those afternoons that never get fully light, yet the office seemed somehow gloomier with the lights on. Tom didn't notice the tall figure of Yannick Morrow in the doorway to his office until the latter spoke.

'Well, my man, you've nailed it!' said Yannick.

Looking up from his laptop, Tom saw Yannick grinning widely. 'What, the NZO pitch?' he asked uncertainly.

'Sure, the NZO. Julia O'Leary just called me. You got it.'

'Wow.'

'Yeah, Fran told me you were on fire in the pitch. Said she'd never seen anything like it. Hey, you need balls to take the kind of risk you took, but you're the man, Tom.'

'Well, you did say…'

'I know, I know. But winners don't play it safe, right?' Yannick, having delivered the good news, was about to return to his office, but added, 'And no big deal about Conch.'

'I'm still pretty pissed off about that, being the

incumbent…'

Yannick shook his head, 'Nah, we dodged a bullet there.'

'What do you mean?'

'Check out the FT. The regulator's kicking Conch around the room for paying its call centre people less than minimum wage. You being ESG lead and all, working for them, and our reputation goes down the tubes. Gotta go, but take the team out somewhere. You all did good.'

After a fruitless morning in his studio, Frank meandered into the drawing room, where Louise was trying to finish the last few chapters before the evening's meeting of the Book Club, despite knowing it unlikely as wouldn't Polly stay watching CBeebies all afternoon.

'I won't do those damned murals, Lou, I really can't bring myself to do them.'

Irritated at having her reading interrupted, Louise said sharply, 'Oh, Frank, I do wish you'd make up your mind.'

'It just doesn't feel right to me.'

'Well, that will be music to Tom's ears.'

'Tom?'

'Yes, don't you remember? He's picking up Polly. Lizzie's got a dentist's appointment.'

'Oh, right, Tom. Hmm.'

It was gone six thirty by the time Tom arrived, just as Louise was leaving to discuss the latest winner of the silver dagger for crime fiction. He sat across the drawing room from Frank as Polly munched celery sticks and hummus.

Tom hesitantly broke the silence before it became awkward, and asked, 'How are the new paintings going?'

'Oh, well, to be honest…'

'You being a Cumbrian and all, I suppose it sort of makes sense for them to ask you to do them.'

'I suppose it does…'

'Thing is, we've been doing some research into nuclear power at SHM, and it's looking like there really is no alternative. That is, if we want to keep the lights on.'

'I see,' said Frank warily, wondering what new line of argument his son-in-law might be developing.

'So, I guess I can see why the NZO need to educate people about it. And your paintings are bound to be an important part of that. Like they say, a picture paints a thousand words.'

'Yes, so they say indeed. But…'

'So, I'd be really interested in seeing them.'

'Ah well, they're not really…'

'You see, we're going to be doing some work for the NZO and it makes sense if what we do kind of dovetails with what you're doing. We don't want to come up with something that looks sort of inconsistent with your paintings.'

'I see. Well, of course, but as I say…' Frank was flabbergasted. So that's what Tom was up to in Penrith. It didn't explain the hug he'd received from the pretty, Black girl, but Frank felt oddly reluctant to mention it, surprised as he was at his son-in-law's apparent volte-face.

'No rush, though. And now I'd better be getting young Miss Polly home. It'll be past her bedtime.'

When Tom and his granddaughter had gone, Frank was in a daze as he carried the remains of Polly's snack into the kitchen. Tom's volte-face had astonished him and he was glad that he had not revealed his own misgivings about the NZO's motives. If Tom had got over his objections to nuclear power, then Frank could think of no reason why he should feel uncomfortable about the commission. There was the deposit and three months' rent on the studio, and there was the possibility of some useful PR that both Max and Julian had mentioned. Frank again mulled over the perks that come with a gong. Yes, he could paint the murals, except for one small snag.

Louise returned just before eight, pleased to see that her husband was not accompanied by a drink, but surprised to find him sitting quietly with a baffled expression.

'Late supper tonight, Frank.' On getting no response, she continued, 'Everything all right, darling?'

'Oh, sorry, miles away. Yes, of course. Fine, fine, fine, thanks,' Frank answered absently.

'You and Tom didn't fall out again, did you?' Louise asked cautiously, not wanting to have to act as peacemaker over yet another family row.

'Oh no, he was fine. It was all fine.' Frank finally came to. 'No, we had a very interesting chat.'

'Oh yes?'

'Yes. Lou, that boy is full of surprises, you know. He gave me pretty much a ringing endorsement to do the murals.'

'Goodness, whatever next?'

'It seems his lot are also going to be working for the Net Zero people, and so...'

'So, you're going to do them then?'

'Well, yes, I suppose so, but...'

'But what?'

'Lou, it's not that I don't want to do them, it's just that I simply can't. I haven't the foggiest idea of how to come up with what those blasted people want.'

'Why not have a word with Georgia? She should be here in a minute,' said Louise, keen to delegate the job to her daughter.

Ten minutes later, Georgia walked in, 'I'm ravenous. What's for supper?'

'Ahm, before we eat, I wonder if I could pick your brains, darling?' said Frank tentatively.

'Sure, Dad. What can I do for you?' Georgia was always delighted at the rare occasions when her advice was sought, rather than that of her elder sister.

'Well, you know what you said about my sketches for the murals? Don't think you thought much of them, did you?'

'Well…'

'It's all right, darling, I can take criticism as well as the next man.'

Louise stifled a guffaw, and added, 'Or woman.'

'Well, yes, or woman. No, you see, what would be incredibly helpful would be any ideas for them. I'm having a bit of a…'

'A bit of an artist's block, Dad?'

'Oh no, nothing like that. But perhaps in a way…'

Georgia thought for a moment. 'How about if you did a series of scenes of what the world would look like without, what is it, clean energy? And then some other ones about how much better the world would look with it? You know, forests, the sea, animals, stuff like that.'

'Yes, I think I see what you mean. But what about the nuclear stuff? They're hellbent on having that included, but goodness knows how I'm supposed to do that.'

'Maybe you could have the first lot showing lots of chimneys with thick smoke pouring out of them…'

'I remember what that was like back in the fifties and sixties. There was smog everywhere…'

'Smog? Anyway, you could then put the nuclear…'

'The reactors.'

'Yes, include them but, unlike the other ones, there'd be no smoke coming out of them. You, know, by doing a sort of compare and contrast.'

'Right, well, there's a casserole in the oven,' said Louise. 'That is, unless your father has changed his mind about that, too. If he has, there's only some soup left over from lunch.'

Gerald took his painting of the pheasants to Julian's gallery, hopeful that it would appeal to the usual clientele who bought his pictures of lions and elephants, despite knowing a pheasant was bound to be worth less than a large jungle beast. He thought about treating himself to a good lunch, but another idea sprang to mind. He crossed Bloomsbury and walked into The Curzon Gallery. It was a long time since he had spoken to Jane McNab, at least as Gerald Graham rather than Mister Melchior. Although he had been at Martin's preview, he wasn't sure she'd remember him. She did.

Jane was surprised to see Gerald, after she had refused to exhibit his paintings all those years ago. He was delighted to see Martin's painting, *The Art Lovers*, remained on show, its red dot removed and now available to buy.

'Gerald Graham! Well, this is a surprise,' said a genuinely surprised Jane.

Gerald opted to start the conversation with a bright and breezy tone, 'I was in the neighbourhood, so I thought I'd pop in and see how young Martin's exhibition is doing.' He lowered his voice, and added, 'I suppose you've heard about what happened to the poor lad?'

'Oh yes, wasn't it terrible?'

'Absolutely shocking. And it seems we're still none the wiser as to what happened to him.'

'Is he still in hospital?'

'I'm afraid so. Not come round yet. We can only pray that he'll be on the mend soon. Incidentally, how did you come to hear about Martin?'

'The police called round.'

'Did they, by God?' Gerald could barely supress his glee at hearing the police had got involved.

'I was astonished when they said they couldn't rule out it being an accident. So I told them about the argument he had with Frank Armstrong.'

'You told them about Frank?'

'Yes, they wanted his address, so I imagine they wanted to speak to him. But, surely it was just a terrible accident?'

'Oh, that's exactly what I thought too, but I suppose if the police aren't entirely satisfied...'

'Well, it does seem rather odd.'

'I daresay they must have their suspicions, now that they know about that brouhaha at the preview.'

'I do wonder if I did the right thing telling them about that.'

Gerald waved away Jane's remark. 'No, you really mustn't blame yourself. Mind you, I find it impossible to believe that Frank was in any way involved. He is one of my oldest friends, you know, as is young Martin. The entire matter is simply inexplicable. By the way, I see the picture, the one that caused all the kerfuffle is still here. Thought you'd got a buyer for it.'

'So did I, but it doesn't look like I'm going to hear from him now.'

'Bad luck. There are some absolute stinkers around, aren't there? Oh, by the way, would you be interested in one of my earlier daubs? A large abstract. I know my recent stuff isn't quite to your taste…'

'I am sorry about that, Gerald, but they didn't really go with what we were showing.'

'Oh, never mind about that. All water under the bridge or something like that.' Gerald grinned, 'So, might you be interested?'

'I would, but I thought they'd all been sold years ago? And, anyway, isn't Julian Furnell your dealer these days?'

'Well, there is one I can lay my hands on. Here take a look.' He found the photo on his phone and held it for Jane to see. 'And I don't think it would be old Julian's cup of tea, do you?'

'In that case, I certainly am interested. And as I recall, they used to command quite a price.' Jane thought about the sizeable commission. The Curzon could do with it.

'A few of them got into five figures,' nodded Gerald.

'Well, do bring it round when you get chance.'

'I will indeed.'

With that, Gerald left Jane with one of his sinister "cheery byes", and began considering what might be his next move on the way back to Ealing.

Frank had been busy. He had sketched out a series of small panels, each showing a desolate world, with stunted trees, filthy rivers, chimneys belching out thick smoke, and dead animals that were even more hideous than Gerald's dead pheasants. He then overlaid them with grisaille, in watercolour that he seldom used since realising he would never make a living painting landscapes. He was exhausted, and carried his work from the studio at the bottom of the garden and arrayed them on the dining room chairs. Louise and Lizzie were chatting in the drawing room, while Polly played a game and Theo, for once, dozed in his buggy.

'You've been in there a long time,' said Louise as he put his head round the door, pleased that her husband appeared to have been working.

Frank nodded and said, breathing heavily, 'Want to see what I've been up to?'

The two women followed him into the dining room. Both looked at the pictures in silence.

'Goodness,' said Louise at last. 'They're a bit of a departure.'

'I had no idea you could come up with stuff like this,' added Lizzie.

'But do you like them?'

'They're really powerful,' said Lizzie.

Frank was thrilled at hearing his daughter's sudden and unaccustomed enthusiasm for his painting, and gave her a kiss.

'Well, it was Georgia's idea,' said Louise, only slightly dampening Frank's mood.

'Yes, I really do think she's come up trumps.'

In the days that followed, Frank worked on pastoral scenes in vibrant colours, with tiny nuclear domes tucked away in the distance. Children played with kites, dolphins leapt from the waves, deer and foxes peeped out from behind lush vegetation. Louise and his daughters approved, but preferred the images of a grim, polluted future. She arranged an appointment for Frank to have another meeting with Julia and Barney. The Sunday before, Frank went down to The Duke of York, as usual, and found Gerald and Doug deep in conversation. On seeing him approach, they stopped talking and moved apart.

'And what are you two old rogues plotting?' Frank asked, trying to sound jovial, but uncomfortable that they were clearly talking about him.

'Oh, just wondering how poor young Martin is getting on,' said Gerald casually.

'Aye, still no news, I'm afraid,' added Doug.

Max came over with the drinks. 'I was in the neck of the wood and saw that Martin's painting remains unbought. How mysterious, don't you think? And Jane McNab is pulling her hair about it.'

'It's been a truly awful time,' said Frank cautiously.

Gerald was unable to keep to himself the question he had been wanting to ask ever since Frank walked in, and blurted out, 'How's the nuclear job going, Frank? Off to the place of your ancestors any time soon?'

'Yes, since you ask. I'm going this week.'

'Well, that'll keep you out of harm's way, I suppose.'

'What on earth can you mean by that, Gerald?'

'Oh, just that I'm sure it will be a relief to be away from everything that's been going on down here. And how long will you be staying up there, if you don't mind my asking?'

Not exactly mollified, Frank replied, 'It's really rather hard to say, but I expect it will be for a few weeks or so, perhaps longer. One never knows.'

'Well, good luck, old lad. I must say I do rather envy you,' said Gerald, knowing full well that admitting envy was the quickest way to placate Frank.

Louise was poring over her laptop. 'I'm very glad it's furnished,' she said as Frank returned from the pub. 'But there'll still be rather a lot for us to take up.'

'I suppose so. Hang on, you said there'd be a lot for *us* to take up?'

Louise eyed her husband cautiously, 'I did indeed. Don't you think it would be a good idea if I knew where you'll be living?'

'Well, yes, perhaps, but there's really no need...'

'I think there's every need. Anyway, I've made out a list of what to take. We can pick up the groceries when we get there, but I think it'll be at least two or even three suitcases, as well as your painting things.'

Frank went over to look at the laptop, 'Good grief. You really think I'll need all this stuff? I mean to say, a travel iron and what on earth is a microfibre cloth when it's at home?'

'I don't want you living like a pig, Frank. And you'll be having meetings with people, so you'll need to run an iron over anything creased, won't you?'

'I've never used a blasted iron in my life.'

'Well, it's perhaps time you did.'

Frank stomped off to his studio, with the pleasant imaginings of convivial evenings spent in a cosy pub replaced by visions of himself iron in hand beside a pile of washing.

Dominic's mobile went off while he was teaching. Martin had regained consciousness. It was the last period, so after the bell, he dashed straight over to University College Hospital. Martin was as pale as ever, and attached to a linguine of pipes and tubes, but awake. He smiled as his husband arrived, then regretted the action and winced at the discomfort.

'Oh, thank God,' said Dominic breathlessly.

Martin opened his mouth as if to speak, but Dominic spoke first, 'Don't say anything, Martin, love. You've been through such a lot.'

Martin smiled and nodded gently.

'Now, love, the only important thing that matters is for you to get better. And I'll look after you. No, don't talk. You must rest.'

Martin put his hand on Dominic's and pulled it towards him. He was determined to speak, and Dominic leaned forward to hear him. 'The studio.' Martin was almost inaudible and the effort was distressing him. 'You need to go to the studio. Jane wants the sketches…'

'Never mind about that now, please, just rest.'

'Please, Dom, get the sketches and take them to Jane. Please.' The effort had worn him out and Martin leaned back heavily onto his pillows.

'Okay, of course. Yes, of course, I'll do that. Is there anything else I can do, anything at all?'

Martin gave a brief shake of the head. The two men sat and held hands. They didn't need to talk and both were simply glad to be able to look at each other. When it was time to go, Dominic kissed Martin's forehead and Martin squeezed his husband's hand.

On the way home, Dominic remembered that the police telling him they'd locked up the studio. He got off the Tube a stop early and made his way to Islington police station. It was quiet inside; Dominic told the desk sergeant about Martin and asked if it would be possible to have the keys to the studio. The policeman scratched his head, 'Do you know which officer was dealing with this, sir?'

Dominic couldn't think of the name, then DS Davis came down the stairs. 'Brian, do you know who's looking after this... What was it sir, an artist friend of yours who had an accident? Clerkenwell, did you say?'

'That'll be me, Terry,' said DS Davis. He turned to Dominic, 'What can I do for you, sir?'

Dominic explained that Martin had come round, and repeated his request for the keys to the studio. The policeman nodded, 'Ah yes, you'll be Mister Robertson's partner? We've spoken on the phone a couple of times. You must be Mister Talbot, yes?'

The two men shook hands.

'Now, if you've some ID, sir, I can get the keys for you. We won't be needing them anymore.'

Dominic handed his driving licence to DS Davis, who handed it back, then started to go upstairs again, but stopped after a few steps. 'Ahm, perhaps it would be more comfortable in my office, sir, if you'd like to follow me.'

They went into the DS's office and the policeman left Dominic to get the keys. He was back quickly. 'And how is Mister Robertson, sir? He regained consciousness today, you say?'

'That's right.'

'Well, I'm sure that's a relief to you. We will, of course, like to speak to Mister Robertson. Just to see if he can shed any light on what happened to him, you see.'

'Of course. I'm sure he'll be happy to help, though I would like to be with him, if that's okay.'

'I'm sure something can be arranged, sir,' said Davis. He looked down at Dominic's feet and smiled, 'Let me guess. Are you a sportsman, Mister Talbot?'

'What?'

'I'm sorry, sir, I just noticed your trainers. My lad wants a new pair, and there are so many it's hard to know the best ones to get.'

'Oh, just Pumas. I do some running now and then. Not much recently, though.'

'No, of course not. I don't suppose you would. Pumas, eh? Any good?'

'Yes they're fine, but why…'

'I'd say my lad has about the same size as you. What are they, about tens or elevens?'

'They're size tens. You don't want me to take them off so you can check, do you?'

'No, of course not, sir,' Davis smiled. 'It's just a bit of a coincidence, that's all.'

'A coincidence?'

'Yes, you and my lad taking the same size trainers.'

Dominic was puzzled by the small talk, and relieved when the policeman handed over the keys to the studio. Back home, he got a celebratory beer from the fridge, put a pizza in the oven and crashed out on the sofa. It was gone nine before he rang his friends, and then Doug to let him know the good news.

And it was the following morning before Gerald heard from Doug. He had begun a small painting of a trout and, as Doug spoke, he mimed casting a line then reeling it in. He could not help wondering which day Frank would be leaving for Cumbria, and was barely able to intersperse the news about Martin with the necessary noises of relief and hope for his full recovery. He decided not to strike too soon. Gerald would wait until Friday, to be sure that Frank would be away from London by then.

It was the afternoon before Frank and Louise were ready,

cases packed. They took a cab to Euston, and spent the journey north doing the Telegraph crossword. Another cab took them to the flat in Penrith. While Frank lugged the cases up a narrow staircase, Louise walked around the flat, wrinkling her nose at the musty smell, tired furniture and hideous wallpaper.

'This is it?' she said at last, as Frank deposited the third case in the small sitting room.

Out of breath, Frank merely nodded.

'My God, it smells terrible in here. We'll have to get some air fresheners, but let's open the windows for now.'

Frank lifted the catch and sent a row of jackdaws packing from the window ledge.

'And they didn't have anything else?'

'Darling, if they had, do you think I'd have taken this place?' asked Frank testily.

'Suppose not. It isn't exactly a Lakeland cottage, is it?'

'I know, I know, but...' Frank felt even more depressed than his wife. 'But, come on, Lou, let's find a pub. I'm starving and I could do with a drink.'

Louise, for once, agreed. 'I'll just hang a few things up, though they're bound to end up covered in mould.'

Half an hour later, they headed into The Old Smithy. They paused momentarily on the threshold as they heard loud music playing while a group of bald headed men played darts. The choice of wine was limited to a red or a white with no further information than that, and the pub's special on the menu was lasagne. They opted for glasses of red and Cumberland sausages with mash, the former cold, the latter white hot, and consumed them under the curious gaze of the landlord and the darts players. Frank paid the bill and they were about to leave when one of the darts players, arms folded across his chest, blocked their way out.

'Best pub in the town, this one,' said the man.

Frank nodded in agreement.

'So, why're you going then, eh?'

'It's been a long day,' said Frank wearily. 'We've just arrived from London.'

'London, is it?' the man scoffed. 'Hey, lads. What did I tell you? They're from London, these two. The big smoke, eh?'

'So, we're tired and need to have a rest,' said Louise.

'Not very sociable, are you? Why don't you want to have a friendly drink with us, eh? We not good enough for you, us up here, is that it?'

'Well, I suppose we…' began Frank.

'Will you please let us pass?' broke in Louise.

The landlord came round from behind the bar, 'All right, Dean, you've had your fun. That's enough.'

With an exaggeratedly courtly bow, Dean waved them past, and said, 'We'll be seeing you again, won't we?'

They walked back to the flat in silence; Frank lit a small cigar which Louise chose to ignore. While Louise sat on a hard chair, unconvinced the corduroy sofa was anything like clean enough, Frank rooted inside his case.

'Thank the Lord I remembered the hip flask,' he said, pouring a stiff measure into a foggy tumbler. 'Want one?'

Louise shook her head, 'Better stick to just the one, Frank, you're meeting the NZO tomorrow.'

Frank nodded, 'What a bloody place. Wish you'd let me bring my stick. Never thought for a moment we'd be subjected to a reception like that.'

'Oh, he was just trying it on. Had too much to drink, I expect.'

'You're very calm and collected, my dear.'

Louise turned to her husband, 'Of course I'm not. But it is a reminder, you know.'

'A reminder of what?'

'Well, for one thing, not to act too much like the London snob, or the flamboyant artist, come to that.'

'I am an artist, but you can't call me a snob. And I am a Cumbrian, you know.'

'All right then, but at our age it rather makes sense not to go courting trouble.'

'I'm not…'

Louise sat gingerly on the arm of the sofa and patted Frank's hand. 'Perhaps not, but you might rein in the bohemian look a little. Just to be on the safe side.'

Back at Islington police station, DC Kelly brought two coffees to DS Davis's desk, then closed the door behind him. The latter took a sip and winced. 'We need to tread a bit carefully here, Errol,' he said at last. 'Now, I don't suppose that Dominic Talbot is the only man to wear a pair of Puma trainers, but the pattern on the soles and the size of them are a clear match with the footprints on the wet floor of Robertson's studio.'

'So, why are we having to pussyfoot around, Sarge?'

'For one thing, he's Robertson's partner. And for another, the Met's had enough complaints about being homophobic. So, we don't go rushing in. At least, not without the DCI's say so, we don't.'

'But, are you saying it's just a domestic that got out of hand?'

'Maybe, maybe not. But we need to think about a way of having another word with Talbot without scaring the horses. Right? First, though, we need to speak to Robertson.'

The bed was anything but comfortable and Frank had to concede that Louise was right to have insisted on bringing their own sheets, pillowcases and a duvet, even though it meant taking an extra case. While he unpacked, Louise went to a corner shop and picked up enough for breakfast, warily watching The Old Smithy across the street, now closed and unlit. The meeting with the NZO was at eleven thirty, and Louise picked out a tweed jacket and flannels for Frank to wear. He ambled south through the town centre and weaved his way past the castle to the hotel. It was further than he remembered, and the warm jacket and the weight of his portfolio caused a band of sweat to roll down his forehead. Frank was glad he arrived early, and splashed some water on his face in the gents. Settled in the lounge by the fireplace, he considered taking his jacket off, but the idea seemed both too modern and out of character, apart from revealing the damp patches on his shirt.

Julia O'Leary led the way in, with Barney Brady trailing behind her like a modern-day Sancho Panza. She strode across reception and shook hands with Frank, while Barney fiddled with something in his shoulder bag.

'I've booked a room for us,' she explained, leading the way to a meeting room beyond the bar. 'There've been a few protests, you see.'

In a room with a steeply beamed ceiling that overlooked a motorway junction, Julia poured herself a glass of water, tea for Frank, and left Barney, still making his way up the steps, to fend for himself.

More out of breath than Frank had been, Barney spoke first. 'Okay, Frank, whatcha got for us?'

Frank opened his portfolio, and arrayed the sketches along a horseshoe-shaped row of tables.

Barney wiped his forehead with the back of his hand. 'Hey, now, I like this. Yeah, this is way better than those old guys, Tommy Tune or whoever...'

'Tom Tuohy,' said Frank with some asperity.

'Yeah, Tuohy, right. What d'you say, Jools?'

Julia slipped on a pair of glasses and peered at the pictures, her head lowered, to Frank's mind, ridiculously close to them. She nodded, 'I think we can go with something like this. That's to say, I think I can get the NDC to give us the nod, but...'

'But?' said Frank.

'Couple of things. First, the PWRs we're looking at...'

'PWRs?'

'Sorry, Frank, alphabet soup. Pressurised water reactors. No, ours won't be having domes.' She pointed at the tiny golf ball-like structures that Frank had placed in the middle distance. 'We're going with ones that look more like, ahm, Barn?'

'Sure, sure, Jools.' Barney fished a laminated folder from his bag, that showed a row of canister-shaped buildings with narrower tops, like Thermos flasks.

'And, we're going to need them a whole lot bigger. The NDC has got to get the message across that nuclear isn't just the junior partner alongside solar and wind...'

'Yeah, but, Jools, we've got to, you know, accentuate the positives here. We gotta hook the kids, the deniers and the don't knows, and they're just not gonna buy it if we go all heavy on nuclear.'

'Sure, Barn, but don't forget who's paying for the NZO, right?'

Frank sipped his tea and enjoyed their squabble, glad not to be on the end of their combined disapproval this time. 'So, you're happy for me to carry on, then?'

Barney nodded vigorously, and Julia replied, 'Sure, but if you can just make those few changes, then I can get the designs signed off, okay?'

'Certainly,' said Frank, relieved. 'You said something about protestors?'

'Oh, it's nothing new,' replied Julia airily, 'but we've been advised to take care, just in case.'

'I see,' said Frank, although he did not, and neither did he want to find out why. He couldn't help wondering, though, what "just in case" meant, and who it was that had advised them to take care.

Julia and Barney picked up their things and left Frank mulling over what to do next. Looking out of the window, he saw the pair of them still bickering, with Barney protesting, arms flailing, but Julia apparently having the better of it. He quickly made his mind up that a drink would be in order before returning to Louise and the depressing flat. Protesters, that confrontation in the pub, Barney having no idea who Tom Tuohy was all made Frank think about how much the place of his birth had changed as he ordered a second glass of sauvignon blanc.

8

DS Davis and DC Kelly took the lift to the second floor of University College Hospital and found Dominic already there, sitting on a hard, plastic chair.

Dominic was holding Martin's hand and saying to him, 'I've been so worried and couldn't stop thinking that what if our last words to each other had been an argument. I'm so, so sorry. It was so stupid and childish of me.'

The two policemen exchanged a glance. On seeing them enter the room, Dominic stopped talking and turned to face them. Davis tapped Kelly's arm, reminding the younger man as to who would be doing the talking.

'Afternoon, Mister Robertson. How are you doing?' he began, then remembered that Martin had never met them before. 'Sorry about that, sir, I should have explained. I'm DS Davis and this is my colleague, DC Kelly. If you feel up to it, I wonder if we could ask you a couple of questions about your accident?'

Kelly flipped open his warrant card, and Martin smiled wanly, 'My husband said you might want to talk to me.'

'And that would be all right, would it, sir?'

Martin nodded.

'You've had a very nasty bump on the head, but can you remember anything about what caused it?'

'I'm sorry, it's all a bit of a blank,' said Martin wearily.

'I see. All right. But I wonder if you can remember if anyone was with you when it happened?'

Martin shook his head, then grimaced at the pain. Dominic stopped staring at the floor, and looked up at the policemen, and said quietly, 'I was with him.'

'Oh yes? I was wondering…'

Dominic looked down at the floor again, 'We argued…'

'And it had been raining when you arrived?'

'Raining?'

'Yes, I wonder if it was your umbrella that you left at Mister Robertson's place of work?'

Dominic nodded, 'Sorry, yes, of course. I'd forgotten. It was broken.'

'This argument, sir?'

'I was being stupid. I was angry and got up to go. Martin tried to stop me, but I pushed him away and left.'

'You were angry?'

'Yes.' Dominic's tears began. 'But I would never do anything to hurt him. It was just…'

'But you pushed him away?'

Dominic nodded, 'Yes, just to get away so I could leave.'

'And you didn't push him to the ground?'

'No, of course not. I would never…'

'So, perhaps Mister Robertson slipped on the wet floor after you pushed him?'

'I don't know. I really don't know. Maybe. Oh God, what have I done?'

Martin watched, horrified at his husband's distress, and reached out a hand to comfort him.

'It's starting to look like you must have been the last person with Mister Robertson that day,' said Davis calmly.

'All this,' Dominic sobbed. 'It's all my fault. I'm to blame. Oh God, Martin, love, I never meant to…'

'It's all right, Dom,' said Martin. 'Really it is.'

'Let me see, just so that I can be sure of all this. We

know that Mister Frank Armstrong visited you on the day of the accident but he had left well before three and it wasn't raining then,' Davis said to Martin, before turning to Dominic. 'So, can you remember what sort of time it was when you got there?'

'It would have been after school, sometime between four and five, I suppose.'

'Yes, that sounds about right. I thought you must have been there. You see, there were wet footprints…'

'Oh, that's why you asked me about my trainers?'

Davis ignored the question and turned to Martin, 'Well, sir, that would seem to be everything. Unless you have any questions, Mister Robertson?'

Martin spoke softly, 'No. I can't think of anything. We've both been through rather a lot. I just want everything to go back to normal now.' He smiled tenderly at Dominic, who nodded and squeezed his husband's hand.

Late on Saturday morning, Gerald drove over Putney Bridge. He went up and down Exmoor Gardens twice before parking his car at the end of the road. It took him a while to recover from a coughing fit that left his eyes watering. He had thought about flowers, but decided against them, both in case Louise was out and to avoid appearing too eager. After straightening his tie, wiping his mouth and running a hand through his hair, he rang the bell of number 14. He was about to turn and leave when he heard someone bounding down the stairs. It was Georgia, hopeful that it was her Amazon delivery. It was a very long time since she had seen Gerald and didn't recognise him.

'Ahm, I'm an old friend of your parents. I was just in

the neighbourhood, so I thought I'd drop by to say hello,' he said cautiously.

'Oh, they're away at the moment,' replied Georgia.

'Of course, of course. Your father told me, Cumbria, isn't it? Silly of me to forget. Sorry to have bothered you. Don't suppose you know when they'll be back, do you?'

'I could let them know you called,' said Georgia, still unaware of the identity of the man standing on the doorstep.

'No need, thank you, I was just calling on the off chance. I'll try again another day.'

'All right, Mister…?'

'Graham. Gerald Graham.'

'Oh, I remember now. You're one of Dad's artist friends, aren't you?'

Gerald smiled, 'That's right. We've known each other for years.'

'Well, Mum should be back later on today, but Dad's going to be working up there for a bit. Don't know how long, though.'

'Ah, I see. Yes, of course. Well, very nice to meet you. Cheery bye.'

And with that, Gerald walked back to his car while Georgia, knowing nothing of why he had called, went upstairs to her laptop. Gerald was in a quandary as he drove back to Ealing. He hoped Georgia wouldn't tell her mother that he had called, but felt it was probably unavoidable. Perhaps next time, he should ring first, Gerald wondered. *Then again, there was much to be said for the element of surprise. But what about the daughter?* He had no idea Georgia lived at home, and that certainly complicated matters. More thinking was needed, but Gerald resolved to try again soon. *Perhaps after the usual*

Sunday afternoon gathering at The Duke of York would work; it would certainly be a genuine reason for saying he was in the area.

It was late by the time Louise returned to London. Frank had seemed in good spirits after the NZO meeting, but she couldn't help wondering how he'd get on in the dismal flat, and hoped he would give The Old Smithy a wide berth and not go wandering around Penrith acting the flamboyant artist. *Still, he had a fridge full of food, a couple of bottles of wine, and no meetings in the offing to require a freshly-ironed shirt. He is a grown man, after all*, she told herself doubtfully.

It had been an odd sort of Monday at the office for Tom. The two o'clock catch up for account directors had been the usual run through of where the agency's accounts were up to, then Yannick Morrow dropped the bombshell, announcing that Craig Richardson was leaving. Tom and Craig had joined SHM at the same time, and become account directors within a few weeks of each other. They had become close friends and, immediately after the meeting, Craig called in to Tom's office to say that he hadn't just left; he had been sacked. They both knew that SHM was preparing to be sold to an American agency, but Yannick hadn't said at the meeting that they were being told to make cost savings if it the sale was to go ahead. Tom and Craig agreed to keep in touch, and Tom said he'd keep his eye open for any half decent opportunities. He was astonished and quickly realised that there was no reason why he might not be next in line for the chop. Although the macho culture of staying as late as possible at the office had disappeared long before the pandemic, Tom thought it might be wise to remain at his desk until most of his colleagues had gone home. By five thirty, after an unproductive afternoon, he decided it was just plain silly to sit there doing next to nothing and started to pack up his things. He could always do some work for a couple of hours over the weekend. Tom had reached the door when his mobile rang.

'Tom? Hi, hi, it's Julia O'Keefe from the NDC,' said the voice at the other end.

Tom dumped his bag and returned glumly to his desk. 'Hi, Julia. How's it going?'

'Yeah, fine, fine. Look, I just wanted to ask you something, you know.'

'Sure, what can I do for you?'

'Well, here's the thing. We're going to be looking for a new Director of the NZO. And I was wondering if you might…' Julia left the rest of the sentence hanging.

'No problem. I can look around and see if there is anyone.' Tom thought of Craig.

'No, that's not what I meant.'

'No?'

'Ah, no. You see, Barney's going. Wrong fit, wrong chemistry, I guess. Don't think he settled too well over here either. No, what I meant was, well, I just thought you might be interested.'

'Me!' Tom was astounded.

'Sure, why not? We think you'd be the right guy, and we'd get along great too.'

'Wow. Well, look, thank you very much, Julia. It's a lot to think about.'

'Sure, of course. So, why don't you think it over and maybe give me a call sometime next week? But we do kind of need to make a decision soon, you know.'

Tom put the phone down and left the office, hardly noticing the rain that had begun as he walked across the city to Blackfriars. On the train home, he decided to make his own mind up about the job before mentioning it to Lizzie.

Frank had spent Friday refining his designs for the murals. At just after five, he decided to finish for the day. He cut himself a slice of game pie and inspected the contents of the fridge, but nothing appealed. Well, it is Friday evening, he said to himself, despite the fact that, at his age, it made no difference that it was the start of the weekend. Instead, he ventured out, ignoring Louise's pleas to eat what they had bought, but accepting her advice to dress more soberly than usual. In tweeds and thick corduroys, he walked the half mile into town, making mental notes of important landmarks: restaurants, cosy and well-kept pubs, and fish and chip shops. Cumberland sausage and chips would be his dinner, but after a few drinks first. Finally, he settled on The Church Inn. It was perfect, with a fire in the hearth, three tweedily dressed men of late middle age, two couples, and no-one over forty. Frank smiled to himself at the prospect of being able to tell Louise that he'd started to go to the church regularly. He went over to the bar where a large man in a cardigan was polishing an already gleaming glass, and asked what sir would like. Frank plumped for a large glass of Haut Medoc and, on tasting it, immediately regretted not buying the bottle. He found a corner, unfurled his copy of The Telegraph and was scanning the obituaries when one of the group of three came over.

'Excuse me,' the man said, 'but I wonder if you could

settle a wager for us?'

'Certainly. But a wager…?'

'Aye, well,' the man gestured to his two companions. 'He says you're a doctor, the other says you're a lawyer. But I say you're in property. So, who's right?'

Frank smiled and shook his head, 'None of you, I'm afraid. I'm a painter.'

'Didn't have you down as a painter and decorator. Dressed like that, you know.'

Mindful of Louise's advice, Frank answered carefully, 'No, I paint pictures.'

'Artist, then?'

Frank nodded. The man turned round, 'We're all wrong, lads.' He turned back to Frank, 'You're welcome to join us, if you like, you being on your tod.'

Unsure of the invitation at first, Frank quickly saw the benefits of making a few friends with the locals. 'If I wouldn't be intruding.'

'No, come on over.'

Frank stowed his paper, picked up his glass and pulled up a chair next to the three men. 'The name's Cyril,' said the man who invited him. 'Worked at Sellafield before it was called that, then me and the wife retired here, to be near the grandkids. Can't play bloody golf, so got myself on the council instead. He's Eric,' he pointed to a heavy set man with long sideburns and then to a thin man with thick glasses. 'Farmer. And that's Trevor, used to be bank manager before they closed the branch down. We were just having a craic about bloody tree huggers.'

'A what about what?'

'We were talking about those tree huggers, you know, greenies.'

'Like I was saying,' the man called Eric returned to

what they had been discussing. 'They were all for diversification after foot and mouth. Holiday homes, chalets and all that for them farmers that lost the lot. Anyway, that's all changed now. Just because half our land is in national park, I'm having to plant two hundred bloody trees to make up for one piddling holiday cottage. They're calling it "nutrient neutrality" or some bollocks. It's not bloody right.'

'And don't get me started on all that anti-nuclear rabble that's pitched up on the west coast,' retorted Cyril. 'Protesting about things they haven't a clue about, and not one of them's from round here, for a kick off.'

'May I buy you gentlemen a drink?' asked Frank.

Cyril grinned at him. 'Now, it might seem odd, Cumbrians refusing a drink, but no thanks. We don't do rounds. Keeps it simple, see.'

Frank didn't know quite how to take that and felt it might be too soon to say that he too was a Cumbrian. In any case, it might be awkward if any of them put two and two together and worked out that he was the son of the Armstrong who had laid off half the workforce when he sold the Kendal factory to the Americans.

'Anyway,' continued Cyril, 'what sort of stuff do you paint, friend?'

'Oh, mainly portraits, I suppose, but…'

'Yes?'

'Well, I'm currently working on some pictures for the, ah, nuclear industry,' Frank thought better of mentioning they were for the NZO, unsure as to whether or not they counted as greenies or tree huggers.

'Portraits of the top brass, eh?'

'Oh, no, not this time. Nothing like that. No, it's a, ah, series of murals on the benefits of nuclear power.'

The three men nodded enthusiastically.

'You said something about there being anti-nuclear protesters…'

'Oh aye,' said Cyril. 'Standing outside the gate with banners and that, shouting at people going in and out of the site.'

'That's not the worst of it,' said the taciturn Trevor darkly.

'He's right,' continued Cyril. 'What makes my blood boil is they've started following mums and dads who work there when they're taking their kiddies to school. Even heard they've waited outside people's houses as well.' He shook his head at the outrage of it all.

Not wishing to risk a breathalyser and anxious for dinner, the group soon began to break up and head home. After a third glass of wine, Frank left, too, and made his way back to the flat with a takeaway.

It was after lunch before Martin was allowed to leave the hospital. The taxi took an age to wind its way through the Saturday afternoon football traffic. At last, they reached the house. Dominic picked up Martin's overnight bag, and helped him to the pavement. 'Is there anything I can get you?' he asked.

'A small glass of wine would be nice.'

'Well, if you're sure… Perhaps just the one glass then,' said Dominic solicitously, and went into the kitchen to fetch the glasses. When he returned, he saw his husband wiping his eyes. 'What's wrong?'

Martin pointed to Frank's painting of Barceloneta that hung above the mantelpiece. 'You really needn't have,' he said.

'I thought you'd like it there, where you can see it better.'

'Oh, I do, and thank you my love. But…'

'But what?'

'Well, I suppose I don't really want to think about Frank and all the trouble I caused.'

'You didn't do anything!'

'But if I hadn't painted *The Art Lovers*, none of this would have happened, would it?'

'That's all in the past, Martin, love.'

'I know, but it did make everything go wrong.'

'Maybe it would help to patch things up if we have Frank and Louise round for supper?'

'I don't know. I think maybe we should wait a while before doing anything like that. And I don't know if it's possible for things ever to be the same again.' Martin took a sip of wine. 'Oh, I meant to ask, did Jane say anything about the drawings?'

'She said she'd give you a call about them when you were back. But, never mind about that, you need to take it easy for now.'

On Sunday morning, Tom dropped off Polly at a birthday party. Meanwhile, a relieved Lizzie had managed to get Theo to finish a bottle and settle down for a nap. Tom made coffee and sat down next to his wife. He had decided that he wanted the NZO job, but had spent much of Saturday wondering how to broach that with Lizzie.

'Don't think I mentioned it, but Craig's been sacked,' he began.

'God, poor Craig. What for?'

Tom explained about SHM having to make savings in order for the acquisition to go ahead, then added, 'Thing is, I don't think he'll be the last. Doesn't seem to matter whether you're any good or not, it's just about cutting the wage bill.'

Lizzie thought carefully about the implications of what Tom had said, then began, 'Are you saying what I think you're saying?'

Tom nodded, 'I don't know. I got the NZO account, but they could still decide to get rid of me. But…'

'What?'

'Well, this is really weird, but I think I might have been headhunted.'

'Well, go on then. And why have you waited till now to mention it?'

Tom felt awkward at having to explain the delay, 'It's just that I wasn't sure what you'd think... No, well, what I mean is, I didn't know whether just to forget about it or take it seriously.' He bought himself a few seconds with some coffee. 'Okay. Suppose I should have mentioned it before now. Anyway, it's the NZO. They rang and asked how I'd feel about being their director.'

'So, what do you think?'

'I've got to say, it'd be nice not to be in a place where you were you're only as good as your last campaign.'

'Are you telling me you'd want the job?' probed Lizzie.

'I wanted to talk to you first,' said Tom blandly.

'But you want it? Yes?'

'I suppose so, but I know it wouldn't be easy. It'd be disrupting for Polly and Theo for a start, and we don't know anyone up there…'

'And I will be going back to work in a few months.'

'That too, of course.'

'I don't suppose there are as many jobs in Cumbria for a radiographer as there are in London.'

'No, well, I don't know. But, on the other hand, property is so much cheaper up there…'

'You've looked?'

'Well, yes, but... We'd be able to afford somewhere bigger and have a car each. And it might be good for the kids to grow up in the Lake District, too.'

'There's a lot to think about, Tom.'

'Ah, yes, I know. Trouble is, they want an answer this week.' Tom felt crestfallen at Lizzie's lack of enthusiasm. 'But, tell me what you think. If you don't like the idea...'

Lizzie shook her head. 'No, it isn't that. This is just all a bit sudden. The Lake District would be really nice, I can see that, but we'd be giving up a lot too. Can I think it over for a bit?'

'Of course you can,' said Tom, relieved that Lizzie hadn't absolutely ruled out the idea.

Dominic called Doug to say that Martin was now out of hospital and doing well, but felt too embarrassed to tell him about his meeting with the police. Doug was glad to hear the news, but had been feeling out of sorts. His paintings were no longer on sale in London, and he was making next to nothing from the couple of galleries in the north east that showed them. The flat was getting him down too. Doug felt cooped up, hardly seeing anyone during the week. He also knew he drank too much. But, most of all, after so many years on his own, he was lonely.

Despite Frank being in Cumbria, the artists met for their usual Sunday afternoon drinks at The Duke of York rather than anywhere more convenient for them all. They raised a glass to Martin, relieved that he was on the mend. Afterwards, Gerald walked up from the river to Exmoor Gardens. As he turned the corner, he saw to his delight the figure of Georgia hurrying off in the opposite direction. Gerald could see Louise through the drawing room window as he walked up the drive. He rang the bell.

'Gerald!' said a startled Louise.

'Hello,' Gerald smiled broadly.

'What are you…?'

'Just thought I'd see how you're bearing up, you know, with Frank away and after all that trouble with… Do you think I might come in for a moment?'

'Yes, of course,' said Louise regaining some of her composure. She showed him into the drawing room.

Gerald looked through the French windows and saw two young men on ladders against the side of Frank's studio. 'Got the builders in? On a Sunday too?' he asked.

'The roof was starting to leak,' replied Louise. 'It was the only day they could fit us in.'

'Can't be an easy time for you, I imagine.'

'Oh, we're coping well enough, thanks.'

'I'm so glad. I just thought if there was anything I could do. You know, change a lightbulb or a fuse, or something.'

'That's very kind of you, Gerald, but I'm sure I can manage.'

'Well, if you're sure…' began Gerald. 'You see, you've always been rather special to me, ever since…'

'Gerald, that was a very long time ago.'

'Yes, but, there never was anyone quite like you, Louise.'

'There is Betty. Your wife, you know.'

'Yes,' Gerald looked down at the carpet. 'Poor girl has never been the same since Andrea died.'

'That was awful for you both, I do know that, but…'

Gerald reached out and grabbed hold of Louise's shoulders, pulled her towards him and kissed her on the mouth.

'For God's sake, Gerald,' snapped Louise.

He lunged forward, pushing Louise down on to the sofa. 'Come on, Louise, you always used to like a bit of a tussle, didn't you?'

'Get off me! Now, Gerald!' yelled Louise.

'What's the matter with you? Don't you like proper men, these days? Happy with that pretentious milksop of a husband of yours, are you?'

Louise slapped Gerald's face and shouted, 'Get out, Gerald. Now!'

He rubbed his cheek and sneered, 'Just as you wish, my dear. But you must wonder sometimes if Frank still has yearnings for younger men, mustn't you?'

Louise stared at Gerald, silent and furious.

'Oh well, nice to see you again, Louise. And don't hesitate to call me when you realise you need a real man.' He closed the drawing room door and called out from the hall, 'I'll see myself out. Cheery bye, my dear.'

Back in his car, gasping for breath, Gerald thumped the steering wheel with both hands, berating himself for his clumsiness. There was blood on his handkerchief, but it was nothing to do with the slap he'd received. 'Home, James,' he said aloud, 'whatever the hell home is.'

Louise sat on the sofa, shaking with anger rather than shock. She didn't hear Georgia come in.

'I forgot to tell you, Mum. One of Dad's artist friends called while you were up in Cumbria. And I just saw him walking down the High Street,' said Georgia, depositing on the carpet a bag of baby clothes for her nephew.

Louise nodded and said quietly, 'Yes, he called to see me.'

'I thought he was Dad's friend?'

'He was. Is. I think he just wanted to see how we're doing.'

Tom didn't want to rush Lizzie into making a decision about whether or not he should accept the job with the NZO, and was pleasantly surprised when she mentioned it on Monday evening.

'I hadn't realised there were quite so many hospitals up there,' she began.

'Really?' Tom was encouraged, but by no means certain that Lizzie was agreeing to the move.

'Yes. Seems they have some difficulties recruiting too. There is one thing, though.'

'Oh, what?'

'Well, wherever we end up living must be near to the hospital. I don't want to be driving for hours after work and having no time with the children.'

Tom nodded vigorously, delighted at his wife's tacit approval. 'So, I can ring Julia about the job?'

'All those years in advertising have certainly made you incredibly perceptive,' smiled Louise, as Tom leaned over and kissed her.

Gerald had spent all of Monday brooding in the conservatory that served as his studio. While Betty was getting dressed, the GP had called yet again, reminding Gerald of the options open to him, and had been puzzled by the flat refusal to them all. He racked his brains to think of a way of repairing the damage he had done with Louise. Nothing came to mind. He doubted she would tell Frank, but couldn't be sure. Betty drifted in and out. Gerald looked at the slice of Battenburg she had brought him, half of him wanting to hurl the cake across the room, while at the same time feeling close to tears at the tragic banality of it. He was angry with the rejection from Louise, with Frank's smug, good fortune, with the dullness of his own life, but mainly with himself. Briefly, he thought about having some more mischief with Jane McNab, someone else who had rejected him, but could think of nothing that would adequately satisfy his mood. There was only one thing that mattered, and that was the longing he felt for Louise. But, what was he to do?

On the train to work on Tuesday morning, Tom thought about his contract with SHM. As an account director, it stipulated a minimum of three months' notice, but if the agency needed to cut costs quickly, would they want to let him go sooner? After all, if he were to move to a competitor, then it was usual to be asked to leave straightaway. Then again, he and Lizzie would need the time to find somewhere to live, a job for her when Theo was ready for nursery, a school for Polly, and they would need to sell the house, and… The list of things to do was endless. And, he also wondered if, by his going, SHM might agree to reinstate Craig…

With Dominic at school and finding himself at a loose end, Martin felt he couldn't wait any longer for her to ring, and called Julia McNab. She was pleased to hear that he was making a good recovery, but there was something in her tone of voice that suggested to Martin that all was not well.

'I was going to call you,' she began tentatively. 'You see, sales have gone pretty well, but I'm sorry to say that *The Art Lovers* has not been sold.'

'What do you mean?' Martin was shocked. 'I thought you'd got a buyer for it before the show opened?'

'The man who reserved it never turned up to pay for it. The picture's still here, and I've been wondering what to do about it.'

'He didn't pay a deposit?'

'No. I know that was silly of me, but he was offering a good deal more than the asking price. The gallery hasn't been doing especially well this year, you see, so I am afraid I must have come across as rather too keen.'

'But what are you going to do?'

'Well, the only thing I can think of is to look into some of the mixed exhibitions coming up and see if it could be included in one of them, and maybe with a couple of others that we haven't sold yet. Perhaps in a gallery that is rather better known.' Jane did not like having to admit that The Curzon was no longer the fashionable place it had once been. She added, 'But don't worry, I'll make sure that it doesn't affect what you'll get for it.'

'Jane, I'm not worried about the money but, if you can't sell the painting, I'm not sure that I'd like it on show somewhere else. After everything that's happened, I think it might be better if we just put it behind us. I really need to get on with my life now, so maybe I should just come and pick it up.'

'Well, I understand, Martin. But what would you do with it? Do have a think about putting it in a mixed show. But I won't do anything without talking to you first.' Jane was loath to miss out on a sale, but knew better than to press Martin too far.

Martin's first thought was to paint over *The Art Lovers*, but then he reflected that we was really rather proud of it. Although Dominic had been so kind, hanging Frank's little landscape in their sitting room, he wasn't sure what his husband really thought about *The Art Lovers*, and that maybe he would rather it were destroyed.

At lunchtime, Tom rang Julia O'Leary to discuss NZO job. The salary was more than generous, there was the possibility of temporary accommodation until they found a place to live, and she agreed to email him details of local schools and nurseries.

'We'll be needing you to come for an interview,' she said. 'It's not like we'll be seeing anyone else, but when it's public money, you know… And, I know you'll have a notice period, but see what you can do about that. I've got to liaise with some people, but I'll email over some dates for you to come up later this week, and the job description and person spec as well, okay?'

Later that day, after several fruitless hours painting a fruitless still life, Gerald knew what he had to do. He remembered seeing the two young men working on Frank's studio roof. He decided to go and see Frank, even if it meant having to travel up to Cumbria. But, this time, he knew he would need to tread much, much more carefully than before, and definitely bide his time.

Louise was in a quandary as to whether or not to tell Frank about the visit from Gerald, as she had never mentioned the very brief affair they'd had, even though it was well before she and Frank got together. She felt awkward at the hypocrisy of not telling him, especially after she had insisted Frank be more open and honest with her. Yet, if she were to, how would Frank react? After all, he and Gerald had been friends for years. Would Frank end up abandoning the murals and come home to have it out with Gerald? She vacillated between the only two options. While she procrastinated, her eldest daughter did not. Lizzie had sent her CV to the HR departments of three hospitals in Cumbria saying she would be available in about three or four months, identified places to live that were nearby and still in reasonably easy reach of the NZO, and was astonished to find that a four bedroom detached house would cost less than half than their semi in Denmark Hill. *There may be something to be said for moving north*, she admitted to herself.

Meanwhile, in between evenings at The Church Inn, and a daily phone call with Louise, Frank spent the week working hard on the murals for the NZO, but on Wednesday evening he felt he needed a break.

'I know you said you might come up this weekend, darling, but I hope you haven't bought your ticket yet?' he asked Louise.

'I haven't. Why do you ask? Has something happened?'

'Oh, nothing. Nothing at all. Work's going well, and I'm at a sort of natural break, so I thought it might be rather nice to come down for a day or two, see the girls, the grandkids, that sort of thing. And you, of course.'

'But what's brought this on? We'd all be glad to see you, of course, but it's a long way to come for just a couple of days, don't you think? The girls do understand you're working, you know.' Louise suddenly felt uncomfortable, knowing that she might have to decide what to say about Gerald more quickly than she had hoped.

'I know, I know. I just rather fancy a few, ah…'

'Home comforts? Is that it, Frank?'

'No, well, yes. But one does get a bit lonely stuck up here all alone, you know.'

'All right, Frank. I suppose you'd like Sunday lunch, a joint with all the trimmings?' The mere prospect of roast beef would at least soften Frank up if she had to tell him.

'Well, that would be lovely, but I don't want to put you to any trouble, darling.'

Although Julia wanted Tom to start as soon as possible, he decided to wait until he received her email before talking to Yannick about resigning. It arrived on Friday afternoon as Frank's train approached Euston.

9.

Louise let Frank sleep in at the weekend. At least he had been getting down to some work on the murals, she told herself, but she was still undecided as to what to say about Gerald and rather hoped that Georgia wouldn't mention his calling round. When he finally surfaced on Sunday morning, Frank pottered off in his dressing gown to admire the work that Mister Sweeney's two sons had done to his studio's roof. Lizzie and Tom came round with the grandchildren while Frank dressed hurriedly and emerged, drawn in by the aroma of roasting beef and then delighted at the sight of a bottle of Graves that Louise had cannily placed on the dining room table.

Frank was feeling even more expansive than usual, prepared to talk at length about the murals. 'Yes, I knew it wouldn't take long to get the people up there round to my way of thinking,' he said grandly, as Louise and Georgia exchanged a glance. 'You see, they really don't know what they're talking about when it comes to painting, and nuclear power for that matter. Take that funny little Yank, for instance…'

His flow was cut short by Tom. 'While we're on the subject, we've got some news,' Tom began.

Frank had welcomed his son-in-law warmly, recalling their last friendly exchange, but could hardly contain his irritation at being interrupted. He helped himself to a glass of wine, even though lunch was still over half an hour away, and swirled its contents crossly.

'And what subject might that be, Tom?' asked Frank, fully expecting it to have nothing whatsoever do with what he had been talking about.

Lizzie passed Theo to Georgia and stepped in to help

her husband, 'It's about the NZO.'

'Oh yes?'

'Tom's been offered a job with them.'

Frank almost choked on his wine. 'I assume that's not the initials of one of your advertising agencies?'

'No, Frank. Barney, that funny little Yank you mentioned has left, and Julia O'Leary rang to say they want me to come in as Director.'

'But the NZO isn't anything to do with advertising, Tom.'

'Well, it sort of is, when you think about it. You know, getting the message out that nuclear power is a key part of the clean energy mix.'

'I think that's rather stretching the point, Tom,' said Frank with growing annoyance at being contradicted.

Louise was no less shocked than her husband, 'But that would mean living up there.'

'We know,' said Tom. 'But wouldn't the Lake District be a great place to bring up the children?'

'And property prices there are peanuts compared to London,' added Lizzie.

'But what about *your* job, Liz?' asked Georgia.

'I've already put out some feelers. They do have hospitals up there, you know.'

'It's miles away, Liz,' protested her younger sister. 'We'd never see Polly and Theo.'

'We aren't going to the North Pole, George, for goodness' sake.'

Trying to regain his composure, Frank asked, 'And just where do you propose to live?'

'We thought Keswick would be nice, or somewhere central that's not too far from the hospital.'

'Oh, you'll never get to live there,' said Frank

highhandedly. 'No, I tried to find a place in the Lakes, but you just can't do it. There's some rule about not letting in people to the national park. It's the, ah, local thingy…'

'Local occupancy clause,' said Lizzie. 'I've checked it out and of course we'd be eligible because we'd working there. So, that's okay.'

'And I suppose trying to make a living as an artist doesn't count as working, does it? huffed Frank.

'Oh, don't be ridiculous, Frank,' said Louise. 'You'll be moving back as soon as you've finished the murals. It's hardly the same thing.'

'I suppose not,' said Frank.

Despite the wine and beef, he barely said a word over lunch, and Louise put it down to Frank sulking. After coffee, he suggested to Tom that the pair of them take a turn around the garden. Neither man said anything until they reached the studio. Tom was surprised when Frank ushered him inside, pointed to a canvas chair, then pulled out a half bottle of Scotch from a cupboard and poured them each a drink.

'Right, Tom,' he began. 'There's something you really ought to know.'

Tom waited.

'I take it you haven't formally accepted the job yet. Is that right?'

Tom nodded, 'I've got to have an interview first, but they've said it's just a formality.'

'Be that as it may, there is something else.'

'Yes?'

'Julia, that woman from the Nuclear Development Commission, was telling me just this week that there've been anti-nuclear protesters in Cumbria.'

'Oh, I know, it's been all over the news.'

'Yes, but what you may not know is that some of the protesters have been intimidating the families of people who work there. And I do not like the idea of Lizzie and the grandchildren having to run the gauntlet every time they leave the house.'

'Oh, I'm sure it's not half as bad as all that.'

'Well, I am. All I'm saying to you, Tom, is that, for the sake of your family, you really must think long and hard about whether working for the NZO is such a good idea.'

Tom smiled, 'You aren't just saying this because you don't like the idea of me working for your client, are you?'

Frank was angry, even though he knew there to be more than a grain of truth in what Tom said, but reined himself in, 'That's preposterous, Tom. I am simply concerned about the welfare of my family. And you too, come to that.'

'Well, I would understand it if you did think that. I'm not sure I'd like it if I were in your shoes,' said Tom emolliently.

With a kind of truce, they returned to the house, Frank unsure that he had been sufficiently persuasive, and Tom wondering what to say to Lizzie. After Tom and Lizzie had collected all of the children's belongings and ferried them to their car, Louise correctly assumed that Frank would want to spend an hour or two with his friends at The Duke of York. She would have liked to spend the rest of the afternoon with him but reasoned that, if she were to mention Gerald's visit, it might be better received by a nicely lubricated Frank.

As he walked down towards the river, Frank was puzzled. The beef had been a delightful surprise, but why had Louise been so accommodating, saying nothing about his health, and why, for that matter, was she so relaxed about his going to the pub? It all seemed so oddly out character. And, if Lizzie and Tom were adamant about going to Cumbria then, as Tom had pointed out, there was the little matter of having his son-in-law as the client for the NZO's murals. Frank did not relish the prospect, especially if that might mean having to change the designs yet again. But, the worst of it was the thought that Lizzie and the grandchildren might have to come face to face with protesters. He didn't like the idea of it one little bit, but made up his mind to say that to Louise when he returned. Maybe she would have more influence on them. After all, Lizzie listened to her more than she ever did to him. His small cigar tasted bitter and Frank hurled it into the gutter as he climbed the shallow steps into The Duke of York.

Max was facing the door and the first to see him come in, 'Now, this is certainly a turning up for the books, Francis. We didn't hold out our hopes to see you today.'

Frank took his glass over to the table to join the others. 'Just us old buggers,' said Doug. 'Thought you were supposed to be up north, Frank.'

Gerald was taken aback, and realised he had to make a series of swift calculations. Knowing the man as he did, he was sure that, if Frank knew about his visit to Exmoor Gardens, it would come out soon enough. But, what possible explanation would he be able to come up with? If he knew, it would certainly make it difficult to put into action what he had been planning. And, although he had been rehearsing almost every day what he wanted to tell Frank, what would be the best way of putting it to him here and now? To his relief, it was clear from Frank's demeanour that Louise had said nothing to him, though he did seem oddly preoccupied.

'No, it's all been going swimmingly,' said Frank. 'So, I thought I'd treat myself to a weekend with the family.' He saw no reason to mention Tom's job offer and its implications, the anti-nuclear protestors, or to give any indication that even a single cloud existed on his particular horizon.

Gerald remained silent as he considered his next steps, while Frank regaled Max and Doug with how he had got his way with the commission, in what he described as his "triumph of art over the philistines". He decided that, since Louise mustn't have yet said anything, it would be best to tell Frank that he had visited her, in case she were to get round to it. A heavily edited version of events might introduce admirably what he wanted to say. As the four men left the pub, Gerald stopped Frank and asked, 'Give you a lift, Frank?'

'No, thanks, Gerald. I rather like to walk it off with a cigar.'

'Look, have you got a moment? There's something I think you ought to know.'

They said their goodbyes to Doug and Max, and Gerald led the way back into the bar. 'Give me a minute, just need to pop to the gents.' He came back and ordered a cognac. 'I'd have one too, Frank, but I'm driving.'

'You're being terribly mysterious, Gerald, what on earth's this all about?' asked Frank, warming the glass in his hand.

'Well, after drinks last Sunday, I popped round to see how you and Louise were faring. After all that business with the police and you being away, I thought the girl might be rather brooding on things.'

'That was very thoughtful of you, Gerald.'

'Not at all. What are friends for? No, what I wanted to say was, well, this is rather difficult…'

'Oh, come on, Gerald. We're both grown men. No need to tiptoe around. Come on, let's have it.'

'All right, yes, I suppose so. Well, now don't take this the wrong way, but when I got there I found two young men…'

'Yes, I know. Our handyman's lads were repairing the studio roof.'

'Yes, I'm sure they were, but…'

'But what?'

'At first, I thought Louise was just being, ah, rather over-friendly with one of them.'

'Eh?'

'Well, I thought nothing of it at first. Just Louise being her usual charming self. But, as I was leaving, I caught sight of them through the window, Louise and one of the young men with their arms around each other.'

'Louise and one of the young men? Nonsense! You must be mistaken. Louise would never do anything like that.'

'And that's what I thought too, but there they were, clear as day. I'm sorry even to mention this, Frank, but I really thought that, as one of my oldest friends, you have a right to know.'

'Of course, of course. Thank you, Gerald.' Frank was stunned. He finished the brandy and got up. 'Yes, that was the right thing to do, Gerald. Thank you. I suppose I had better get to the bottom of this.'

Walking back to Exmoor Gardens, Frank felt weary. Now, Louise's lack of protestations about the wine, the roast beef, and his going to the pub all made sense. They were the actions of a wife with a guilty secret. What a fool he had been, he told himself, not to pick up any of that before now. And he should never have taken on that blasted commission for the NZO. If only he had stayed in London. He had never liked those Sweeney boys, with their transistor blaring all the time while he was trying to work, and the endless mugs of tea they demanded. He would have to sack Mister Sweeney, but how could he do that without explaining why to Louise? And what on earth was he to say to her?

Meanwhile, on his way back to the car, Gerald kicked a stone into a puddle and said to himself, 'Time to wait and see where the ripples end up.'

Frank hung his coat up and went into the drawing room with no clear idea about what to say or do next. Louise put down the Sunday paper, got up and put her arms around her husband. Frank flinched. Was this unexpected display of affection nothing more than another sign of her infidelity?

'You really are a most surprising man, Frank Armstrong,' she said.

'Really?'

'Yes, Lizzie rang and told me about your conversation with Tom.'

'Oh, that.'

'Yes. She was very touched, and so am I, that you were so concerned about their safety.'

'Well, it was just…'

'No need to be modest, Frank. It was a lovely thing to say.'

And, with that, Frank felt unable to say anything to Louise about what Gerald had told him, and Louise had decided to say nothing about Gerald's visit. They spent the rest of the day in an odd sort of calm, not exactly a stalemate, more an awkward over-politeness towards each other. They both knew that something unsaid was preying on the mind of the other. By Monday lunchtime, neither of them was any closer to saying anything. They kissed goodbye, as usual. Frank concluded that sacking Mister Sweeney could wait, but caught his taxi to Euston filled with apprehension at what might happen while he was away from home.

Julia O'Leary called both Tom and Frank on Monday afternoon. The recipients of both calls sounded awkward. Tom had been thinking about what Frank had said, even though Lizzie saw no reason for him to change his mind about the NZO job, saying they wouldn't be living anywhere near the site of the proposed power station, so there really was nothing to worry about. He also had not fully worked out what to say to Yannick.

'So, tell me your thoughts, Tom. You've not changed your mind?' she asked.

'No, I don't think so,' Tom replied, knowing he sounded equivocal at best.

'Okay, so just so I'm sure, you're telling us you're definitely in, then?'

'Yes, I am. Thanks, Julia. And the information you sent over was a big help.'

'Great, great. So, the interview. Stuff's come up, so we can't make all the dates I sent over now, but we've a window later this week, Wednesday lunchtime. How does that work for you?'

Tom hesitated. Should he resign before or after the interview? He could take a day's leave; he was owed plenty. 'Just checking my schedule,' he lied. 'Yes, that should be okay.'

'Okay, great. Penrith's good for us. I'll send a calendar

invite.'

Frank, on the other hand, was on the train and, having been shushed as he took the call, found himself wobbling about in the gangway between two carriages, far from happy with what Julia was proposing.

'You want me to do what?' he yelled above the rattle of the train.

'We think it's time you came and had a look at the NZO for real.'

'Do I really need to? I mean…'

'Think it'd be a good idea, Frank. Don't you want to see where the murals'll be going?'

'I suppose so. Oh, very well, if you insist. How do I get there then?'

'I'll email the directions. It's only an hour or so's drive from Penrith…'

'Drive? I don't drive.' Frank had no problem admitting that, but wasn't prepared to reveal as well that he didn't do emails, and relied on Louise to receive them for him.

'You haven't got a car?' Julia was incredulous.

'I live in London. What could I possibly want with a car in London?'

'Jeez. Ahm, there's a bus service. Well, you'd need to take two buses, actually. Or there's the train, but that takes forever and you'd have to…'

'You expect me to catch a bus?'

'I don't know. But I'll let you figure out what you want to do. We were thinking Thursday morning, ten thirty would be good for us.'

'I'll see what I can do,' replied Frank glumly.

'Good man. Oh, and it'll be just me. Barney's not with us anymore.'

'So I've heard.'

'What, you know already? Did Barney ring you? Wow, news travels fast. Look, got to go, someone's calling me. I'll email you the directions to the NZO. See you Friday, okay?'

Frank tramped back to his seat, wondering how on earth he was going to get to the NZO, and he wasn't too keen either to ring Louise and ask for the directions. With a miniature of Scotch, he settled himself down and opted for a taxi, and Louise could worry about the expense.

In Islington, Martin listened wearily as, yet again, Dominic tried to persuade him to let *The Art Lovers* appear in a mixed exhibition. 'I just want to forget about it all,' he said at last.

'You don't have to commit yourself yet, love. It isn't as if Jane has found a show for it to go in, now is it?'

'Oh, she will, Dom. She's like a terrier, is that one. Any day now, she'll ring and tell me she's found somewhere.'

'But, you told me you thought it was one of your best works, didn't you? So, why not let her find somewhere that'll show it?'

'You're being very sweet, Dom, thank you. But it caused such a lot of trouble for us, and now I only have bad memories of it.'

'But, Martin, I've already said it was all my fault. I was being very childish and…'

Martin put an arm around his husband, 'And I know you feel bad about it, but it doesn't get over the fact that you were very hurt at the time.'

'I'm over it. Really. And, anyway, there was nothing to get over. It was just me being stupid.'

Martin looked at him quizzically, 'Are you sure?'

'Just think about it, love. What if, in years to come,

you realise it should have been shown? That would be such a pity, and you'd be kicking yourself.'

Tom had still not got round to resigning and caught the train north on Wednesday morning, wondering if he should have done and, if by not doing, he was less than committed to taking the NZO job. He arrived early at the same hotel where Frank had met Julia and Barney, and sat in the lounge with a coffee. At 12.30, Julia O'Leary walked in, accompanied by two men of differing heights, but otherwise identical with bald heads, light beards and suits with open necked white shirts. She gave Tom a wave, and beckoned for him to follow them to a meeting room down the corridor.

'All rightee,' she began once they were all sitting at a round table that already had four glasses and a carafe of water in the middle. 'This is Bill Rice,' Julia pointed first to the taller of the two men, 'he's my boss and in charge of project delivery for us at the NDC and his team are looking after the build. And this is Vernon Nelson, from DESNZ, and our link with Treasury. He's the money man. Vernon controls our air supply.'

Neither man smiled, but Tom thought it best to, before asking, 'DESNZ?'

'Sorry, sorry. It's the Department for Energy Security and Net Zero,' she gave a half rueful smile at Vernon Nelson. 'We forget that we're the only people who use all the bloody acronyms.'

Tom was annoyed with himself, realising too late that he should have known it already, or kept his mouth shut.

After a few routine questions from Julia that were, as she had promised, not remotely challenging, she threw it open to Bill and Vernon.

'You're pretty new to our world,' Bill began. 'So, what can you bring, and what made you want to work for the NZO?'

Tom had expected a question along those lines and, in his preparations, opted for a high risk approach. It had worked for the pitch. He explained that he had once been against nuclear power, though never a protester. That got a smile from Julia, but not the others. He went on to say that, in researching the pitch for the NZO account at SHM, he had learned a great deal and come to realise the critical need for an effective and robust base load that could only be fulfilled by nuclear power. Bill nodded and took some notes, before nodding to Vernon Nelson to take over.

'At the Department, our priority is energy security. So, how do you see your role in enabling that?' he said.

Tom had not expected that and needed to think quickly. If in doubt, he told himself, go with a few assumptions, and see if any of them hit the spot. 'I think there are quite a few strands to that. You need the new power stations to go ahead, right? And you want more people to accept the need for nuclear power, yes? So, the NZO has a key role in getting that message across. And that's where I come in. I've senior level experience in advertising and marketing, and that's what I'll be bringing.'

Vernon frowned. 'Yes, I suppose so.' He thought for a moment before continuing, 'Yes, that's all very well, but you've not said anything about exactly *what* you'll do. All right, let's take an example. I assume you know there are plenty of people who are dead against nuclear power? People who are up here protesting about it. Okay, so what would you do, as Director of the NZO, to address that *proactively*?'

'I know that the NZO isn't just there to show pretty pictures of clean energy,' Tom felt an odd pang of disloyalty towards Frank as he said it. 'If I were to get the job, I would meet with the protesters, get them round the table, listen to them, but put forward the case for nuclear. I don't believe that they have much of an idea of how we'd struggle to keep the lights on without it.'

This time, Vernon, still frowning, nodded a sort of approval.

Julia laughed, 'That's right, Tom. Better to have them in the tent pissing out of it, than outside and pissing in to it.'

Neither men laughed with her. They conferred in whispers, then Bill Rice turned to Julia then to Tom, 'We've no more questions. Is there anything you want to ask us?'

'There is just one thing. Can you tell me if SHM will keep the account if you offer me the job?'

Bill shrugged. 'That's up to you, Julia. Right, I think we're done. Thanks for coming; we'll let you know our decision in a day or two.'

She didn't answer Tom's question, but got to her feet. The interview over, Tom shook hands with Bill and Vernon, and Julia showed him out. She walked alongside him to reception and said quietly, 'You did great, Tom. You've got it.'

'Well, thanks, Julia. But what about SHM?' he ventured.

'Sure, sure. No problem. Call you soon, okay?' she replied, shaking his hand before heading back to the meeting room.

That evening, Louise called Frank and gave him the directions to the NZO. He didn't mention how he planned to get there, and she didn't ask. It was a cordial conversation, but little more than that, as they tiptoed around each other. The following morning, a gale roared through Penrith so, when he heard the taxi sound its horn, Frank, dismissing Louise's advice, donned his heavy coat and large hat and went downstairs. 'Ahm, how much are we thinking?'

'It's up to you, marra,' said the driver after a slurp from an energy drink.

'I'm sorry, I don't follow you.'

'Well, you can take your chance on the meter and it'll cost what it costs. Or it's a flat fare. Just past Whitehaven, hey? I reckon a ton should cover it.'

With a sigh, Frank checked his wallet and opted for the latter. After an hour, the car pulled up outside the Net Zero Observatory. Frank looked across a muddy field filled with dumpers and diggers to a building that looked for all the world like a giant, lopsided daisy made out of wood and slate. There was a large, round central building with a sloping roof, surrounded by six smaller, circular structures. Along the main road were a succession of banners, each from a different group, protesting about the nuclear power station. The one nearest to him read "NZO = nuclear zone only."

He crunched his way across a rough gravel track to the entrance, wondering if he should have asked the driver to wait for the return journey, whatever that would cost, then remembered he had less than a hundred pounds left in his wallet. Inside, there were men in hi-vis jackets who were drilling. Wires hung out of the walls, and the place smelled of freshly cut timber. One of the men glanced up at the confused-looking visitor and pointed to a paper sign on a door that read "Office".

In a large room devoid of anything other than a desk and two chairs, Julia O'Leary was poring over her laptop. She looked up as Frank walked in, 'Ah, you made it. Good man. Welcome to the NZO.'

Frank sat down opposite her.

'Now, don't you be making yourself too comfortable, Frank, I'm going to give you the guided tour.' Julia led them through a maze of rooms, ticking off each one with a single word, 'office, store, toilet, kitchen,' before opening a pair of double doors that led onto an auditorium. She pressed a panel of switches and spotlights that revealed a stage and tiered seating. 'Like it?' she beamed at him.

'It's, ahm, very nice. But where do…?'

'The murals? Sure, course you'll be needing to know where they'll be going. Come on.' She led the way into a large, oddly-shaped room with skylights and floor-to-ceiling windows that faced a chain link fence, behind which a vast army of men and machines were at work. To one side of them, a row of caravans and motorhomes were parked, with banners fluttering above them bearing rainbow stripes or the CND symbol on them. 'There you go, Frank.'

'The view…?'

'Oh, yeah, we chose where the murals are going to go. They'll be facing the site of the power station, you see. We want people to put two and two together, renewables and that and the power station all as one, so they can kind of see for themselves that nuclear isn't this big, scary monster.'

'It does look rather intimidating right now, what with all those workmen, not to mention those people over there.' Frank pointed to the banners.

'Don't be worrying about that. Bill says it'll all be nice and tidy before we're ready to open. And we'll be getting that lot moved on, too.'

'Well, you know best.'

'Anyway, come on, what do you think?'

Frank had to admit it was an excellent space for the murals and said so.

'Glad about that, Frank. Let's grab a coffee.' In the kitchen, she switched on a large and expensive looking machine that ground the beans and discharged two cappuccinos. 'Oh yeah, I was meaning to ask you. How come you heard about Barney? He didn't call you, did he?'

Frank smiled at knowing something that Julia did not, 'Oh no, it's just that I gather you've offered the job to my son-in-law.'

'Tom Wilson's your son-in-law? Wow, small world, eh, Frank?' Julia grinned back at him. 'Keeping it all in the family, then. How about that?'

After a more detailed look at the exhibition space, and a supermarket sandwich each, Julia said she needed to go to a meeting.

Frank felt uncomfortable saying it, but couldn't think of what else he might do, 'Ahm, I hate to ask, but I don't suppose you could lend me a few pounds? It's for the taxi, you see.'

'A taxi? To Penrith? Jeez, you're something else. How much d'you need?'

'Ahm, I think forty would be enough with what I've got. If that's all right. As soon as I get back, I'll send you a cheque…'

'Sorry, Frank, I can manage a tenner, but that's it. I'm like royalty these days. Hardly carry any cash, pay for everything on the card.'

'Oh, never mind. Sorry to have mentioned it.' Frank was crestfallen, and had no idea how he'd get back to the flat.

'Tell you what, though, I can drop you off in Workington. You can get a bus all the way to Penrith from there, and its only two quid for as far as you like. Unless you've got a bus pass, that is.'

Frank remembered the bus pass in his wallet, but was unwilling to admit to being old enough to have one. Despite his earlier protestations, a bus would at least get him back. 'Oh, that would be most kind of you, Julia,' he said gratefully. 'I can manage the two pounds all right.'

As they walked across the car park, a middle aged man with a pony tail rushed towards them and took a photo of Frank on his mobile phone. 'You're one of us, now, Frank,' said Julia with a grim smile. 'Welcome to my world.' Frank was all set to remonstrate with the man, but Julia pulled him back and urged him to get into her car. 'It'd only make things worse. Best to do nothing.'

He didn't have to wait long for the bus, but his thoughts about the NZO and Louise were interrupted by a tiny, bird-like woman with two Bedlington terriers that kept wandering up and down, ignoring the woman's cries of "come to mummy". It was over an hour and a half before he made it back to Penrith. Frank was exhausted, convinced he deserved a trip that evening to The Church Inn, but too tired to venture out.

Meanwhile, with his appointment now approved by Bill Rice of the NDC and Vernon Nelson of the DESNZ, Julia called Tom, 'Good news, Tom. It's all sorted.'

'Great, so…'

'So, I need to know a start date so we can get you

DBS checked and arrange a P4 pass for you, too.'

Tom was reluctant to ask what the latter was, after his embarrassment at the interview, but thought it best to. 'A P4 pass?'

'Yeah, that gets you on site. Okay, so let me know as soon as when you can start.'

It was gone four when Tom saw Yannick return to the agency. He had been tentative about tendering his resignation but, with the NZO job now confirmed, he walked into Yannick's office confidently with an envelope in his hand. 'Can I have a word?'

'Sure thing, what's on your mind?' Yannick cracked his knuckles and leaned back.

'I'm leaving, Yannick.'

The tall Ulsterman came forward, elbows on his desk, 'Really? You going to say why?'

'I've been offered a job running the NZO.'

'Going client-side? So, the NZO, eh? No other reason?'

'Well, I guess no-one round here is safe, with you having to make cuts.'

Yannick looked hard at Tom, 'Is this about your buddy, Craig going? The chemistry was all wrong there. Good guy, wrong agency, wrong fit.'

'No, it isn't, but you are having to make people redundant, aren't you?'

'Sure, but not you, Tom. The guys and me see you as one of our rising stars. So, the NZO. You chase them or they chase you?'

Tom was momentarily thrown by the question and being described as a rising star by a man almost ten years younger than him, and wondered why Yannick wasn't making much of an effort to persuade him to stay. 'Yeah, they called me. Anyway, I don't see any problems in SHM keeping the account,' he said without much conviction.

Yannick gave Tom a less than joyful smile, 'Good of you to say so, Tom, my man. But we won't be able to let you go until you've made sure the NZO stays with us. That's probably going to be pretty much the full three months, right?'

'If you're having to make cuts, don't you want me to go early?'

Yannick laughed mirthlessly. 'That's a good one, but no, we're not in that much of a hurry. And it wouldn't look good to the Americans if we lost an account we've just won.'

'What about who'll take over as account director?'

Yannick shrugged, 'Well, I haven't had much time to think about that, have I? Still, I reckon Fran could handle it okay.'

'What, Fran? I mean, yeah, she's good, but she's had no experience at that level. Surely, you're going to need someone more senior.'

Yannick shook his head, 'No, I don't think so. She was on the pitch team, and she did the research so, yeah, I think we'll run with Fran. Anyway, it's over to you, my man. We're relying on you. Just train her up so she's ready.'

'But what about getting Craig back in? He's senior enough, and he'd be ideal.'

Yannick stretched, 'Ah, thinking about your old buddy again, eh? Nah, Craig's good, sure, but he's too much of an FMCG man for the NZO. Anyway, he's gone. Just get Fran up to speed, right? Sooner you do that, we can kick around how much notice you'll need.'

Tom dropped the envelope on Yannick's desk and left.

10.

After his visit to the NZO and with little more to look forward to than a lasagne ready meal for two and a couple of glasses of wine, Frank nodded off on the sofa in the fug of his overheated flat. It took him some seconds to realise that the ringing noise was his mobile phone, but he was glad to have been woken. He'd had such a horrible dream. In it, Frank had been swallowed whole by an enormous plant, a Venus flytrap or perhaps a pitcher plant. Inside, it was unbearably hot, as if he were in a furnace, except that the flames and billowing clouds of smoke were bright green. Everything, in fact, was green. Then there were distant voices getting louder, and people appeared decked out in green, carrying banners, dancing and singing. Frank looked around and he was the only one without any clothes. The green horde then turned and pointed at him, laughing, before throwing him out of the plant completely naked.

'Dad? Are you there?' the voice said for a second time.

'Uh, yes, just a mo,' drawled Frank dozily before straightening himself. 'Sorry, darling, yes, I'm here. This is an unexpected…'

'Is everything all right?' asked Georgia.

'Yes, of course. I was just in the, ah, other room.'

'Right, that's good.'

'So, how are you, darling?'

'I'm fine, Dad, but that isn't why I'm ringing.'

'No?'

'No. It's Mum. I'm a bit worried about her.'

'Ah yes, she did say she's got a bad cold and wouldn't be coming up this weekend. Has it turned nasty?'

'No, nothing like that. It's just a cold. No, it's just that she doesn't seem quite right.'

'What do you mean, not quite right.'

'Well, it's ever since that friend of yours, Gerald someone called round a second time…'

'A second time?'

'Yes, she was out the first time, but he came back again and she's been really weird since then.'

'How do you mean "weird"?'

'Oh, you know, sort of like she isn't really there. It's like she's on another planet.'

'Perhaps I'd better come down this weekend.'

'I don't know, Dad. Maybe I'm worrying about nothing, but I just thought you should know.'

'Well, I'm glad you called. But, if you could keep an eye on her and let me know how she is, I'll come down straight away if she's no better. Oh, by the way, have Mister Sweeney and his lads been round this week?'

'Don't think so, Dad. I thought they were just fixing the studio roof.'

'Oh, of course, of course. Just wondered if your mother had them doing any other odd jobs for her.'

Frank was in a quandary. Part of him wanted to catch the next train to London, but another couldn't help wondering if Louise's apparently remote behaviour was because she was thinking of, or God forbid, pining for that Sweeney boy. Or, then again, was it because she was going over ways to end their marriage? He also couldn't make up his mind as to whether or not he wanted to know the answer. Frank decided he would stay put unless Georgia called again. Anyway, he was tired. His mind turned to Gerald. Yes, he had told Frank that he'd visited Louise after The Duke of York, but he'd said nothing about calling round before that. And what reason would

Gerald have to be in Putney apart from the Sunday afternoon gathering? Maybe Gerald hadn't told him everything? In any event, there was something about all this that didn't add up.

That morning, Gerald had nicked himself shaving. He looked at himself sourly in the bathroom mirror, dismayed at the blotchy face and the trickle of blood that kept dripping from his cheek. He shook his head, as if trying to dismiss the image, saying to himself, 'What a bloody wreck'. Gerald didn't feel much like painting. He was tired and irritable, and spent the day leafing through his art books, vainly trying to find some inspiration. He was glad of the distraction of his mobile phone ringing, though hoped it wouldn't be the GP again. But, on seeing Frank's number come up, his mood changed. He quickly switched the phone off. He waited a few minutes before turning it back on, and listened to the message.

'Gerald, hello? Hello, are you there? Oh blast it. Anyway, ahm, it's Frank here. Look, could you give me a ring? I've been wondering if you told me absolutely everything on Sunday, and it's been rather preying on my mind. I'm in all day.'

'Looks like the cat's about to climb out of the bag. What the hell was I thinking of?' Gerald said to himself grimly. He waited until the morning, remembering that Betty would be going to the shops as usual. She would be gone for at least an hour or more. There was a ring binder in the conservatory. Gerald took out the most recent bank statements. Although he knew roughly how much was in each account, he double checked, and satisfied himself that the combination of his current account, savings and pension would give him more than enough to live on for the best part of a year. There was plenty in the joint account too, and he had no need of that. Betty could have it. He made a phone call and booked a room. Hauling himself upstairs by the banister, he pulled the pair of leather grips from the spare bedroom cupboard and filled them with clothes and toiletries. The exertion had taken its toll, but he couldn't waste time. With his keys, diary, wallet and mobile phone pocketed, Gerald stowed the bags in the back of his car. But, he then doubled back into the house, and took a sheet of Basildon Bond from the bureau, wrote a short message, folded it once, and placed it on the dining room table propped up against the fruit bowl. He took a last look at his studio, shrugged, then set off.

The M25 was as busy as ever, and it was well over an hour before Gerald picked up the A21 just outside Sevenoaks to head south. With the window open and the radio blaring, he was managing to stay awake but he had barely cleared ten miles before he knew he had to stop. He had no appetite whatsoever, but pulled into a roadside café and drank two cups of coffee. It was another hour's drive, so Gerald crossed the road to a petrol station and bought a packet of cigarettes. It didn't really matter now, and they might help him stay awake for the rest of the journey. Crossing The Weald, he couldn't remember if he was a Kentish Man or a Man of Kent. Growing up in Faversham was years ago.

Mornings were always quiet at the gallery, and this Friday was no exception. Jane McNab didn't know why she bothered opening when there was no-one around, but a closed gallery sends out the wrong signals, and there was always the remote chance of some passing trade. She skimmed through Art Market, and saw an announcement that a new gallery had just opened in Soho. The more she read of the article, the more convinced she became that it would be the perfect place to show Martin's painting.

Chloe rolled her eyes as Jane asked her to mind the gallery for an hour or so, but she knew there were precious few jobs where one got paid for doing next to nothing. Jane walked through Fitzrovia then down Dean Street. It took her a couple of false starts to find the gallery, tucked away in an alley off Romilly Street. Like most of the newer establishments, its frontage was painted white, but large red letters above the doorway read POLARI GALLERY. Jane was delighted, and smiled broadly. Inside the gallery, two large men were being supervised by a young woman as they filled a row of wooden packing chests. Jane had barely crossed the threshold when a harassed-looking man came over. 'I'm sorry, we aren't open today,' he said.

'Oh, I just wanted to ask someone about what exhibitions you have coming up,' replied Jane.

'Sorry, come in,' the young man smiled. 'We're all a bit at sixes and sevens, I'm afraid,' he pointed round the room. 'We're between shows, you see. But how can I help you?'

'Well, I saw in Art Market that you're concentrating on mixed shows, yes?'

'That's right. We're about celebrating London's gay art scene. Hang on, you've seen our piece in Art Market,' he looked at her quizzically. 'Aren't you Jane McNab?'

Jane smiled at him, 'Yes.'

'God, it's so good to meet you. The Curzon was such a legend…'

'I hope it still is…'

'Oh, God, sorry, yes of course. Oh,' he thrust out a hand. 'Tony Quinn. My Dad was a regular at your previews. He used to talk about them all the time.'

'Alan Quinn's your father? Oh yes, I remember him. Such a nice man.'

'But, Jane, what can I do for you?'

'Well, I'm just exploring a few ideas for now. I've a few paintings that haven't sold, and I was just wondering if you'd be interested in including them in one of your shows.'

'Hmm, if they aren't selling, that might not be easy…'

'Oh, I should have said he is gay, if that helps.'

'Well, it might, but who is it?'

'I shouldn't really say, because I haven't mentioned this to him yet, but between you and me, it's Martin Robertson.' Jane handed Tony a copy of her catalogue.

'Martin Robertson! Wow, yes please. We'd love to have some of his work here.' Tony turned the pages and stopped at *The Art Lovers*. 'That's amazing. Oh, do try and get it, and anything else by him too.'

'That's marvellous. I'll have a word with him and get back to you. Perhaps we could share the commission?'

'Absolutely. Yes, having his work on show here is about the best marketing we could ask for.'

Three cigarettes kept Gerald going until he reached Winchelsea. He parked in the yard at the back of The Anchor Hotel, and lugged his bags to the reception desk. He stood there wheezing until a woman came from behind the bar, where she'd been dealing with the last of the lunchtime rush. She flicked through a large desk diary, 'Graham, Graham. Ah, yes, you're the gentleman that called this morning.'

Gerald nodded.

'And you're with us for…' she paused uncertainly. 'Um, how many nights did you say, Mister Graham? I don't seem to have it down here.'

'I don't really know at the moment. But I expect it will be for a few weeks at least. At least, I hope so.'

'Oh well, that's fine. It's always nice to have people who stay here for a while. We get to know them, you see. But if you could let us know when you're thinking of moving on.'

Gerald stifled a hollow laugh, 'I certainly will. As soon as I know, that is.'

She saw the sweat on Gerald's forehead and asked, 'You're on the first floor. A nice room with a view over the garden. Would you like a hand with your bags?'

Gerald did, but replied, 'No, I should be able to manage.'

He made his way upstairs, and lay on the bed. It was almost an hour before he woke. There hadn't been another message from Frank. It was still just about light, so Gerald didn't bother to unpack, and went for a walk. He remembered the town well. He had come as a teenager, and been there with Betty more than once. It was no more than two hundred yards to the church. 'Incomplete and half-ruined,' he said to himself. 'Just like me.' He thought he might do some sketches of it, but soon dismissed the idea. Inside, there were two women attending to the flowers, so he found a pew at the back and looked around the strange, half-finished church, before taking out a notepad and pen.

Frank was at a loss as to why Gerald hadn't called him back. He wasn't going to call him again; he didn't want to appear panicky or desperate. Instead, he made his way across Penrith to the cosy comforts of The Church Inn. His new friends were already ensconced, and Cyril greeted him cheerily, 'Ah, it's the man of the moment! Come on over, Frank, and tell us what's been going on.'

A puzzled Frank took his large glass of Haut Medoc and joined them. 'Very nice of you to say so, Cyril, but what's all this "man of the moment" stuff about?'

Cyril unfurled a copy of the local paper, licked his thumb and turned the pages. 'Here we are, look. There you are.' He passed the paper over to Frank, who looked with horror at the photograph and the article beneath it. A single word headline blared out 'CYNICAL!' above a picture of Frank glaring from beneath his voluminous hat.

'Good God,' murmured Frank and took a long drink, then proceeded to read the first few lines aloud:

'*According to anti-nuclear protester, Pete George, A London-based artist, Frank Armstrong, has taken the nuclear industry's shilling to work for the so-called "Net Zero Observatory" which is nothing more than a PR stunt to get support for the proposed new power station. Has he been naïve, or is he as cynical as the people funding the NZO, the Nuclear Development Commission?*'

He handed the paper back to Cyril, and exhaled loudly.

'Good on you, Frank lad,' said Eric, the farmer, clapping him on the back. 'Anyone who gets up the nose of them protesters is doing summat right.'

'Calls for a drink, this does,' said Trevor. 'Same again, Frank?'

'I thought you didn't do rounds?'

'This is different. Anyone who puts two fingers up at that shower deserves a drink.'

'Well, thank you,' said Frank uncertainly. He was grateful for the effusive reaction and another glass of claret, but this was anything but the sort of PR that he had been hoping for. Max was completely wrong; of course there was such a thing as bad PR, and this article was hardly going to help him get a K. He also wondered why Julia O'Leary hadn't rung him about the article. Back at the flat, he thought about ringing Gerald again. Maybe he and Betty had gone away somewhere? Then again, these days, Gerald and his wife hardly went anywhere. No, while it would certainly be difficult, he decided it would be far better to speak to Louise, but face to face.

That evening in the sparsely populated dining room at The Anchor, over a bowl of soup which was about all he felt able to eat, Gerald pondered on how he was going to spend his time in Winchelsea. For one thing, he hadn't brought with him even a sketch pad, let alone paints and canvas. He could drive around the pretty villages along the coast, but driving would soon be a non-starter. And why hadn't he packed any books? First, though, he needed to finish the letter he had begun in the church, and that was not going to be easy. He thought about Betty, too. He knew he hadn't been much of a husband to her, especially after Andrea died. It wasn't as if he had set out to be cruel to her, he told himself, it was just that there was nothing left between them. And he knew it was wrong of him to leave Betty without a word. But, of course, he had never stopped longing for Louise. Back in his room, Gerald opened his wallet and took out the photograph he had kept there for years. 'I won't be needing that any more, and we don't want anyone finding it when the time comes, do we?' he said to himself, as he tore it into quarters.

Dominic had not stopped badgering Martin about letting *The Art Lovers* go on show, but he was beginning to be convinced that his husband was right. But, if he were to agree to it, the last thing Martin wanted would be for it to reopen an old wound. He would have to find a way of healing the rift with Frank. An idea had begun to take shape when Jane McNab rang on Monday morning. She told Martin about her visit to the Polari Gallery, and their enthusiasm for having the paintings she had not been able to sell in a forthcoming exhibition. Martin could not help being excited by the idea, but was not going to let that run away with him.

'So, what do you think, Martin?' Jane asked at last.

'It sounds wonderful, but there is just one thing…'

'Yes?'

'It's about Frank. Frank Armstrong, my old tutor. After all that unpleasantness at the gallery, I would like some of his work to be in the exhibition too. It's the least I can do.'

'But, Martin, he isn't gay.'

'Well, not as such, perhaps. But, they're hardly likely to object, seeing as he was one of the subjects in *The Art Lovers*.'

'I suppose so, but…' Jane was far less sure that Tony Quinn at Polari would agree to including Frank's paintings. 'But, Martin, his paintings are very conventional. They don't exactly celebrate London's gay art scene.'

Martin dug in his heels, 'I'm sorry, Jane. This is important. And, if they won't have anything by Frank, then I am afraid *The Art Lovers* is not going in their show.'

Jane thought about the commission. Tony had been so keen on having Martin's work; maybe she could convince him. 'Well, I suppose I could at least see what they have to say.'

'Jane, I really need to put things right again with Frank. Please, it would mean such a lot to me.'

'All right. I'll have a word with Julian Furnell at The Snicket, too. He still handles Frank, doesn't he?'

Jane poured herself some coffee. Maybe Tony Quinn would agree to Martin's demands, but what if there simply weren't any paintings by Frank to be had? After all, his work almost exclusively comprised commissioned portraits. If she was unable to track anything down, it would hardly be her fault, but Jane knew how stubborn Martin could be. Not only that, but there was also the little matter of somehow persuading Frank to have his work exhibited alongside the painting that had caused the argument with Martin in the first place. Rather than go back to Polari, she decided that the first thing to do was speak to Julian Furnell and find out if he had anything suitable. Or, for that matter, anything by Frank at all.

Jane knew nothing of Frank's commission from the NZO, and that might have given her some encouragement, as well as the fact that he was well on with it and had only three remaining panels to complete. Despite his worries about Louise and seeing his photograph in the paper, Frank spent the next few days working solidly. How they would be transported from the flat to the NZO had not yet crossed his mind.

In the bar of The Anchor, Gerald had another go at writing the letter. The waste paper basket in his room was filled with unsatisfactory drafts. It was proving to be an almost unbearably difficult task, but it had to be done. His labours drew no more attention from the locals than a glance or two in his direction, but the landlady came over to see how he was. Gerald was surprised to find himself pleased at having a few moments of someone's company. He realised he had become lonely. He took a break from writing the letter, and asked her to bring them both a brandy, and to put the bill on his room. But, in almost no time at all, her duties behind the bar called his companion away again.

On Friday morning, Julian Furnell announced to his wife, Joan, 'Shan't be in for lunch, my dear.'

'And who is it this time?'

'Ahm, I'm meeting Jane McNab of The Curzon.'

'I see,' replied Joan tartly, as she divided the correspondence between bills that were overdue and those that could wait. 'I daresay you'll be taking her to somewhere suitably lavish.'

'Oh, just a little bistro, I expect.'

'We both know that's rubbish. You'll have booked a table already, won't you? I bet it's that new place you've been going on about. What's it called? La Girolle. It is, isn't it?'

'Well, I haven't seen her for ages,' replied Julian defensively. 'And she mentioned something about a spot of business…'

'Funny business, I'll be bound…'

'Joan, really!'

'And, like all those other men, you'll be there with your tongue hanging out as she flutters her eyelashes at you and orders caviar and champagne.'

'No, I hardly think so, she is over seventy, you know. And do remember, her salad days were all a very long time ago, Joan dear.' Julian fiddled with his tie as his wife looked on disgustedly.

'Well, it's all leopards and spots if you ask me. Don't suppose I'll see you much before three. You could pick up a pint of milk on the way back. That is, if it isn't too much trouble.'

Julian kissed the top of her silver grey bun of hair, and sauntered out of The Snicket Gallery. He waited until he reached the corner of Southampton Row before hailing a taxi, knowing that Joan would disapprove of such extravagance almost as much as taking Jane McNab to lunch. It would be the last straw for her.

Gerald had slept badly, and was oddly anxious that his constant coughing might have woken up the hotel's other guests. He need not have worried, had he known that only two couples were staying, and they were at the opposite end of the corridor. But he felt washed out, far worse than just a day ago, and the sight of blood on his pillow meant that explanations would need to be given. In the late morning lull before lunchtime, Gerald sought out the landlady. 'I wonder if I might have a word?'

'Certainly, Mister Graham,' she said brightly.

'Gerald, please. I'm afraid I don't know your name.'

'It's Dorothy, Dorothy Nicholas. What is it I can do for you?'

'Well, you asked if I could let you know when I would be, ahm, moving on.'

'Oh, you aren't planning to leave so soon are you, Mister… Gerald? Are you, by chance, a military gentleman? Called away?'

'Ah, the moustache. No, I'm afraid not. Just one of those little changes, you know, that one makes when life takes an unexpected turn. As for leaving, though, I'm afraid there are circumstances beyond my control. You see, I'm in really rather poor health. And I'm sorry to say that one of your pillows has borne something of the brunt of it.'

'Ah, yes, one of the chambermaids did say she saw some blood. She thought you must have cut yourself shaving and gone back to bed.'

'I'm afraid not.'

Dorothy nodded, 'We do get quite a few convalescents here. It's the sea air, I suppose.'

'I'm afraid I've rather gone past that. So, you see, the business of my moving on isn't altogether in my hands.'

'You poor man,' she said softly, and put a heavily ringed hand on his. 'I understand. Well, please be sure to know, Gerald, that we will do everything we can to make sure you're comfortable here.'

Julian arrived early at La Girolle, one of his foulards, a mauve one, flapping louchely from his top pocket. When Jane arrived, dead on time, he leapt to his feet, bowed low to kiss her hand, and pulled a chair back for her with a flourish. 'Yes, he's creepy,' Jane told herself, 'but he's harmless, just old school. At least he's never tried it on with me.' She knew Julian would insist on paying but, despite the state of The Curzon's finances, said, 'I think it would be best if we go Dutch.'

'Oh, there's really no need, Jane, my dear,' protested Julian.

Jane shook her head, 'No, Julian, this is a business meeting and, remember, I called you.'

'Very well, if you absolutely insist,' he gave in easily with the pretence of a disappointed sigh, knowing it would avoid at least confrontation with Joan about the cost of their meal. He ordered a large glass of Mâcon-

Villages after Jane had plumped for mineral water and a Tom Collins and, with the waiter gone, said, 'This is all very intriguing, Jane. It isn't often our paths cross,' and couldn't resist adding, 'professionally-speaking, that is.'

'Have you heard about the new gallery that's opened? It's called Polari.'

Julian shook his head, 'A new one on me, I'm afraid.'

She explained that, while the owner as keen to include his paintings in a show, Martin had insisted that they also exhibit work by Frank.

Julian gave her a broad, yet baffled smile. 'What a very interesting dilemma. And you're wondering if I've got anything of Frank's in the basement? Well, let me see. There may be an oil sketch of one or two of his portraits, but I'll have to check. From what you say, I gather they may not quite fit the bill?'

Jane nodded, 'No, I don't suppose they would. That is a pity.'

'Hang on,' Julian sat up straight, 'I wonder…' He told Jane about the commission from the NZO. 'I wonder if a couple of his sketches for them might do the trick?'

'Well, that would be better than one of his dusty old portraits.'

He raised an eyebrow and gave her a knowing grin. 'They do help me to keep body and soul together, you know.' Then he frowned. 'But there is one other thing. Two, come to think of it.'

'Go on.'

'Well, he'll need to be persuaded to let his work to go in the same show as *The Art Lovers* – delicious title, and so naughty of Martin, too. And, even if he does agree to it, what if the NZO people won't let us use any of the sketches?'

'Hmm, yes. And, even if they do, I'll still need to convince Tony Quinn to include Frank.' Jane took a sip of her Tom Collins. 'Anyway, I don't suppose Frank has to know that *The Art Lovers* will be in the show. We could just say that there'll be a few paintings by Martin.'

Julian leaned forward. 'What a wicked girl, you are, Jane McNab. And how absolutely marvellous!'

They split the bill and agreed that, first of all, Julian would speak to Frank. It had been an enjoyable lunch, but not a long, boozy one and, the sun being out, he decided to walk back to The Snicket. Julian's delight at spending a conspiratorial hour with Jane soon evaporated, replaced by a feeling of disappointment at it being nothing more than that, something he always experienced after time spent in the company of a beautiful woman. He completely forgot about picking up the milk, and rang Frank from a bench in Bloomsbury Square. 'You're not the only art dealer who knows all the tricks of the trade, Ms McNab,' he said to himself, as he waited for Frank to answer. Smiling mischievously, he didn't see the need even to mention that there might be a few paintings by Martin in the show, let alone *The Art Lovers*.

Frank was glad of a break from the murals and a call from Julian was usually good news, at least for his bank account. It had been a while since he last had an exhibition and Frank was delighted at the possibility of being with what Julian described as "a group of highly fashionable, contemporary artists". But he was nervous about approaching the NZO. What if they refused? Still, Julian had said there was no tearing hurry, since it was still only a possibility and nothing had yet been agreed. All Julian needed for now were photographs of the sketches that he could take to the gallery. So, Frank decided to wait until he had finished the last mural; the NZO might be more amenable then to letting him do as he pleased with the preliminary sketches.

It hadn't been a particularly bad cold and Louise was over it soon enough but, by Tuesday, she felt she couldn't wait any longer and rang Frank to say she was coming up the following day. The situation was becoming intolerable; one of them had to make the first move and she felt certain it wouldn't be her husband. Frank had made good progress, so he chose to spend Wednesday morning going over what to say to Louise. He vacillated between not wanting to know if she was having an affair and the need to face up to reality, knowing that both options would be painful. Louise, too, spent the train journey trying to think of the best way of telling him about Gerald's visit, not to mention events long ago, without causing Frank to go off the deep end. Unlike her husband, she did not travel first class but wished she had. It was not until after the carriage became emptier at Preston that she was able to concentrate sufficiently to reach some sort of conclusions.

Despite lacking any evidence for it, Frank had been getting increasingly upset at what he might or might not discover, but thought it might do him some good to meet Louise at the station if their marriage was not already a lost cause. He arrived early and Louise was surprised to see him standing on the platform. That and the hug she received disconcerted her, and Louise began to doubt whether she would be able to tell him what she had finally made up her mind to reveal. Her reluctance only increased as Frank picked up her overnight bag and insisted on carrying it back to the flat. He had spent part of the morning tidying up too, and arranged the completed murals in a row against the living room wall. While Louise unpacked, he made tea, even though he would have preferred a hefty Scotch if there was a difficult conversation to be faced. It would have to wait.

Despite noting Frank's little touches of chivalry and domesticity, Louise's resolve survived. Joining her husband again, she began, 'Frank, I think we need to talk.'

They were the words he had been dreading, knowing they invariably meant only one thing. He nodded, 'Yes, I suppose there is. I should have told you before now.'

Louise was taken aback, having expected to be the one with explanations to make, 'Oh. Told me what?'

'But was there something you wanted to say, Lou?'

'Well, yes, but you go first.'

'Where to start...?' Frank wished he'd poured something stronger than tea. 'Gerald told me something at The Duke of York...'

'Gerald?' Louise was alarmed. *How much did Frank already know?*

'Yes, he buttonholed me and said he'd been round to see you.'

'He did?'

'Yes. And he told me he'd seen you...' Frank struggled to complete the sentence.

'Well, he would have done, wouldn't he? But what about it?'

'Oh, Lou,' he said at last, 'he told me he'd seen you and one of those Sweeney boys...'

'They were fixing the studio roof, I told you...'

'In a passionate embrace.'

'What!'

Frank exhaled loudly and leaned forward, his elbows on his knees, unable to do more than nod.

'That's the most ridiculous thing I've ever heard,' Louise cried. 'One of those Sweeney boys and me! You can't possibly believe something so utterly preposterous.' She then realised her protestations about what Gerald had said would be nothing to how Frank would react when he heard what she had to say.

Frank felt a degree of relief and said, 'There was something you wanted to say too, wasn't there?'

'It's to do with Gerald.' Louise steeled herself. 'Yes, he came to see me. I wondered if he might have had a bit too much to drink…'

'He isn't much of a drinker…'

'Well, perhaps not. Oh God, there's no easy way of saying this,' Louise sighed heavily. 'Let's get it over with…'

Now Frank was alarmed. If it wasn't one of the Sweeney boys, was there someone else? Was she about to say their marriage was over?

'All right, Frank. The fact of the matter is that Gerald tried it on with me. There. He grabbed me and pushed me onto the sofa.'

Frank was astonished, the stuffing knocked out of him, and said in almost a whisper, 'Gerald really did that?'

Louise bit her lip and just nodded.

'But, why on earth would he do that?'

There was no point in concealing anything else now. 'A long time ago, Gerald and I…'

'What, you and Gerald?' Frank expostulated.

Louise nodded again, 'It was a long time ago. We had a fling for all of about a fortnight, and he seemed to think there was still something between us. Of course there wasn't, and actually there never had been. Truth be told, I didn't really like Gerald. I never have. But, back then, things like that just seemed to happen, and there didn't seem any harm in it. Anyway, it was all long before you and I got together...'

'The bloody bastard, I'll kill him...' Georgia's call, that Gerald had been to the house twice, now made sense to Frank.

Louise had regained her composure. 'I think it was about the time that you and Martin...'

The pair of them sat in silence for a few moments.

Frank's new realisation of his hypocrisy suddenly calmed him. 'Oh God, this is awful,' he said at last. 'Gerald...'

Louise reached out and put her hand on Frank's.

He breathed deeply, 'Thank God. I can't tell you the relief.'

She kissed him, and he put his arms around her. They held each other close, then Louise spoke, 'I don't suppose you could pour us a drink, could you?'

It was all behind them now, but Frank returned to it later that evening. 'I'll have to speak to him, you know. I'll have it out with him at the pub on Sunday.'

Louise knew he would get round to saying it, and that there was no point in trying to dissuade him. On Friday, they caught the train to London together, with a new lightness between them as they put to the back of their minds what might happen when Frank met Gerald.

It was a late, leisurely breakfast for Louise and Frank, after a couple of hours doing the Sunday crossword together in bed. The hours appeared to dawdle as Frank thought more and more of his confrontation with Gerald that afternoon. He had by no means scripted or rehearsed what he was going to say. No, he would merely ask Gerald what he had to say for himself, and take it from there. When three o'clock came at last, Louise kissed her husband and said, 'Good luck'. She thought it unlikely that the two men would come to blows but Frank could be unpredictable and she hardly knew Gerald at all. Louise comforted herself, knowing that Doug was bound to be there, and he towered over both men. He would keep the peace.

At The Duke of York, only Doug and Max were there. Sean had gone out to make a phone call, but there was no sign of Gerald. Frank wondered if he had got wind of his being there. 'Odd for Gerald not to put in an appearance,' he said, hoping one of the others might know something.

'Yes, odd is very much the operative, I would say, Francis,' agreed Max.

'Dunno,' shrugged Doug. 'Must have had a better offer.'

With no clue as to why Gerald hadn't turned up, the conversation reverted to art and their usual gripes about who was doing well. After half an hour, a slim, blonde woman walked in. She scanned the room anxiously, looking about a foot and a half above the heads of the drinkers as if what she was looking for might be suspended from the ceiling. At last, her gaze settled on the three artists. She remained rooted to the spot then, as if a switch in her had been pressed, hurried towards them.

'Hello,' she said, sounding breathless.

'Betty!' said Doug, 'Come and sit down, love. Is everything all right?'

'Indeed,' added Max, pulling a chair back for her. 'We were somewhat agog at not to clap an eye on Gerald.'

'It's about Gerald that I've come,' Betty hesitated. 'Oh, I am sorry. I don't mean to interrupt your meeting.'

Her apologies waved away, she agreed to a small Tio

Pepe, so Frank went to the bar to fetch it, and to give himself a moment to think about what he might want to ask Betty.

The three men pulled their chairs closer to the table to hear what she had to say. Betty rummaged in her handbag, eventually pulling out a small piece of writing paper. 'It's this, you see. And I remembered that this is where he goes on Sundays, so I thought I might...' She took a hankie from her sleeve and pressed it to her eyes.

'What's it say, love?' asked Doug when she finally lowered the hankie, clasping it in her lap with both hands.

She handed him the note which read:

GOING AWAY FOR A BIT. WILL BE IN TOUCH.
YOUR LOVING HUSBAND, GERALD.

Doug passed it to Max and Frank.

'Bloody rum, that,' said Doug, without adding that he'd always thought Gerald to be a bit of a rum bugger.

'And you've no idea where he's gone?' asked Frank.

Betty shook her head. 'He never said a word. And he hasn't even taken his paints and brushes and things.'

'How very curious, if I may say so,' mused Max.

Betty seemed to come to life after a sip or two of sherry. 'Things haven't been easy for ages. The things he says, sometimes I think he doesn't like me at all. It was after Andrea, you see. He was never the same after we lost her. Something changed in him. But, I never expected him just to walk out on me like this.'

The artists knew just how much Gerald's work changed after his daughter died. They took turns in consoling Betty, reassuring her that Gerald would surely return. Not taking his materials with him must be a good sign, they agreed. Sean returned, saying he had to go, as Siobhan was expecting.

'And that, I am afraid, means my leave must also be taken,' said Max, with a courtly bow to Betty. 'Sean had kindly offered me transportation, as I have business matters that will not stand a delay.'

With no further information on Gerald forthcoming, Frank saw no reason to stay any longer, 'I should probably be getting back, too.'

The meeting apparently at an end, Betty half rose from her chair, but Doug said, 'No need to rush off, Betty, love. Stay and have another. I'm in no hurry.'

Frank left them to it and walked back to Exmoor Gardens with no clear plan of what to do about Gerald. Louise was glad to see him return unscathed, but equally puzzled at Gerald's sudden disappearance.

11

Frank had had enough. He was tired of Cumbria, and it seemed nothing like how he remembered it. Flogging up and down from London had become wearisome, the flat wasn't that comfortable, and he wanted to be back home. But he needed to finish the murals first, and the sooner he did that, the sooner he would be back with Louise, so he caught an early train on Monday, vowing to get on with the job. And then there was the exhibition in London that Julian had called him about. He worked steadily all afternoon and with just one left to do and a few finishing touches, Frank then headed over to The Church Inn.

Cyril and the others seemed unusually grim when he joined them.

'What a bloody shambles,' said Eric.

On noticing Frank's puzzled expression, Cyril said, 'Haven't you heard?'

'Heard what?'

'It's been all over the news.'

'What has?'

'That Net Zero place. You know, the one you're doing them pictures for.'

'What about it?' Frank began to sound impatient.

'They've only gone and burned it down,' said Trevor.

'They've what?' cried Frank.

'It's burned to the ground,' explained Cyril, then added, 'Aye, but, hold on, Trevor, they're saying it was an electrical fault that did it.'

'Don't know about that,' muttered Trevor, 'I bet the protesters had something to do with it.'

'Aye, and I bet they wish they had too,' said Eric with a mirthless laugh. 'They'd be right proud of their handiwork, wouldn't they?'

'Let me get this straight,' said Frank at last. 'You're telling me the NZO has burned down?'

'That's what we've been saying. Went down in no time with all that wooden cladding on it.'

'Good lord.' The implications began to dawn on Frank. At least he had received the first three payments for the murals… *But what about the last one? And then there was Lizzie to consider. What would happen about Tom's job now?*

Julia O'Leary hadn't called about Frank having his photograph in the paper, but she did call him on Tuesday morning. 'You'll have heard, I suppose?' she asked.

Frank had seen the charred remains of the NZO on the local news. 'It's completely destroyed?'

'More or less. Bill thinks we might be able to salvage a bit of it, but I don't know.'

'So, what's to become of the NZO? Are you going to rebuild it?'

'I don't think so, but that's up to Bill. Anyway, I was ringing to talk to you about the murals.'

'Yes?'

'Well, we aren't going to need them now, well, not for a while, at least.'

'Oh.'

'But the money's already been allocated in the budget, so you'll get the final payment all right.'

'So, do you want me to finish them then?'

'You might as well. They'll come in handy for the schools outreach we're doing.'

Frank was relieved to hear he'd still get paid, but the thought of his paintings just going in a few local schools was disappointing. 'I see. Ahm, I was going to ask if you might still need the sketches and designs I did for them.'

'No. Do what you like with them. I can't see why we'd want them.'

'And, while you're on, what about Tom's job?'

'He's coming up tomorrow. We need to work out what we can do for him.'

Frank thought about calling Lizzie, but didn't know what he might say to her and decided to wait until after Tom had met Julia and her colleagues. Instead, he called Julian and told him he could have the sketches he'd done. Jane was delighted at the news, but there was still the matter of persuading Tony Quinn to include Frank's work in the exhibition.

Tom's mind went over all of his options as he ate a full English. Could he try to get his old job back at SHM? That seemed unlikely, since there would be no account with the NZO to look after now, and his resignation had probably already been included in the agency's planned cost savings. Or he could join a competitor, though his CV was starting to look rather threadbare, having lost Conch Telecom and now the NZO. They could sell the house in London, buy somewhere cheaper in Cumbria or anywhere outside the M25, come to that, and live off the proceeds for a while until he found another job. But there weren't many agencies up there that could pay him anything like the salary he received at SHM. With no obvious solution to his dilemma, he trudged from the station to the hotel, wondering what, if anything, Julia had in store for him.

His reception was rather different from the interview he had attended only a few weeks earlier. Julia greeted Tom with a sad expression on her face, while Bill Rice and Vernon Nelson shook his hand warmly and thanked him for coming to meet them. There was a buffet on a side table, too.

This time, Vernon spoke first, 'Okay, Tom. Let me tell you where we're up to. We haven't had much time, but I spoke with the Minister this morning and we ran through the situation. The bottom line is that we need to do the right thing for you, but…'

Bill cut in, 'The fact is, Tom, there isn't going to be an NZO as such now. By the time we find out who was responsible and get the insurance, it'll be too late. We'll be on with the project by then. What's left of the building, we'll turn it into a facility for the locals. Yoga classes, mums and tots clubs, that sort of thing. But, for the NZO's comms work, we're now looking at having a mobile unit that can be taken round schools, community groups and so on, and that would be staffed by Julia's team.'

Julia looked at the carpet.

Vernon continued, 'So, although there won't be any need for a Director, we've had a few ideas that we'd like to run by you. Okay?'

'Sure. What have you got in mind?' Tom didn't expect much.

'Well, we'll pay you six months' salary for a start. It's the least we can do. And, Julia?'

'Thanks, Vernon. Yeah, I've been putting out a few feelers. There's the firms doing the build. Bill says there's one that needs a marketing manager. And then there's a kind of nuclear networking group, you know, for all the supply chain that'll be working on the power station. They're after someone to co-ordinate it. If you're interested, there may be a few roles coming up at the

NDC too. It's not much, but there hasn't been much time, you know.'

Tom nodded.

'Look, think it over. We'll see if anything else crops up, but get back to us if any of those appeal,' said Bill.

That afternoon, Jane rang Tony Quinn. 'I've had a chat with Martin Robertson,' she began carefully, 'and he's fine about his paintings appearing at Polari.'

'That's wonderful, thank you so much.'

'But, there's just one thing…'

'Yes?'

'He wants some works by his former tutor to be included too. Frank Armstrong…'

'But isn't he a portrait painter?'

'Well, that's what he's best known for, but he's recently done a series of murals about the need for green energy and he'll let us have the sketches for them.'

Tony didn't want to dismiss the idea out of hand and risk not having Martin's paintings at the gallery, but still hesitated, 'I don't know. It doesn't really sound like our sort of thing, but I suppose if he's a gay artist…'

'I'm afraid not. He isn't really, at least not these days. But you remember that painting by Martin you really liked, *The Art Lovers*?'

'Of course. It's fantastic.'

'Well, Frank is the figure on the right.'

'Oh, I didn't know that! It might work, I suppose.' An idea came to him, 'You know, it's got me thinking. Perhaps we could include Frank's sketches, but tweak the theme of the exhibition a bit. Maybe it could be something that kind of links our celebration of gay artists with them caring for the environment. What do you think?'

'I like it. That's a great idea. So, you're okay if I'll tell Martin and Frank that we're all set?'

'Yes, I think so. Let me come up with a title for the show, and we're good to go. I'll give you a ring about timings too. We're looking at probably round about the end of next month.'

Jane rang Martin and Julian Furnell with the good news, and Julian rang Frank, but mentioned neither Martin nor what the exhibition was about. *There was no point in putting him off*, he reasoned and, much as he valued having Frank on his books, *it would be fun to see his reaction*. It wasn't long before Jane began to think that matters were by no means cut and dried, so she rang Julian again.

'Well, don't expect me to go running around after her, pouring drinks and whatnot for that old tart,' snapped Joan Furnell after Julian informed her that he had invited Jane McNab to come to The Snicket.

'Honestly, Joan, the things you say,' said her exasperated husband.

'I don't know what possessed you to invite her here. Well, yes actually, of course I do.'

'I haven't the slightest idea what you mean,' Julian replied with exaggerated hauteur.

When Jane arrived, Joan scuttled off into the office, leaving her husband to pour two glasses of his usual, middling Fitou. He slid a pile of photographs from a hardbacked envelope and spread them across his desk. There were sixteen in all, since each of the eight murals was in two parts, one showing a series of desolate worlds where fossil fuels still burned, and one of lush landscapes protected by the adoption of clean energy. They agreed that the former would have the greater impact, perhaps even demonstrating, to Julian's great amusement, Frank's new-found commitment to the environment. That, however, was not enough to dispel Jane's concerns. She hadn't touched the wine.

'I think there maybe something we've overlooked,' she said as Julian topped up his glass. 'What if Frank hits the roof and storms out when he sees *The Art Lovers* on display?'

Julian shrugged and pulled the half-moons back up his long nose, 'Not really our problem, is it, Jane my dear? In any case, it will be too late by then. The pictures will already be on show.'

'Well, it would be a problem for me if Martin withdraws his paintings from the exhibition.'

'Ah, yes, one does hate to lose one's commission.' Julian smiled.

'And it may be a problem for you, too.'

'And why might that be?'

'If Frank blames you for this, it will be. You do rather value having Frank as one of your artists, don't you? And what if he also decides to withdraw his sketches when he hears it's about celebrating gay artists?'

Julian sipped some more wine. 'Yes, there is that, I grant you. But what do you propose we do about it?'

'I'm not sure, but, at the very least, we need to make sure that whatever Tony Quinn calls the exhibition doesn't scare Frank off.'

Julian nodded, 'Yes, I see. I rather think it would be a good idea to do that.'

'I'll take the photographs to show him, and see if I can come up with something. How about *Lovers of Art and the Environment*?'

'My goodness, the very idea of it! Jane, at times you really are quite the naughtiest girl,' Julian chuckled. '*The Art Lovers* at the *Lovers of Art* exhibition. Oh, I love it!'

Loath though she was to leave The Curzon in Chloe's sole charge for long, Jane walked down to Polari. This time, the gallery was empty, but for Tony Quinn at his laptop. He greeted her like a long-lost friend, and Jane got out the photographs, keeping the pastoral landscapes in reserve. She need not have bothered; Tony enthused over the grisaille and watercolour sketches. 'I've been looking at Frank Armstrong's work and, I must say, I was starting to have my doubts when I saw all of those dreary portraits, but these really are something else.'

Jane began to feel relieved. Then Tony said, 'And, I've come up with a great title for the exhibition.'

'Oh yes?' she had hoped to get in first.

'*Gay artists and the environment*. What do you think?' he beamed at Jane expectantly, and looked disappointed as she pursed her lips.

'Hmm, I'm not sure. I do think that sounds rather, how shall I say, niche.'

'But it's what we're about,' he protested.

'Oh, I know, but I think you'd get more footfall with something like *Lovers of Art and the Environment*.'

'I don't want all of those people who've supported us, and made Polari happen, thinking I've sold out.'

'You wouldn't. And a new gallery needs the broadest possible appeal if it's going to survive. It's a competitive world out there, Tony. How would your supporters feel if you can't make a success of the gallery?' Jane felt she had gone out on a limb and may have overplayed it, but knew she needed to convince him.

'I think I see what you mean,' said Tony slowly.

'Trust me, Tony. Julian Furnell and I have been running our galleries for years, and we do know just how difficult it can be, and how vital it is to do everything possible to get people through the door.' She decided against revealing the state of The Curzon's finances.

Tony brightened. 'Oh, okay. What's in a name anyway? Potato, potarto. All right. *Lovers of Art and the Environment* it is.'

Frank finished the last of the murals and arranged for a courier to take them to Julia's office at the Nuclear Development Commission. He clapped his hands together as the van drove off, glad that his stay away from home had finally come to an end. Frank made one last trip to the pub to say goodbye to Cyril and the others, packed his bags and sketches and caught a train the following morning. There were a few weeks' rent left on the flat, but he no longer had any use for it. There was now the exhibition in London to look forward to.

While Frank was clearing out the flat in Penrith, Doug was similarly busy too. His friends would have been amazed to see him cleaning and scrubbing surfaces that had been untouched for over a decade. He stowed away his chipped plates and glasses, and even his beloved Sunderland FC paraphernalia. The bathroom received particular attention as he hacked away at tidemarks and doused everywhere liberally with bleach. After several attempts to assemble it, he got the Hoover working, and emptied it half a dozen times before he was satisfied. As a finishing touch, he bought a bunch of chrysanthemums and placed them in a pint glass. Doug wanted the flat to be at least presentable for his visitor.

There being no need, now, to train up Fran to take over the NZO account and having handed over his smaller accounts to colleagues, Tom had nothing much to do at SHM. He was at a loose end, but in no hurry to leave the agency when there were three months of income to be had. When Yannick walked into his office, Tom had a pretty good idea what was coming.

'Well, my man, you're free to go,' said Yannick, reclining in the seat across from Tom.

'I'm in no hurry.'

'I guess not, but you did say you wanted to go early.'

'Yes, but with the NZO job falling through…'

Yannick shrugged. 'Yeah, who'd've thought? Still, shit happens.'

'So, I'd like to work my full notice.'

'Hmm, me and the guys thought you'd say that. Thing is, that doesn't really work for us if there's nothing for you to do round here.' He leaned forward, with one elbow on Tom's desk. 'But, hey, we're not throwing you under the bus, Tom. We aren't like that.' He waited for Tom's reply but, when one didn't come, continued, 'Okay, so here's the deal. You can have a special projects role for now…'

'Special projects! What does that mean?'

'I dunno. Business development, streamlining, efficiencies, stuff like that. But it's up to you to make it into something 'cos we'll need you to come up with the goods if we're going to pay you for the whole three months. Okay? Gotta go, but keep me in the loop. Good man.'

Tom knew all too well what a "special projects" role meant; it was just SHM's way of easing him out of the door without risking an employment tribunal. It would be miserable, trying to find things to impress the directors, with no guarantee he'd be kept on for even three months. But, like Frank, he had no wish to return to Cumbria, and Julia O'Leary hadn't been in touch with any more attractive opportunities. Instead, he set about scouring the recruitment listings for marketing jobs. After her initial doubts, Lizzie, to his surprise, was having none of it.

'I thought we'd made up our minds,' she told him, 'so, we might as well at least go up there. There is a vacancy coming up for a senior radiographer, and you do have six months' salary from the NZO to keep us going while you find something. Now he's back home, we could borrow Dad's flat for a long weekend.'

Martin was glad that Jane McNab and Julian Furnell had managed between them to persuade Frank to include his sketches in the exhibition at Polari, but he was still anxious. Over dinner, he said to Dominic, 'I can't stop worrying about seeing how he'll react to seeing *The Art Lovers* again.'

Dominic nodded, 'I know. You've been fretting about it ever since she called.'

'The thing is, Dom, I don't even know if Julian has told him that *The Art Lovers* will be there. I can't help thinking it was a stupid idea to insist on Frank being included in the exhibition. I mean, what if it just makes everything worse? I don't think I could bear that.'

'I've been thinking about that, too. There may be something we could do.'

Having racked his brains for days to no avail, Martin was sceptical. 'But what could we possibly do?'

'Well, you know how Frank used to go on about how unfair it was that actors and musicians always get the honours, but very few artists do?'

'Oh, yes, it was typical Frank. He just couldn't understand why he hadn't been given a knighthood. We all thought it was ridiculous.'

'Yes, but what about if you were to nominate him for something? I mean, maybe a knighthood is a bit too much of a stretch, but what about one of the other ones, an OBE or an MBE, something like that?'

'Do you really think so?'

'Angela got an MBE for apparently "turning the school round",' Dominic's fingers stressed the inverted commas. 'I mean, if she can get one just for being the headteacher, anyone can. Anyway, she told me the chair of governors had nominated her, and all he had to do was get a few letters of support from the others. Simple as that. Look, love, why not get all of your artist friends involved?'

Martin shook his head. 'I don't know the first thing about all that sort of stuff.'

Dominic was getting impatient. 'Well, if you won't do it, I will.'

'And there is Julian Furnell too,' said Martin, giving in. He gave Dominic a kiss, 'You are absolutely right. It's a wonderful idea. And you're wonderful, too.'

With Tom's job at the NZO falling through, Frank had been surprised when Lizzie rang him to ask if they could stay at his flat in Penrith, and Louise remained puzzled by her daughter's new enthusiasm to move away from London. Lizzie and Tom considered taking the train but, despite being more arduous, opted instead to drive so that they could see more of what Cumbria had to offer them. Although Lizzie was by far the better driver, they shared the driving, making several stops en route to feed the children and change Theo. They were exhausted by the they reached Penrith. On Saturday, they trawled round the estate agents and Lizzie was adamant that moving north was both more than feasible and the right thing to do. Driving back the following day, though, Tom was deep in thought. Yes, they could have a bigger house, somewhere beautiful to bring up the children, and the job Lizzie had found would leave them better off, but what was there for him? As they drove down the M6, he said, 'I suppose I'll end up being a house husband, Liz.'

Lizzie removed the bottle from Theo and replied, 'Don't make it sound like it's the end of the world.'

'I'm not. It's just that I can't see me getting a job up there. Well, not one that pays anything like SHM.'

'There's more to it than that.'

'Walks in the Lakes, I suppose, things like that. When I'm not picking up the kids and doing the washing and cleaning, that is.'

'Oh, for goodness' sake. What century are you living in, Tom? Other people do it, you know. And it'll give you time too.'

'Time for what?'

'Well, you've been going on for years about the novel you want to write. This way, you'll have the time to get round to it, won't you?'

Tom hadn't thought of that and, on the drive home, it now dawned on him that this was an opportunity too good to miss. At Charnock Richard services, with Theo asleep and Polly engrossed with her Gamepad, Tom kissed Lizzie. 'If you're sure...'

'Of course I am.'

'It'll be wonderful. Thanks, Liz, and I really don't

mind picking up the kids and doing my bit around the house.'

She kissed him back and smiled, 'You'd better not. And I expect to see plenty of writing being done, too.'

Earlier that week, with drafts written on the hotel's stationery, Gerald had walked from The Anchor to a newsagent's where he bought two postcards, stamps, a pad of plain paper and envelopes. Back in his room, he decided against sending a card to The Curzon Gallery. Jane McNab would get her commission when she sold his last remaining abstract, assuming Betty had no wish to keep it. There really was no need for an explanation of his elaborate deception as well as that. Mister Melchior could simply remain a mystery. The other card, though, was another matter, and far more difficult to write than his lengthy letter that had already been drafted numerous times. In the end, he was unable to come up with anything better than:

I'm sorry, but I think this was for the best. Gerald.

Copying the final draft of the letter onto the plain paper was a laborious task. Gerald was quickly tired and unable to complete it in one go. Dorothy Nicholas, the landlady, began to notice how much more slowly he made his way upstairs, how he ate less and less, and the changes in his complexion. Then, when Gerald had not emerged from his room all day, she knocked on his door and, on hearing no reply, unlocked it and went inside. He was asleep and his breathing was little more than shallow rasp. Dorothy went downstairs and rang for the GP.

By the time Dr Claudia Marinello arrived at The Anchor that evening, Gerald was awake. Although she wasn't comfortable leaving him, she had a hotel to run, so

Dorothy and one of the chambermaids took turns keeping him company. He said to Dorothy, 'I wonder if you might do something for me?'

'Of course, Gerald.'

He pointed to the dressing table where the results of his labours were, 'If you could post those two, I really would be most grateful.'

'Certainly. But is that all?'

Gerald nodded. 'You'll find some stamps in the drawer.'

She left the room while the GP examined Gerald, and waited in the corridor. Ten minutes later, Claudia emerged and said to Dorothy, 'He's very weak and there's not much we can do for him beyond palliative care. I think a hospice is probably the best place for him.'

Dorothy nodded sadly, 'We would do whatever we can for him, but we're not really equipped…'

'And, of course, you've a hotel to run. No, a hospice would be best.' Claudia Marinello paused, 'But has he mentioned a next of kin, family members?'

'No. He seems a very private man. He has given me a couple of things to post. London addresses. One could be a relative, or maybe even his wife.'

'If you could let me have the address, I'll ask our practice manager to contact her.'

His special visitor had by now called round to Doug's flat several times and didn't seem to mind that his efforts to spruce the place up had little more than scratched the surface. But he lent her a sympathetic ear as she revealed to him how unhappy married life had become since the death of her daughter. She also wondered if her husband had been having an affair, and if it was to a woman that he had gone. Doug's straightforward manner appealed to her, and she remembered what a good dancer he had once been. She knew where she stood with him.

After a few days back home in Putney, Frank was taking it easy, but curiosity was beginning to get the better of him. He wanted to know more about the forthcoming exhibition, and decided he had better risk the hateful Tube and call in on Julian at The Snicket. A letter landed on the mat and that delayed any plans for going into town. It was addressed to both him and Louise. Over their morning coffee, they read it together.

Dear Frank and Louise

I daresay you both know by now all about the unpardonable things I have done. I am truly sorry, but there is probably little need to explain my actions as, I am sure, the reasons for them are self-evident.

Andrea's death was hard for me to bear and, perhaps, harder still for Betty as I paid the woman so little attention. Yes, Louise, I wanted to wind back the clock, foolishly believing I might start a new and happier life for myself with someone I have always admired. All rather selfish and juvenile, I admit. But also rather too late in the day.

You see, while H did for poor Andrea, Big C will soon have done for me. You will notice that I have omitted to include my address, because I don't want you or anyone else to find me. It is not because I am afraid you will, with good reason, want to come and knock my block off, it is because I don't want you to see what I have become.

I can't ask you to forgive me, but would like to ask one small favour. There is the last of my abstracts hanging at the house. Jane McNab at The Curzon is willing to sell it, and thinks it should make a pretty penny. If you could persuade Betty to let it go, the proceeds should make her life a little more comfortable.

Yours, Gerald Graham

12

'Poor Betty,' said Louise.

'And poor Gerald,' said Frank.

They held hands and sat silently as they reflected on the couple they had both known so well.

'It's odd,' said Louise at last. 'I had always thought it was Betty who struggled to cope after their daughter died, but I suppose it can't have been any easier for Gerald too. It's just that he never let on about it.'

Frank nodded, 'And it probably explains why his painting changed so drastically too. What do you think we should do?'

'Well, I'll call round on Betty. She must be worried to death.'

'But what about Gerald?'

The following day, Louise drove over to Ealing, expecting to find an inconsolable Betty. To her surprise, Betty seemed remarkably cheerful. Not in her usual pinny or housecoat, she was wearing a smart, tailored suit and in the middle of putting on lipstick.

'It's nice to see you, Louise, but I have to go out in a little while, so I can't stop and chat for long. Sorry, I should have said when you rang.'

Louise had thought carefully about what to say, and how much to tell Betty. She decided not to reveal the full contents of the letter, but said, 'I thought you should know that we've heard from Gerald.'

'Oh yes?' said Betty, sounding barely interested, as she brought Louise a cup of tea.

Louise explained that Gerald had said he had cancer and that it sounded as if he hadn't long to live, but left no address where he could be found.

'I knew he was taking tablets for something or other, but he never said what for. Oh dear, I do hope he isn't making one of his dramas out of it. He does do that, you know. But it was very kind of you to go to the trouble of coming all the way here to tell me.'

'If there's anything we can do, Betty…' Louise was at a loss as to what to say next.

'Oh, I suppose someone will be in touch when there's some news.' Betty looked at the wall clock. 'I'm terribly sorry, Louise, but I really ought to be going.'

Driving back to Putney, Louise was baffled by Betty's reaction to the news.

Meanwhile, Frank had gone into town to see Julian Frnell. The thought of mentioning Gerald had gone completely out of his head. He settled down with a glass of Fitou in hand to find out more about the exhibition. Jane had already called Julian to let him know that Tony Quinn had agreed to call it *Lovers of Art and the Environment*, and he had plenty of time to plan the answers to give to the questions he was sure Frank would ask.

'I like the title,' said Frank, starting to think of the PR it might generate. 'Yes, there's a nice ring to *Lovers of Art and the Environment*. But I assume this gallery does have a name?'

'It's a new place, called Polari.'

'Good God, it seems I can't get away from all things nuclear these days,' chortled Frank. 'Fancy naming an art gallery after a nuclear submarine!'

Even though he was certain Frank wouldn't know the real meaning of the gallery's name, Julian thought it best not to mention that there was an 's' too many in his interpretation. 'Indeed. Hasn't been open long, but they're delighted with your sketches.'

'I suppose that's why they're keen to make a bit of a name for themselves with a few well-known artists like yours truly,' said Frank smugly, as Julian topped up his glass. 'Well, as you know, Julian, I'm always more than happy to give my support to new ventures in the art world. By the way, where did you say it is?'

Julian smiled, knowing Frank might think rather differently when the exhibition opened. 'Oh, a little place in Soho. Just off Romilly Street, as I recall.'

'Soho, eh? Unusual sort of place for a gallery, don't you think? Ah well, no matter, I might just pop along and take a look.'

As Frank made his way across Bloomsbury, Julian began to worry, just as Jane McNab had. Despite knowing Frank's dislike of venturing into town, Julian knew that just one look at Polari, and there was every chance that he would run a mile. Not that Julian could have possibly known, Frank did not head for Soho. Instead, pleased with himself and at the possibility of some very positive PR, he treated himself to a lavish lunch, with oysters, a rare T-bone, and a hefty bread and butter pudding, washed down with most of a bottle of Pauillac. By the time he reached Putney, Frank was gasping for breath. It was all he could do to make it up the slight rise to Exmoor Gardens, stopping several times, and wishing he had brought a stick with him.

Back from looking after the grandchildren, Louise was startled to see Frank, recumbent on a sofa, groaning. His eyes were bloodshot and she could smell the drink on his breath from several feet away.

'I think all the excitement of this exhibition has rather got to me,' he gasped.

'And I think you've had rather too much to drink. You'd better sleep it off and if you're no better in the morning, you're going round to Dr Schwarz.'

'Oh no, not Schwarz. I don't like him,' said Frank pettishly.

'He's a doctor, Frank. You don't have to like him. Now, off to bed with you.'

While Frank was dozing, the phone rang. 'I'm afraid Frank's not too well. He's in bed right now, Julian.'

'Nothing too serious, I hope. Well, there's no need to disturb the poor chap in his bed of pain,' said Julian Furnell. 'You see, it was you I was rather hoping to have a word with, Louise, my dear.'

'Oh, you do surprise me.'

'Yes, a slightly knotty little problem has arisen. Well, not a problem as such, at least not yet, but I would be grateful for your wise counsel on the matter.'

'Wise counsel! How very mysterious you're being.'

Julian explained his concerns to Louise, that Frank might react badly to having his sketches in the same exhibition as Martin's painting, and that it would be in a gallery for gay artists too. 'Now, I'm most terribly sorry to trouble you with all this, and I hope I haven't put you in something of a spot. But it's been rather a long time since his work appeared in a show like this, and it really is such a marvellous opportunity for Frank that I would hate for him to miss out.'

'And there is your commission to consider too, Julian. I imagine you'd hate to miss out on that too.' Beneath the tart response, Louise did all she could to keep her amusement to herself.

'Well, naturally, but I just thought that, if anyone could make sure Frank doesn't storm off or do anything silly like that, you could.'

'I can't promise anything, Julian, but I will see what I can do.'

'That's splendid. You really are a brick, Louise. And if you could do what you can to avoid him going to Polari before the exhibition opens…'

'I did tell you he's under the weather at the moment, so I doubt he'll be going anywhere for some little time.' As Louise put the phone down, tears of laughter poured down her face.

After a fruitless day at the office, spent trying to dream up any sort of special project that might impress the directors and getting absolutely nowhere, Tom arrived home with the kind of debilitating tiredness that comes from not having enough to do. Lizzie closed her laptop as he arrived and said, 'Well, I've done it.'

He slumped into a chair and said wearily, 'Done what, Liz?'

'Put the house on the market. I thought it would be best to do it sooner rather than later, just in case you have another wobble.'

'What do you mean, "another wobble"?'

'About becoming a house husband. Well, at least for the time being.'

In the morning, Louise bundled a reluctant husband into her car and drove the short distance to the GP's surgery. Dr Schwarz was business-like and, once he had satisfied himself that there was nothing seriously wrong with Frank, he took the opportunity to remind him to take better care of himself. 'I'm pleased to hear you've stopped smoking,' he said, 'but you must remember that a stent won't enable you to live like a twenty year old. You really must cut down the drinking…'

'I hardly touch a drop these days, doctor…'

'And overindulging in general is not a good idea for a man of your age.'

A morose Frank trooped out the surgery. 'The cheek of it! Man of my age, indeed,' he muttered. 'If he was any good, he'd know I'm in rude health.'

'I'm glad to hear that,' said Louise. 'With all that time you were away in Penrith, there's all sorts of things that need doing now. I've a list as long as my arm.'

Doug was the first of his friends that Martin called to discuss his plan to nominate Frank for an MBE, after he and Dominic had agreed that it might have a better chance of success than anything more elevated. Martin liked Doug, but couldn't help sometimes feeling intimidated by the large, laconic Wearsider, and was a little nervous about putting the idea to him. He wasn't surprised by Doug's response.

'Yeah, no problem. I'd be happy to write a letter of support. Mind you, what is it they say about an MBE? Massive bloody ego!'

On Sunday morning, Frank knew he'd have to put on a good show, if Louise was to let him go down to The Duke of York that afternoon. Unlike his usual Sunday routine, tottering into the kitchen in his dressing gown for tea and toast, he showered and shaved before joining Louise and Georgia in the drawing room.

'Lazarus is risen', he declared to them grandly.

'Oh, Lord above,' murmured his wife, all too aware of the play acting before her.

'Feeling better then, Pa?' said Georgia, looking up from her mobile.

'Indeed I do, darling. Positively fighting fit.'

'It's a simple lunch, Frank. No roast today. I thought soup and a salad.'

'Whatever you say, my love,' said Frank, wholly unaware that the more compliant his behaviour, the less plausible it appeared.

At three o'clock, Frank got his coat from the hall cupboard, but found the front door blocked by Louise.

'Oh no, you don't, my boy. I'm not having you going to and from Dr Schwarz like a yo-yo every time you have too much to drink.'

'I don't have to drink, you know,' said Frank loftily. 'I will be quite happy with a glass of tomato juice or some such delight. I go to the pub to see my friends, not to get drunk.'

'Tomato juice, my eye. It's me you're talking to, Frank Armstrong, and it'll be half a bottle of wine at the very least.'

'Louise, I promise you…'

'All right. One glass of white wine, and that's your lot. And I'll know if you've had more than that. I can always tell, you know.'

Frank kissed Louise and swept out into Exmoor Gardens, exhaling loudly with relief as he made his way down to The Duke of York. He pulled out his box of small cigars, but returned them to his pocket. *It just isn't worth fighting every battle*, he told himself. Unusually, Frank was not the last to arrive, and he joined Max while Sean went to the bar. He had debated with himself whether or not to say anything about Gerald and the letter, but Frank was wholly unable to keep such a piece of news to himself. Nevertheless, he thought it best to wait until Doug had arrived, since he was the one member of the group who never missed a Sunday afternoon and was bound to turn up.

Minutes later, Doug walked in. With a pint in hand and his usual greeting to Frank of 'Now, here's a man who looks like a real painter,' he was much the same old Doug, but there was something different about him. For a start, he had lost weight, but more surprising to his friends was that he had discarded his usual battered jacket, paint-splattered jumper and voluminous corduroys for a blazer, polo shirt and chinos.

'What a sight for my sore eye you're looking today, Douglas,' said Max, turning an unlit Balkan Sobranie cigarette round and round between his slim fingers.

'Very dapper,' added an equally puzzled Frank, mildly irritated that his friend's appearance might delay the news he had to impart.

'Just thought it was about time,' replied Doug, without offering any explanation.

The others were shocked when Frank told them about the letter he'd received from Gerald. Max raised a solemn toast, and Sean kept muttering 'Jaysus'. Doug, although hardly the most voluble of men, remained strangely silent, taking in Frank's report with little more than a few nods. *It was an odd sort of afternoon*, thought Frank as he returned home, having had just two glasses of sauvignon blanc. Louise was relieved to find her husband had consumed less than usual, though more than he admitted to, and that it seemed his visit to Dr Schwarz had been something of a false alarm.

The exhibition at Polari drew nearer. Jane McNab and Julian Furnell arranged to visit the gallery and see how the hanging was coming on. 'Rather different from my old-fashioned little place,' said Julian, half amused and half envious. 'Yours too, come to that, Jane dear.'

Two young women were emailing their contacts with details of the preview night, and Tony Quinn had a stack of flyers to send out. Both Jane and Julian were relieved to find no mention of *The Art Lovers* on it, and that it simply invited the recipients to come along for fizz and canapés.

Martin had continued to worry about meeting Frank again. He had avoided the Sunday gatherings ever since Frank's outburst at The Curzon, but he would have to see him when the exhibition opened. He also doubted whether Dominic's plan would work. Then, an email arrived, followed by a letter from the Honours and Appointments Secretariat, informing him that they had received Frank's nomination for an MBE. That calmed him a little, but did not fully put his mind at rest.

When the flyer from Polari arrived, Louise was in a quandary. She had found Julian's subterfuge amusing, but now felt uneasy at keeping the details of the exhibition from Frank, not to mention the thought of him having one of his tantrums at the gallery. But, it was too late to do anything about it now. She resigned herself to having to smooth things over if the worst came to the worst, but then an idea occurred to her. Having to explain *The Art Lovers* to them wouldn't be easy but, although Lizzie and Georgia had always been reluctant to go along to one of their father's increasingly infrequent exhibitions, Louise knew that Frank was less likely to behave badly in front of his daughters. She and Georgia drove round to Lizzie's that afternoon. They were surprised to see a "For Sale" sign outside the house. 'I've a favour to ask,' said Louise, and told her daughters about the exhibition. 'I'd really like it if you could both come along to the preview.'

Lizzie nodded, half distracted by Theo crawling towards the television, but Georgia roared with laughter. 'Oh my God. I can't believe it. Dad's going to be shown at a gay art gallery,' she hooted.

'You've heard of it?'

'Yeah, course. There's this random cousin of Toby's, and he's invested in it. This is just too hilarious. What was the old man thinking of?'

'Ahm, well, he doesn't actually know it's a gay gallery…'

'You haven't told him! Oh my days, the look on his face…'

Having retrieved her son and put him on his play mat, Lizzie said, 'Hang on, George. You know what's going to happen, don't you? He'll hit the roof, then go on and on about it like a spoilt brat. I can just see how it's going to end up. He'll be in a colossal sulk for weeks. Why on earth didn't you warn him, Mum?'

Louise explained about Martin insisting that Frank's sketches had to be included in the exhibition. While Georgia still found the whole idea too funny for words, Lizzie said resignedly, 'Yes, Mum, I'll come. But you know full well, we'll be the ones, as usual, who'll have to put up with the fallout.'

On the day of the preview, Frank was like a cat on hot bricks, and kept fussing about what he should wear. Contrary to expectations, Louise did not ask him to tone down his garb, reasoning that it wasn't worth risking an argument when a bigger one was on the horizon. With Tom's parents drafted in to look after Polly and Theo, Lizzie came over to Putney so that all four of them could go together. The sight of their father in a lime green linen suit and indigo fedora almost convinced the girls to make their own way to the gallery.

Martin was as agitated as Frank and, when Dominic returned from school, it took him a good half hour to persuade Martin to go to the preview. Jane McNab and Julian Furnell, the latter unaccompanied by Joan, got to Polari early, and found a nervous but beaming Tony Quinn giving the hangings a final check and asking, for the umpteenth time, if there were enough glasses. He had hung *The Art Lovers* at the far end of the gallery, feeling that would make it the climax of the exhibition.

The taxi stopped on the corner of Greek Street, and Frank bounded out ahead of Louise and their daughters, stopping only to point out L'Escargot, 'We haven't been there for ages, Lou. And, once upon a time, we were almost regulars.'

Louise considered calling to book a table for later on, but thought better of it, not knowing how the evening would unfold. It was a warm evening, and a crowd had gathered outside Polari. Frank looked it up and down before exclaiming, 'Well, it does rather look like le dernier cri, don't you think, with all of these bright young denizens of the demi-monde milling about?'

Louise and the girls said nothing, Georgia grinning, while Lizzie and her mother remained resolutely straight-faced. They followed Frank as he made his way through the throng. He spotted Jane and Julian deep in conversation. Helping himself to a glass of wine, he joined them. 'And what, may I ask, are you two plotting?' Frank asked, much amused. With no more than bland denials from them, he continued, 'Ah, my sketches do look rather well, I think.' He paused to admire his work.

Martin saw Frank arrive and hurried off to the opposite end of the gallery. It took a few minutes of chivvying from Dominic before he allowed himself to be prised away from behind Tony Quinn's desk. He emerged just as Frank turned to look for Louise. They couldn't avoid speaking to each other.

'Martin,' said Frank with clipped civility.

'Frank,' replied Martin in the same tone, as Dominic watched him anxiously.

'Nice show.'

'Yes. Nice to see a new place open up, isn't it?'

'You've recovered all right?' ventured Frank.

'Yes, thank you. No lasting harm done.'

'Good. I'm glad to hear it.'

As more people entered the gallery, Frank and Martin had little choice but to make their way further and further from the door until, at last, they found themselves standing in front of *The Art Lovers*.

'Oh, not that bloody picture again. Martin, of all the underhanded…' began Frank, before a large figure presented himself alongside the pair of them.

'Evening, lads,' said Doug. 'Enjoying the show?'

Louise, meanwhile, turned to her daughters and said quietly, 'Thank God for Doug. There won't be any punch-ups while he's around.' What neither Louise nor Frank and Martin had at first noticed was that he was holding the hand of a slight, blonde woman who couldn't stop smiling.

'You know Betty, of course, don't you?' said Doug with a broad smile.

'Of course. But Gerald…' was all Frank could splutter.

'Yes,' replied Betty, 'I'm afraid we've only just heard, so we haven't had chance to tell anyone yet. No, they called to say Gerald died last night.'

'Aye, we'll be going down to Winchelsea to sort out the arrangements,' added Doug.

'Good God!' Frank patted Betty's hand, 'Betty, I'm so sorry.'

'Well, it's sad, I suppose, but I'm not sorry. No, you mustn't think me heartless, Frank, but things hadn't been right between Gerald and me for years. Ever since…'

'I know, I mean, I can imagine.'

'But this lovely man has made such a difference to my life.'

'Come on, love,' butted in Doug, forestalling any further embarrassment, 'let's get ourselves a drink.' He led Betty away as Louise came over, before Frank could get round to telling them what Gerald had said about Jane McNab offering to sell the last of his abstract paintings.

'Would you believe it?' said Frank. 'Whatever next?'

'They look very happy together,' replied Louise.

'But, so soon?'

'You're sounding very Victorian all of a sudden.'

Frank shook his head and tutted, 'I just don't know what to make of it. Goodness me, the beauty and the beast.'

'Frank!'

Louise went off in search of the girls, while Frank and Martin looked at each other in baffled silence until Frank resumed, 'Now, Martin, about this bloody picture…'

Before he could continue, Julian Furnell and a tall, bespectacled young man with a notebook, approached him. Julian introduced his companion as Luke Jensen, a reviewer for *The London Art Gazette*. 'Forgive us for barging in like this,' he said to Martin. 'But Luke, here, would like a few words, if you've got a moment.'

'Oh well, certainly…' Frank never could resist an interview, scarce though they had been. It might be the right kind of PR at last!

Julian cocked his head on one side, 'Listen to them, they're all raving about your sketches. You're the talk of the town. Frank Armstrong, the, ah, enlightened artist who cares about the future of the planet. Whoever would have thought?'

After Luke Jensen did indeed confirm Julian's enthusiasm, and promised a glowing review of the sketches, Frank made his way back to Martin. He was about to continue his tirade, but was interrupted again, this time by the arrival of Dominic, who whispered to his husband, 'Come on, Martin. Show him the letter.'

'Oh, yes, of course, right.' Martin delved into his pocket, while Frank looked on, wondering what was about to take place. 'Here it is,' he continued, unfolding it carefully and handing it to Frank.

'What's this all about?' said Frank crossly.

'Read it. Go on.'

Frank scanned the letter, confirming receipt of his nomination for an MBE. 'Oh, my goodness. And you've done this for me?'

'It isn't definite yet, but…'

'All the same, I…'

'Well, we thought… you know, after all your years of…'

'I don't know what to say.' Frank shook his head, overwhelmed by the emotions of the evening.

Louise and the girls came over to where the two men stood. She turned and said to her husband at exactly the same time Dominic said to Martin, 'For God's sake, kiss him.'

About the Author

Apart from three years studying History of Art and Philosophy at University College London, I have lived my entire life in the North West – born in Warrington, lived and worked in Manchester, and fourteen years ago moved to north Cumbria.

After several years of freelance arts journalism, I ran a North West-based public relations agency called Lawson Leah in the 1990s, then worked for various organisations in the construction industry, as CEO of Construction for Merseyside Ltd and then Director of the Civil Engineering Contractors' Association. I have been a guest lecturer on urban regeneration and chaired a housing association for three years, and now work part-time as a consultant.

I have had articles on a range of topics, including the arts, construction, engineering, housing and economic development published in numerous magazines, as well as poetry and a guidebook to waterway walks in the North West.

My approach to writing tends to involve identifying a problematic situation and then finding a means of resolving it. I derive particular pleasure from finding the right words to achieve that. I was first inspired to write, as a teenager, after reading *The Catcher in the Rye*, and latterly find inspiration in the daunting novels of Bellow, Nabokov and Pynchon.

www.blossomspringpublishing.com